EARTHRISE

JEFF BUCHANAN

Pitcairn Press

EARTHRISE

Pitcairn Press

Buchanan, Jeff

Earthrise / by Jeff Buchanan

ISBN 10: 0-9969279-7-2
ISBN 13: 978-0-9969279-7-0

Cover Design by Jasser Membreno © 2019

E·A·R·T·H·R·I·S·E

Pitcairn Press

Chapter 1

THE SURFACE OF MARS had been stirred to a violent fury, the virulent winds rousing the sands in blinding wrath, blotting out the sun and making mad the riot with red. The thrashing tumult made cruel play of a chain-link fence, threatening to uproot its poles from their deep moorings of cement. Clinging to the rungs in rebellion against the assault a tin sign rattled in metallic staccato. In descending order down its sandblasted and scarred face, six languages warranted the myriad, towering smoke stacks beyond streaked with rust and spewing acrid plumes that flattened against the wind. Arabic tiered the order, followed by Farsi, then Hindi in Devanagari script, the distinct symbols of Chinese, then Russian. Lastly, the faded letters of English:

NO TRESPASSING
TERRAFORMING STATION NO. 344

The brutal winds reshaped the dunes in their harsh play, revealing long dead plants buried beneath the ocean swells of sand. The various species of seedlings, imported long ago from across space, were harsh reminder of man's failed attempts to green the great elsewhere of Mars. The ceaseless winds pounded the brittle forests with a tireless ebb and flow of burials and exhumations.

Today, the winds were mischievously uncovering something else hidden in the sand. Entwined within the decaying undergrowth the fingers of a human hand, frozen in rigor mortis, reached statuesquely skyward, the ashen skin drawn taught against the bones in a diaphanous glove.

✝

The mad play of the winds had subsided. They had taken their folly elsewhere. The calm of the new Martian day, just begun, had awakened to perfectly groomed dunes of sand-muted quiet, as still as the bottom of a deep and waterless ocean. It was but an ephemeral gift, existing only briefly in the lull between tumults.

Out of the immaculately brushed sand, barely discernible among the small forest of dead branches, rose the alabaster hand, the delicate fingers frozen in grotesquely elegant posture against the dawn. The winds had further exposed the forearm, which was wrapped with a length of oxidized chain that anchored it in puzzling malice to the thick roots.

Leaving cascading trails in the sand, a group of scientists descended the slope from where their rover was parked, fanning out into the ancient riverbed in private paths of study. They came once a week, dressed in their white jumpsuits and wide-brimmed sunhats in anticipation of the water that was slowly coursing its way down from the Martian pole to wake this riverbed from one million years of sleep. Advancing in her work, one of the researchers was unwittingly headed to imminent discovery of the mystery the Martian winds, in their childish play, had ruefully uncovered; a mystery that would inevitably beg answering.

✝

------------------------------Chapter 2

T HE SOFT RUMBLE OF treated air coursed the labyrinth of ventilation shafts, driven by the monotonous din of generators deep within the bowels of the mammoth spacecraft. In the darkness of the first class cabin breathing rose and fell to rhythms of sleep. The delicate chimes of a clock reached out into the darkness to gently stir the sleeper from his dreams.

In the bed, passenger Enerson Drinkwine gently stirred and, half sleeping, silenced the clock. He blinked his way to consciousness as the LED lights began their slow, programmed rise to brightness, illuminating the small cabin of brushed aluminum walls and artificial wood accents. There was just enough room to take two short strides in any direction. The single bed, declined from the wall in a retractable frame of titanium, took up the majority of the cabin. There was a writing desk, the accoutrements secured with Velcro. Drawers were fitted into all available slivers of space, making efficient use of the limited economy of room. The tiny bathroom was comprised of a combination toilet and shower, with an aluminum sink that held barely more water than what Drinkwine could hold in his large, cupped hands. The cabin was tastefully appointed with flowered wallpaper, intended to remind one of home. But this was a long way from home.

Collecting his thin wire-rimmed bifocals from the nightstand, Drinkwine brought the room into focus. He ran a hand through his thinning hair and, still in bed, reached across the small space to slide the window shade up. Beyond the two-inch thick glass of the porthole, freezing to the touch, the wild reaches of space pooled as if submerged in an ocean of ink. The sunlight that came through the porthole crawled down the wall of the cabin as the enormous craft rotated on its axis, the great, spoke wheel structure in a slow and constant spin to generate centrifugal force, mimicking gravity in the outer perimeter where the main operational area and first class cabins were situated.

Drinkwine remained in bed for a moment, tracing the patterns of sunlight that slid down the wall and bent at the floor before sweeping across the carpet and ascending the adjacent wall. Round and round, a continuing kaleidoscope of oscillating patterns of light that made play of the room. It was all the spectacle of the massive spacecraft, waltzing its way through the weightlessness of space.

Further down the giant spokes of the craft, in declining values of gravity, were the second class cabins. At the center of the hub, where centrifugal force had no influence, were the mechanical machinations of the ship. Immune to gravity the churning nuclear turbine drove the beast, the electrical main panels and computer brains navigating the endless reaches of space with infallible precision. Also down there, among the stowage, sharing the devalued space, plagued by the uncomfortable effects of weightlessness, was the steerage.

As the craft gently rotated on its axis it brought into view, in sweeping arcs outside the porthole, brief glimpses of the perimeter of Mars. The planet shone as a rust-colored orb streaked with shadows cast from tall mountain peaks across its barren plains. The six-week flight from the Moon, following the three-day layover from Earth, was coming to a close. Now only the final leg remained; the shuttle that would rush him to the surface of Mars. Drinkwine wished he could go on into the black abyss of space—continue traversing the solitude. But work was at hand.

The trip had been uneventful. Drinkwine had spent the majority of the time in here, preferring to take his meals in the privacy offered by his cabin as opposed to dining with the other first class passengers, with their condescending stares and vaguely insulting inquiries into who he was and what line of work he was in. After all, he was an oddity; a Caucasian, an American, traveling in first class. For many of them this was the closest they'd ever been to a white person.

A gentle female voice came over the intercom. It spoke in English, heavily accented with a Middle Eastern inflection. "Good morning, Mr. Drinkwine. Boarding for the Mars shuttle will commence in one hour. Please notify your valet of any personal items you require assistance with."

Beset with morning stiffness, Drinkwine draped his legs over the side of the bed and let out a sigh. He gazed at the planet, still some four hundred kilometers off, glowing red against the gathering Martian dawn. Mars; the newest and most promising outpost of humanity. Down there, spread across the surface, fully automated terraforming stations, hundreds of them, had been spewing out a concoction of chemicals for eighty years. Rich in fluorocarbons, specifically Tetrafluoromethane—otherwise known as CF4—when congealed with the existing composition of atmosphere resulted in a breathable facsimile of oxygen. It was putrid and thin, and scratched the throat, but Mars had air. He'd read all about it over the past six weeks.

Drinkwine knew when he received his itinerary and saw the first class passage that the department was attempting to assuage his concerns for what lay ahead. Their efforts only served to heighten them. Drinkwine was a forensics detective. He dealt in homicide. He had the dubious distinction of having solved the Moon's first murder. That was twenty years ago, when the Moon was first being colonized. It seemed so remote at the time, the notion of a murder on the Moon. The novelty had long since worn off. There had been over fourteen thousand lunar homicides since. And now, in strangely similar circumstance, here he was en route to Mars to investigate the red planet's first murder.

Yes, someone had been murdered. There was little to go on. The body of a low-level white American worker had been found. The Martian winds had exhumed it from its shallow grave. The body had been there for some indiscriminant amount of time—long enough for serious decomposition to set in. The deceased went by the name of Michael Byrne and no one seemed to know much about him, except that, under deeper scrutiny, the name turned out to be invented. Perhaps to cover-up some past indiscretion with the law that would negate employment on Mars. Who knows? Well, the front of Michael Byrne's skull was missing. Where normally there would be a face and a brain was a gaping hole. His head had been disintegrated by the blast of a Roches 4.0 service handgun against the back of the head. The Roches was a popular and rugged sidearm for police officers on the Moon. Designed primarily as a subduing weapon for riot situations it had a nasty spray of lethal shotgun-like discharge requiring minimal accuracy of aim—as was evident in the photos Drinkwine had been wired from Mars. He had studied the photos of the gaping hole of obliterated skull and hanging jaw with indifference. To have excavated the front portion of the head while leaving the back half of skull intact, save for the 40mm diameter entrance wound, irrevocably pointed to extremely close range; execution style. Other than that there was only rumor and conjecture.

The classified materials Drinkwine had been studying while en route these past weeks were now neatly filed away in his small aluminum briefcase. The hard copies of materials deemed insignificant or unnecessary had been taken to the furnace in the refuse room of the spaceship in a ritual of burning, always presided over by Drinkwine. The attending technicians resented being watched over by a white man—however, orders had been passed along by their superiors ensuring the detective's wishes.

†

Having shaved and showered, Drinkwine dressed in front of the full-length mirror, smoothing the creases of his white linen suit. To offset the prejudices and uneasiness that his color and nationality provoked, Drinkwine always took measures to present himself in the best light, keeping his wardrobe of finely tailored linen suits immaculately laundered and his personal hygiene impeccable, right down to the daily splash of rose water cologne.

In anticipation of arrival Drinkwine had already packed, his travel bag and aluminum brief set by the door. On the desk sat two unopened cartons of Hollands. He allowed himself the indulgence of five of the thin, rich cigarillos per day. One carton had already been consumed. Another carton would be reserved for the return six-week trip to Earth. That left one carton, roughly a five-week supply, to cover the duration of the investigation. How Drinkwine had arrived at that estimate he had no idea. Confidence perhaps. Or perhaps the shopworn routines of this work had taught him that more often than naught—especially when large corporations had a stake in the outcome—the investigation would meet with some strange strangulation of interference and he would be conveniently relieved of duty in a questionable abortion of ethics and the law. The want of dollars would always supersede the concerns of justice. Money, greed, they were the anacondas of truth. And Mars had proliferated them in spades. There was little use in trying to fight it.

As he self-consciously combed his thinning strands of hair one last time, Drinkwine thought of the questions and suspicion he was bringing with him. The investigation was already seen as a potential stain on an otherwise beautifully embroidered tapestry of commerce by the various entities with a stake in colonizing Mars. Those entities had already made discrete inquiries into how the investigation was going to be handled. When they had learned of the nationality of the detective being assigned to the case they were, accountably, worried. They were intent on diffusing any threat to the promise of the safe and crime free planet they had been selling the past few years. His being white and an American, like the victim, would only add fuel to the fire.

Drinkwine picked up one of the ubiquitous color pamphlets from the desk with an artist's rendition of what the future Mars colony would look like; smiling settlers, all of them dark-skinned; a metropolis of towering glass; tranquil lakes; the air a mild 26 degrees Celsius year round. Murder wasn't mentioned anywhere in the marketing materials. 42,332 people currently populated Mars; engineers, technicians, researchers, investors, bankers. The vast majority, however, were low-level, unskilled workers hired for the backbreaking tasks of extracting the iron ore from the planet to create the new city. Thousands more crawled the skeletal framework of the high-rises, welding and riveting them ever skyward. 42,332 people in all—among them, a murderer. Drinkwine had a hunch there was only one culprit. There was nothing to substantiate that. It was just a hunch. Until he peeled back the layers of what had transpired, they all must be regarded as a possible suspect. It was the best way to work; don't trust anyone. That's how cops died, letting their guard down—believing people. There were 42,332 people on Mars and the only one he knew didn't do it was himself. That's where he was starting from.

After dropping the pamphlet into the trashcan Drinkwine gathered himself. Taking a deep breath, he pressed the button that slid the metal cabin door open on a swoosh of air. Surrendering his precious solitude, Drinkwine exited the safe confines of the first class stateroom, the door closing behind, delivering him into the soft parade of wealthy travelers making eagerly for the shuttle platform. Instantly he encountered the familiar, curious stares as he made his way along the corridor, the token white in a linen suit among a small throng of wealthy, dark-skinned Middle Easterners dressed in beautiful silk thwabs and hijabs. The only sound was the soft padding of expensive shoes against the perfectly groomed carpet.

The corridor funneled the travelers toward the shuttle platform. Through the few windows lining the passenger tunnel, travelers glimpsed with awe the impressive craft moored to the mother ship; the sleek, white fuselage of carbon fiber ribbed with rows of tiny windows. Narrow wings would provide just enough surface area to guide the craft down through the vague atmosphere of Mars in steep spirals of descent to land them in the new world that awaited.

As the procession slowed to a bottleneck at the cabin door of the shuttle, Drinkwine looked out at the gently turning Ferris wheel of the main ship, sunlight playing shadows with the giant spokes of the cathedral-like structure. Barely visible below the first class causeway, Drinkwine caught sight of a pedestrian tunnel where the second class and steerage passengers made their way onto the lower level of the shuttle. Through the few windows that lined the footway, suspended across the narrow abyss of space, he could see passengers, most of them white, bunched together like sardines in a tin. They wore weary and motion-sick faces from weeks of weightlessness, now ambling awkwardly with atrophied limbs against the effect of artificial gravity found in the outer perimeter of the main craft. For one fleeting moment, Drinkwine caught the bewildered stare of a young boy who looked back at him quizzically before being pushed along in the urgent crush of humanity.

As Drinkwine approached the main door of the shuttle he anticipated the change in demeanor that was to come to the two East Indian officers, presently welcoming the passengers warmly in various languages. An American, in the first class corridor, in possession of two cartons of cigarillos was bound to rouse suspicion. It would require explanation, patience, and answering a litany of accusing questions to put them at ease as to what a white man was doing here, for surely they would believe him to have somehow coerced his way. As if by rote, Drinkwine had already retrieved his passport, his boarding card, and his official work papers.

As expected the smiles left their faces as Drinkwine advanced to the cabin door. One of the officers spoke into a lapel microphone as they stepped into Drinkwine's path. With trained efficiency they set their hands upon him in firm, clandestine hold, and ushered him to the side. They rifled accusatory questions in a rapid Indo-Aryan tongue, to which Drinkwine could only answer with the presentation of official papers and polite pleas of, "Pardon me, English, please, I only speak English."

As well-to-do Middle Eastern families and businessmen continued to board the craft, regarding the altercation with curiosity, one of the officers snatched the paperwork from Drinkwine. The other, still with firm hold—as if Drinkwine might spirit off to God knows where—used his free hand to seize the passport, the seal of America only heightening their suspicions. The officer flipped the passport open to the picture, holding it up alongside Drinkwine's face in insulting deliberation. Drinkwine was accustomed to this treatment by passport control officers, policemen, hotel clerks and maître d'. The two officers studied his boarding card with suspicion, looking for discrepancies or fraudulent alteration. They calmed slightly, exchanging questioning looks as they perused the papers with the official seal of law enforcement. Reading the notes in the official box for special circumstances, one of the officers asked harshly in broken English, "You have a badge then?"

Drinkwine nodded, producing his wallet and flipping it open to reveal the gold-plated shield. The two officers seemed disappointed. Without ceremony or apology they rudely thrust the passport, boarding pass, and papers back at him, reluctantly stepping aside to allow him to board the first class level of the shuttle.

✝

The first class cabin was less than half full. Drinkwine reclined in one of the plush leather seats, a five-point safety harness holding him securely in place against the weightlessness that would take over the cabin once it freed itself from its nursing of the mother ship. Several rows forward, a dark-skinned child wearing a finely stitched, colorfully patterned silk coat, continually peered around the tall seat back to look at Drinkwine. Repeatedly the dark, slender, bejeweled fingers of his mother's hand came around the boy's head to gently pull him from his innocent curiosity.

After the perfunctory pre-flight emergency brief the cabin went dark and was immediately filled with the red illumination of warning lights that signaled detachment was imminent. With a whisper of vibration that traveled the length of the shuttle, accompanied by a distant thump of mechanized movement, the craft jettisoned away, instantly confusing the cabin with weightlessness once un-tethered from the centrifugal influence of the main ship. After a brief thrust of propulsion the shuttle dropped without sensation toward the planet below, banking around to align itself with a runway that awaited down there, somewhere, on the red surface.

Craning his head, Drinkwine looked back at the giant spoke wheel of the main craft that had been his home for six weeks, its carnivalesque movement framed in the small porthole, drawing small against the increasing distance. It was so strangely beautiful, the soundless turn of the massive Ferris wheel in tireless, eternal movement, serenely adrift in the infinity of space.

The seats around Drinkwine were empty. His closest traveling companion was an Asian businessman who had already fallen asleep due the strains of motion sickness. He had the appearance of a heavily funded businessman; on his way to Mars to ink deals that would net his company billions. Machinery. Hotels. Tooling. Who knows? Drinkwine thought of the business that had brought him across space. The business of murder. Mars loomed. Down there, beneath the new phenomenon of clouds, was this "thing" that had happened.

The shuttle appeared to be sitting still in silent orbit, betraying nothing of its actual velocity as final preparations were made by the pilots to pierce the flimsy atmosphere of Mars. Drinkwine used the time to listen through an earpiece to what he'd spoken into his personal recorder the previous day. The pocket device streamed somewhat trite mention of the trip along with sparse facts about the impending case that was drawing him in to arrival on Mars. "On the final leg of the trip to Mars from Earth. A homicide, uncovered over seven weeks ago. There's little to go on. A standard-issue Roches riot police sidearm was the murder weapon. It had gone missing just prior, with no traceable paper trail to link to it. The victim was a low-level worker, name; Michael Byrne. Fake name, Caucasian, roughly 35 years of age, no family of record. The body was discovered by scientists monitoring the ancient riverbeds. Most likely the murder was committed elsewhere, the corpse taken to an area that will eventually be flooded with water thawed from the ice caps to form one of Mars' lakes, then chained to dead roots in the hope it would remain forever at the bottom. I'm here to investigate the first murder on Mars."

The digital recording presented a moment of pause, broken by a long, drawn out sigh. Drinkwine's recorded voice resumed in a more contemplative tone. "Perhaps the workload will provide distraction, preventing me any time to think about Celeste. Seventeen years... ended... gone, with only the vague and unsatisfactory words that are offered in the turmoil of waning emotions and the end of devotion."

Drinkwine was pulled from his musing out the window at the retreating spectacle of science in the distance. He reached into his breast pocket to retrieve the small recorder and paused it. He stared at the mother craft drawing smaller and smaller against the ocean of black; a ballerina in white, engaged in a never-ending pirouette. Celeste's forlorn gaze came back to him, stirring the blackness with frightful clarity. So often had she taken that look over their penultimate year together it had invaded his dreams with haunting detail. How often had he caught her in that distant, sad mood? He had given up trying to coax any explanation from her and let her be, soaking up whatever melancholy was about in the feminine pastures of her mind in the hope it would abate and she would return to him. Which she did, but each time with diminishing value. They were now merely man and wife in name only. And that was on the verge of evaporating as well. The paperwork was noted and filed. They would be divorced by the time he returned to Earth.

For the past six weeks his mind had cruelly conjured portraits of her against the blank canvas of space. His mind was stubbornly immune to reason and continued to taunt him with all that had unfolded those oh so few weeks ago on Earth. In the intervening time not a single message had been received in response to his initial communications to her. She had said, in that last evening together, that his years of handling death had seeped a callousness into her being, and that she was afraid of becoming like one of his lifeless corpses. Yet, despite all that was at stake, he had accepted the assignment, understanding full well it would be the last nail in the coffin of their marriage. Awkwardly fumbling with the small device in his large hands, Drinkwine retraced the previous comments, listening intently. He pressed delete, erasing mention of her.

His moment of reflection was broken by the intercom coming to life with a pleasant female voice speaking Urdu. Drinkwine donned the seat's headphones and found the English icon for translation; the words were translated by computer into perfectly enunciated English, replete with charming British accent.

"This is the cabin steward speaking. As we prepare for descent to Mars we wish to draw your attention out the port side windows, where visible against the backdrop of space, the Myoko orbiting mirror can be seen. Though appearing to be rather close, the Myoko mirror is actually one thousand kilometers distance. This is due the Myoko's enormous size, measuring one-hundred kilometers in diameter, the face of which is comprised of over one hundred million square meters of reflective Mylar panels. Set in a gyro-synchronous orbit four hundred kilometers above the surface of Mars, the Myoko is positioned to redirect the sun's rays at Mars' north pole to melt the ice caps, which, in time, will create the Great Lakes of Mars. The satellite was designed to accommodate a working crew of two hundred."

Yes, all very impressive, Drinkwine thought to himself. The huge mirror had been pounding the polar region for sixty years with an intensely focused beam of reflected sunlight, coaxing the reluctant water out of the ice caps, freeing it from a million years of imprisonment. The water was tediously flowing down the ancient mountains into the expansive basins of the Martian plains to form the essential life-giving lakes, breaking down latent peroxides and releasing oxygen into the atmosphere. It was taking its own good time. The projections had been horribly wrong; the lakes were some twenty years behind scheduled flooding. Sun glinted off the distant orbiting structure, a gargantuan framework supporting the mirrored face, suspended in a motionless swim in the ocean of space high above the red planet.

What the steward left out of her eloquent discourse was the fact that the scientific marvel was abandoned. The company that had deployed the trillion-dollar satellite had long since gone bankrupt. The crews that lived aboard her had been pulled off and flown home. Over time, talks had broken down as to whom the responsibility fell to maintain the great debacle. No one came forward. Through it all, with the operation buried in an increasing avalanche of red tape and lawsuits, the orbiting mirror continued its dalliances with the sun, redirecting the unnatural course of its rays at Mars.

Eventually the science community declared that since the unmanned mirror was carrying out its purpose with impressive efficiency and no apparent threat, it was decided to simply leave it be—leave the lumbering giant of abandoned technology be in its solitary, motionless waltz of quiet purpose. Adrift for two decades, its creaking moans had been rendered mute against the vacuum of space, undertaking its task without the troubling, bothersome influence of humans.

The work of the mirror would continue until the lakes had formed and someone deemed it necessary to put it out of commission. That was the parlance of the manufacturer. It translated to blasting the satellite out of its orbit and sending it into the trash bin of the universe, where it would float untroubled for a thousand years until chance put it in the path of an asteroid. The resulting impact would create ten thousand fragments that would jettison off in independent trajectories—on and on, and so forth and so forth.

The arduous endeavor of settling Mars, as was evident with the Myoko mirror—with its vast requirements of time—had created new corporate strategies with projections charted not in years, but generations; business deals with latent maturity to be overseen by the executives' offspring many years hence. The decision-makers who had green-lit the major projects would not live long enough to see the fruits of their labors. Like the work of the pharaohs in the building of pyramids, understanding they would not see the end purpose of their commissions. They were to be but cogs in the noble enterprise that would be enjoyed by future generations. There was, however, as it turned out, enough profit to be made in the interim steps to Martian utopia to satisfy the coffers of many companies. No one was about to go broke, or volunteer financial martyrdom simply for the sake of the future.

Drinkwine noticed that the craters of Mars were becoming more defined. The shuttle was quietly and seamlessly descending toward the red planet, aligning itself for piercing of the thin veil of atmosphere that had blossomed on the remote outpost. With but a trifle of vibration the shuttle broke through, introducing the organic weight of gravity to the craft as it dove toward the Martian surface, bringing the landscape into view amidst a murmur of enthusiasm from the other travelers.

Drinkwine allowed himself one last boyish pleasure of wonder before the demands of maturity required in dealing with murder consumed him. Staring out the small porthole the jagged mountains and reaches of red plain came more sharply into focus with each hundred meters of descent. Drinkwine saw the shadow of the shuttle skirting the mountains in the distance race across the barren flats to meet the descending craft. An infant cried out in confusion against the build of pressure in its tiny ears.

The whir of the landing gear locking into place and the hydraulic hum of flaps lowering was met with a soft alighting upon the perfectly groomed landing strip that stretched for five kilometers. The G-forces of deceleration pressed reassuringly against the travelers. The shuttle's vortices unspooled spiraling pyres of red dust behind that spun off into the barrenness to die. The craft slowed to taxiing speed and steered toward a small terminal, the only structure in sight on the plain. Detective Drinkwine had arrived on Mars.

†

Chapter 3

T HE JETWAY WAS THINNING of passengers. Drinkwine had waited for the shuttle to empty before making his way into the terminal. Brushing past in a hurried state, disheveled by the lingering motion sickness, the Asian businessman nervously spoke to himself in his native tongue. He held his briefcase under his arm protectively, scurrying off and disappearing into the turn of the aluminum tunnel.

Opening onto the lavish first class lobby, the terminal was streaked with rays of afternoon sun pouring through the elaborate architecture of metal support beams. Most of Drinkwine's traveling companions had already dispersed, just a few remnant passengers eyeing goods in the display cabinets of shops that lined the terminal corridor.

Gusts of wind pelted the glass walls of the terminal with lashings of sand. Man had altered Mars' atmosphere. In so doing they had brought about significant changes evidently immune to speculation. Virtually every prediction the science community had made—with their erudition echoed by the politicians—proved to be wrong. The winds had not ceased, but in fact had proliferated. The climate had not stabilized (*"reminiscent of the Mediterranean"*), instead resembling the extremes of Death Valley in California, with stifling heat and bitter cold. Most perplexing was the planet slowly taking on the same gravitational properties as Earth, upsetting all the hype of Mars providing a less strenuous, and therefore, *"life-extending"* atmosphere. Nothing was at all like what science had promised.

As a result the marketing materials slowly excised all references to Mars being a perfect place to retire—due the reduced effort required to move about—and focused their attention on the planet's exploitable resource: land. The marketing firms had seamlessly glided over the previous promises and were now steering the public's interest with proposals of land ownership and attractive appreciation rates—as evidenced in the wall-to-wall advertisements that lined the terminal. Just the thing to seduce gullible humans away from the morbid realities of outlandish real estate prices on the Earth and Moon.

Waiting at the end of a run of velvet ropes, dressed in a finely tailored suit of aqua silk, a white Ascot tied neatly about his neck, stood a slight man of East Indian blood. He had a pretentious upper class mannerism of clutching his monogrammed handkerchief close to the chest. He wore large, black-rimmed glasses fitted with thick lens that magnified the beautiful almond eyes of his race.

"Mr. Drinkwine?" the little man inquired with a refined English accent (remnant of education in the now defunct United Kingdom) and a pleasant smile of perfect white teeth—implants most likely, common among the affluent. "I'm Mr. Kurian, Ambassador to the Mars colony. Welcome to Jannah." Offering his delicate brown hand.

Drinkwine took note of the immaculately manicured and polished fingernails. The man had never used his hands for anything so much as labor in his life. Drinkwine immediately disliked him. After politely correcting him, "Detective Drinkwine," he shook the Ambassador's hand.

"Pardon me," Kurian acquiesced, "but I'm curious, is Drinkwine your actual name?"

Drinkwine was accustomed to this. After all, with everything that a name like Drinkwine conjured, it was to be expected. "Yes, it is," he came back, his eyes staying fixed on the Ambassador, waiting to see if the inquiry was to be followed by the inevitable remarks people made, believing they were being clever or original.

When the small brown man leaned in to allow him to speak in a whisper, Drinkwine was overcome with a strong dose of cologne. Kurian raised the handkerchief effeminately to his cheek, like a gossiping woman in a salon, "When I saw the manifest I thought, being an official police investigation, perhaps it was a code name." Kurian seemed to enjoy the notion of intrigue and giggled girlishly, stifling his laugh with the handkerchief.

"Family name," Drinkwine said curtly.

"My driver is waiting," Kurian offered with an efficiency of nature, "we'll take you to get settled into your room at the Science Center," adding with an approving turn of the head, "a very nice room."

"Ambassador," Drinkwine responded, leveling his gaze, "I'd prefer to get started immediately."

The tone surprised Kurian, absently slowing him in his stride, as if this simple change in his plans confused things. "I've made the journey several times, Detective," Kurian said, arm still poised demurely with the handkerchief. "Surely you must be tired. Why not rest?"

"I've done nothing but rest for six weeks," Drinkwine spoke with simmering agitation. "They said you would clear my service weapon without any delay."

Again Kurian seemed put off balance, unaccustomed to being addressed in this manner—especially by a white. "Yes," he came back after a long pause, as if assessing how each turn of word now would set the foundation for their future relationship. He finished his thought, his surprised almond eyes made all the more large by the lens of his glasses, "all arranged, just as soon as it is removed from the cargo hold of the shuttle."

Drinkwine stared at the Ambassador, intimidating the little man. Kurian turned on his heel and began to walk the polished tile floor, Drinkwine stepping in alongside.

"Where do you want to go?" Kurian asked uneasily, as if Drinkwine's request was an inconvenience.

"To see the body," Drinkwine answered, the aluminum brief, the cartons of Hollands and his small suitcase in hand, walking with urgency, "then the location where the body was found."

"Well, to get out there you need a rover," Kurian said absently.

"A request for a rover was put in weeks ago by the department," Drinkwine asserted, "to be made available upon my arrival."

"Yes, well," the Ambassador came back flippantly, "since that time the Royal Family of Saudi Arabia has arrived for a wedding. All available rovers have been procured for them and their family's needs."

Drinkwine stopped dead in his tracks. When Kurian stopped, the detective spoke with an authority that further troubled the already beleaguered Ambassador. "That needs to be rectified. This is official business."

Kurian cocked his head slightly, regarding the stranger—a prominent official from Earth arrived to conduct an investigation—as if trying to find cracks in an otherwise perfect façade. "I'll see to it."

They were interrupted by a uniformed, Middle Eastern security guard carrying a small strongbox. The officer was slight in physique, his perfectly pressed uniform two sizes too large for him. He studied Drinkwine with uncertainty. Kurian spoke to the man in Urdu. Drinkwine caught only fleeting words in the rapid-fire exchange. The officer wanted to make sure that the Ambassador had the approval of handing over the weapon to a white. Bits and pieces of the exchange ascertained that Kurian was putting the officer at ease, assuring him that; Yes, the gun was to be handed over to this white man. With trepidation the officer unlocked the door to a small office, turning for final approval from Kurian, who reassured with a nod of the head.

The three men entered the small station room, locking the door behind. The officer then unlocked the strongbox revealing a service handgun and a well-used leather shoulder holster. The officer handed it over to Kurian, who, acting as if it might soil his hands, quickly handed it to Drinkwine. The detective took the handgun, adeptly turning the battery-powered weapon on to check its charge. The needle was just touching the lower portion of the green scale. Removing his linen jacket, Drinkwine donned the shoulder holster, drawing the straps snug against his aging body, sliding the weapon in and securing it. The holster was old school, but Drinkwine had gotten used to it, the same way he'd gotten used to a lot of now defunct aspects of his work. He often wondered if he was too sentimental for this job.

Kurian and the officer watched as Drinkwine pulled his jacket on, smoothing the fine linen over the slight bulge of holster to help conceal it. He met eyes with the two men who were still marveling at the rare sight of a weapon.

"Shall we?" Drinkwine proffered, to snap them out of their trance.

†

<hr>Chapter 4

THE AMBASSADOR'S LIMO SWOOSHED down the main avenue of the budding metropolis of Jannah, sharing the six lanes of perfectly poured pavement with sparse few other vehicles. The city construct was comprised of but a small crosshatch of wide avenues that went nowhere, the six lane thoroughfares merely vague promises of a future of fast and efficient commuting. For now they ended abruptly in barricades of flashing warning lights with only desert beyond. The city planners were optimistic. They foresaw a time when these roads would connect the whole of the planet in a bustling of superhighways.

Feeling the eyes of the driver on him in the rearview mirror, Drinkwine gazed out the window at the blur of industry. Everywhere he looked construction cranes were in motion. Jannah was a metropolis being born out of the oblivion of the vast Martian landscape. The clatter and stamp of hydraulic hammers resounded through the steel canyons with the imperious cry of progress. An urgent pace busily crafting a city out of the desert to accommodate the coming settlers of the red planet. From the arid, barren plains, skyscrapers of glass and steel were rising up, coaxed out of the nothingness, a strangely incongruous patch of modernity among the oceans of sand and rock. Armies of workers, mostly white, like him, toiled in tasks of physical labor on the open floors. The sparks of welding on the upper levels cascaded the structures like white-hot waterfalls pouring into canyons of concrete and steel. In the passing slivers of space between the buildings the red sands of Mars were visible just beyond the pale. The majestic structures met the undisturbed sands of Mars in an abrupt collision with antiquity.

"Look, Detective Drinkwine," Kurian spoke, his delicate hand gesturing proudly the view of the advancing metropolis, "the future." He smiled broadly, repeating enthusiastically, "The future," as he snatched the air with his delicate hand, his perfect white teeth clinched with pride.

Drinkwine's gaze drifted back onto the burgeoning city. It was impressive, no doubt. He considered the immense gambles of corporate fortunes being poured into the red planet to secure a foothold in this new frontier. He considered the hopes of so many humans that would make the costly, dangerous trek across space to find new lives here. There was a great deal riding on this. The grand experiment of the Moon had long been eclipsed by the sad realities of its close proximity to Earth, being too easily attained by too many. It was already showing signs of bursting at the seams. And the Earth? The Earth had suffered the changes that had long been predicted and was struggling under cataclysmic overpopulation. Twenty billion inhabitants and growing. Humanity, spilling out over onto the Moon, into every conceivable patch of lunar ground. Twenty-five billion humans in total, all in search of a life. The next logical step was Mars. The powerbrokers were betting on it. And they were intent on not repeating the mistakes they'd made now on two previous planets.

Find a new life on crime free Mars. That's what the marketing materials were so ardently proffering. Life, Drinkwine thought to himself. It's what all of this reaching into the cosmos was about. However, it was the circumstance of death that had brought him here. The unfortunate incident threatened to undo a lot of the utopian promise that was being orchestrated. Intrinsically, Drinkwine knew there was brewing concern behind many boardroom doors about how the news of a murder could undermine their folly, their fortunes, the 'future.' He knew they would be watching him, his every move. He also knew that this man beside him, this Kurian, with his overly pleasant demeanor and accommodating manner, had in fact been dispatched by the powers that be to keep an eye on things, and certainly to report back to them. His every movement, his every action was certain to be conveyed to others.

"Your book precedes you, Detective," Kurian said, brushing an invisible piece of lint from his aqua silk trousers. "I understand that between the Moon and the Earth there are more than three million copies in circulation. That must have made you well, hmm?"

"The majority of copies in circulation were pirated," Drinkwine responded dryly. Adding, accusatorily, "The same way they were pirated here."

"Well," Kurian began with a chuckle, "being that there are no copyright laws on Mars, you can hardly accuse us of piracy."

The car continued down the avenue, the tires humming against the pavement, filling the quiet. Mention of his book stirred Drinkwine's thoughts. It had been said that he had authored the most comprehensive study of the modern era on the mind of a killer. The book had become a bestseller, enjoying multiple re-issues each time a new murder fascinated the public. The homicides—provided they possessed some unseemly brutality or unspeakable perversion— always sparked the public's interest, the murderers themselves enjoying their own celebrity, sharing the same kind of popularity as that of pop stars and video games. The more gruesome and hideous the murder, the greater the celebrity.

Faddish nature of the public aside, his book, *The Alchemy of Murder*, was a respected Bible among law enforcement and criminal pathologists. The book was a first-hand study of the nature, mindset, and motivation of a murderer, putting forward the theory that modern man had evolved past primal impulse. Modern man had reasoning. Therefore, each murder was bound by some construct of reason, arguing the perspective that there must be motivation, however substantial or brutally trivial. But behind each murder was a calculated motive.

"Hmm," Kurian broke the long silence, returning to his previous train of thought. "The Alchemy of Murder,' I suppose most believed it to be a murder mystery. Not a tome devoted to the dryness of forensic science."

Drinkwine understood then that Kurian had read his book. He purposely didn't indulge the opening to more conversation, feeling the Ambassador's eyes on him.

Kurian was still trying to assess the stranger. "You contend that modern man has evolved past the base, primal responses of his nature, is that true?" Crossing his legs and turning his slight body to face him.

Drinkwine was not a man given to banal conversations, choosing instead to play his cards close to the chest with a good deal of silence. "Ambassador, I'm here to solve a crime, not discuss the psychology of man."

"Yes," Kurain spoke with a hint of bewilderment. "Tsk, tsk, tsk. Our first crime."

The comment surprised Drinkwine. "Surely you've had crimes perpetrated here, Ambassador."

Kurian looked out the window at the blur of heavy industry that was raising the grand towers into the sky and responded smugly, "No, none." The little brown man saw that Drinkwine was not believing him. "Yes, it's true. There has been no crime on Mars—not among the decents anyway. You see, Detective, by preventing the introduction of alcohol, pornography, and guns to Mars, we prevent the seeds of unsocial behavior from being sewn, and by not allowing the tools of violence, we eliminate the incidence of violence."

Drinkwine studied Kurian as he stared out the window of the limo at the rushing scenery, wondering if he truly believed what he was saying. He turned and looked out his own window at the blurring landscape.

†

<hr>Chapter 5

THE THICK DOOR OF the restaurant's freezer was pulled back by one of the restaurant staff, wafting clouds of frosted air into the kitchen. Busboys and waiters banged in and out of the swinging doors, uninterested. The novelty of the body being deposited here for lack of a proper morgue had waned over the previous weeks. The dishwashers, all white like Drinkwine, continued their work, more curious about him and his suit than the circumstance of murder that had worn off its sheen of newness. They watched passively as Drinkwine pulled on latex gloves before pushing aside the drapes of plastic strips that served to keep the chilled air from escaping, and entered the cold climes of the walk-in freezer. Kurian hesitantly followed.

Weaving between hanging carcasses of raw red meat, Drinkwine followed the worker who led him toward the back of the freezer. They arrived at where the body of Michael Byrne had been stored. Wrapped in an opaque sheet of plastic, covered with a layer of frost, it was almost indistinguishable from the surrounding bags of produce. After an exchange of glances between the three, Kurian dismissed the kitchen worker with a tacit nod of the head.

Drinkwine regarded Kurian with a disapproving look as to the use of the restaurant freezer for keeping the body.

"We had little choice but to bring it here," Kurian said in defense. "There's nowhere else where we could preserve it."

"Certainly you will need some facility in the future to handle these types of situations," Drinkwine said as he made study of the frozen features of the body.

"Mr. Drinkwine…" Kurian began.

"…Detective," Drinkwine said without looking up.

"Detective," Kurian corrected, "when people arrive to Mars they sign agreements and a lengthy contract. If they are to die, their bodies are immediately cremated. Therefore, we have no reason to build facilities to handle such things. This is a most unique circumstance."

Kneeling to the frozen bundle of plastic, Drinkwine used a rag to swat away rat droppings.

"What is that?" Kurian asked curiously.

"Rat turds," Drinkwine answered.

"Oh, I'm afraid you're mistaken Detective," Kurian came back, humored, "we have no rats on Mars."

The comment went in Drinkwine's ear and out the other as he forcibly cracked back the frozen folds of plastic, revealing the outstretched arm, frozen in rigor mortis, the fingers pointing skyward. Kurian absently took a step back at sight of the alabaster skin, drawing his collar closed against the cold and sobering aspect of being in such close proximity to death.

Drinkwine discerned his uneasiness without looking. "If this disturbs you, you can wait outside."

Kurian didn't answer, leaning slightly to see around Drinkwine.

Continuing to unwrap the decomposed corpse, Drinkwine drew his bifocals from his jacket, making a rudimentary overview of the frozen cadaver as he wiped the fogged lens. "Who has access to this freezer?"

"Just the kitchen staff," Kurian slowly ushered out, his breath clouding.

"Who brought the body here?" The question went unanswered. Drinkwine turned to see Kurian cringing at sight of the gaping hole that once was a face, the skull partially filled with grains of fine red sand.

The Ambassador was pulled from his stare. He looked queasy. His response came slowly. "Several maintenance workers."

Drinkwine studied Kurian. The Ambassador's repulsion to the body seemed to exonerate him in Drinkwine's mind; one less suspect. "I'll need to speak with them."

"The workers? What for? They merely…," but Kurian's words stopped there as Drinkwine bent to peer into the gaping hole of skull.

"No next of kin?" Drinkwine asked under his breath.

"No," Kurian responded, staring in fascination at the strands of hair hanging down over the missing forehead, wafting slightly on the unseen currents of the freezer.

With an unexpectedly gentle touch, Drinkwine traced his fingers over the brittle gray skin of the victim's forearms. First one, then the other. Pushing the frozen plastic aside with a crack, a cascade of ice fell and shattered against the floor. Drinkwine then repeated the tenderness of touch on the neck of the corpse.

"I'd like to speak to his supervisor," Drinkwine, continuing his strangely gentle probing, "as well as his fellow workers."

"Must you?" the Ambassador fired back. "They won't have anything to say."

Drinkwine turned and looked at Kurian sharply, "Ambassador, I'll be needing to talk to a lot of people." The words spilled out into the freezer as firm declaration. "When did his employer first notice he was absent?"

Kurian sighed, "They aren't sure. About seven or eight weeks ago."

"What about his time cards or work records?" Drinkwine asked.

"There are a great many workers on Mars, Detective, it's difficult to track all of their whereabouts," Kurian offered up defensively.

Drinkwine returned to his contemplative study of the faceless corpse. "His employment papers, his background check, surely there's someone who might have some information."

"Detective," Kurian began with an air of tired wisdom, "as with most of the low-level workers, anything in his file is likely to be a lie; his family, his faith. We know his name was a lie. It's what they do."

Drinkwine held for a moment on Kurian's words. "'They?'"

"Yes, the Americans," the Ambassador shot back unapologetically. He saw Drinkwine register disapproval. "It's the reality, Detective," the Ambassador retorted. "The mines, the platforms, all are in need of unskilled labor. The Americans are eager for the opportunity. They're the only ones who will work for the wages offered. As a result, the hiring firms tend not to scrutinize the background checks."

"How many of the Roches firearms are on Mars?" Drinkwine asked.

"Six," Kurian came back. "Only five accounted for presently."

"When did the murder weapon go missing?"

"Heavens knows," Kurian said with indignation. "We are a colony of scientists, of investors, of builders. There is little concern, or time, for the tracking of handguns."

"I'll need to see the names of all of those who had access to the weapons," Drinkwine said curtly.

"It will serve little purpose," Kurian responded absently. "The only people with clearances that would put them in the proximity of the weapons are all official personnel. I'm certain the weapon was got through thievery."

Drinkwine slowly looked back over his shoulder, repeating, "I'll need the names of all those who had access to the weapons."

"Come now, Detective," Kurian, unfamiliar with being spoken to in this manner, responded defiantly, "we're not barbarians." Teetering back and forth nervously, he stared at Drinkwine a long moment before asking, "And what do you hope to uncover with all of this?"

Drinkwine turned to him, surprised at the question. "A man has been murdered. Someone committed that murder. I intend to find out who it was and why they did it, then arrest them so that the judicial system can try them."

Kurian pouted, wrapping his arms around himself in an animated gesture, like a child who is not getting his way. He shot back. "Surely this was just some petty squabble between workers."

Drinkwine cocked his head slightly, "Why would you think that?"

"Who else?" the Ambassador came back, somewhat perturbed.

"Who knows? This could be linked to some malfeasance or corruption at the corporate level," Drinkwine spoke, studying the body.

"Oh," the little Ambassador said, waving his hand dismissively, adding with absolute conviction, "I am certain this is between workers."

"Really," Drinkwine said, "You're 'certain?'"

"Who else? Why? To what end?" Kurian shot back.

"Money, property, narcotics, sex," the detective rattled off, "you name it." He looked at the frozen corpse. "Maybe a squabble among workers, as you say, or, perhaps an elaborately orchestrated homicide to silence someone. But rest assured, Mr. Byrne was murdered for a reason."

The freezer seemed to be getting colder. Kurian, as if hesitant to break Drinkwine from his contemplation of the dead body—pitifully faceless and frozen in the plastic—offered up softly, "Are you just about done here?"

The words elicited a nod. Drinkwine respectfully folded the frozen sheet of plastic over the corpse before stiffly rising, pulling off his glasses along with the latex gloves. He became slightly lightheaded, reaching out to a shelf for support.

"It's the atmosphere," Kurian offered, "it takes some getting used to. Equivalent to being at 3,500 meters elevation on Earth. You'd best be advised to refrain from moving too quickly or over-exerting yourself."

The brewing tension and uncertainty between the two men was interrupted by the appearance of a rat that crept up to the open freezer door. They both watched as it raised itself up on one of its front paws to quizzically sniff the air before darting back into the kitchen.

†

—————————————————————Chapter 6

I T WAS NEAR DUSK when the limo delivered Drinkwine to the Science Center. The complex had been built to house the visiting scientists, researchers, engineers and executives, with a tawdry elegance more befitting a casino.

The driver had retrieved Drinkwine's travel bag from the trunk, placing it on the walk under the massive façade of the center. Drinkwine took in the opulent entranceway as he emerged from the back of the limo, his aluminum brief and the two cartons of Hollands in hand. The driver swung the door closed and with efficient purpose returned to the driver's seat.

The tinted rear window slid down. Kurian pushed across the leather seat to address Drinkwine. "Your rover will be ready at 9:00am, Detective," he offered.

Collecting up his travel bag, Drinkwine responded dryly, "Thank you." And on that he turned and moved toward the lobby.

Kurian watched after him for a moment, face registering uneasiness to this stranger who had arrived with an agenda that threatened to unsettle the careful routine of the planet. The electric window silently rose to tint out the world.

From afar the Science Center was a sprawling marvel of grandeur, integrating steel and glass in arching sweeps of impressive design. But as Drinkwine drew closer to the front doors the structure took on another persona. The building had an unfinished look about it, as if the carpenters had gone off to some other duty mid-task and forgotten to return. The decorative urns were full of dry dirt, awaiting greenery. The impressive columns were scarred with dried oozings of hardened cement, which had seeped between the gaps in the shoddy wood plank molds during construction. The gold trim of the glass doors was unevenly screwed. Inside, the lobby continued this strange continuity of dubious construct. The carpet had been cut irregularly, the misaligned edges at the wall joints revealing moist swaths of rough cement beneath. A halfhearted attempt had been made to conceal the shoddiness behind velvet curtains and potted plants. In one place, the glass of a large window was so ill-fitted as to allow breezes to pass through at the sill juncture.

As Drinkwine crossed the open expanse of the lobby that towered impressively overhead, he wondered about the structural integrity of the building. Standing at attention behind the registration counter, four dark-skinned employees in matching uniforms welcomed Drinkwine, wearing broad smiles and echoing a chorus of hellos, which did not fully conceal their curiosity.

†

The suite, situated on the fourteenth floor, had a generous view. A large bed dominated, set with a dozen pillows piled high against a somewhat garish headboard of swirling gold trim. The room was bathed in the orange glow of a Martian sunset, the distant reaches of desert clouded with a thin haze of airborne dust that diffused the setting sun to a dull red ball, just touching the horizon.

Drinkwine set his travel bag down on the thick shag carpet, placing the aluminum brief on the desk, the cartons of cigarillos alongside. He flicked on the light of the bathroom to reveal smooth tile and a glass enclosed shower with gold fixtures.

As he crossed the room to the sliding glass door, Drinkwine grabbed the remote and by routine switched on the large flat screen television. It was set to the hotel channel where a looping video showed beautiful, well-dressed Egyptian, Indian, Pakistani and Iranian couples enjoying the amenities; the stately lobby; the opulent guest rooms; fine dining in the restaurant; swimming in both the indoor and outdoor Olympic pools.

He muted the TV and picked up one of the cartons of Hollands, stripping off the plastic wrapper and ceremoniously pulling out a fresh pack. From that he drew the first, thin cigarillo to be smoked on Mars. Pulling open the sliding glass door Drinkwine stepped out onto the balcony, into the warm, thin air that gently breezed the fourteenth floor. The only sound was the evening call to prayer of the muezzin, settling hauntingly over the city. The wailing voice echoed out from dozens of speakers that pierced the ancient song into the budding Martian metropolis, the song slightly obscured by distortion. Taking up at the banister, Drinkwine produced a well-traveled silver lighter from his pocket and lit the Holland.

Breathing in the sweet tobacco, Drinkwine looked out over the burgeoning city of Jannah. The cranes had ceased their work for the day and stood quiet and still, silhouetted against the blushing Martian sky. The workers had repaired to their living quarters, far from the opulence they were creating. Visible beyond the shallow wreath of the city, the vast, barren plains of Mars stretched to the horizon in all directions. The landscape of rock and red seas of sand had been corrupted by the incongruous rise of the skyscrapers.

The call to prayer of the muezzin weaved through the empty streets far below, accompanying sporadic pools of green mercury vapor street lamps snapping on against the approaching darkness. They lined the avenues in strings of sparkling green pearls of incandescence.

Drinkwine had seen the endless parade of marketing campaigns on Earth selling a safe and leisurely life on Mars; future prosperity for pilgrims adventuresome enough to take on the challenge. What a bunch of fools. The brochures left a lot of basic facts on the table. Artists' renderings had transformed the barren stretches of nothingness into alluring properties of luxury high-rise apartment complexes with views of man-made lakes and lush green parks. The written materials were generously peppered with language selling a crime free environment where families were safe. Crime free. He tiredly smiled at the naivety of it all.

Leaning on the banister, Drinkwine looked out at the modern metropolis that clashed with the barren landscape. Fools, he thought to himself as he savored the Holland, wishing all those who were presently selling off their lives on Earth to come here could see this; the endless swells of wind shaped sand and barren flats, as far as the eye could see.

The phone rang, muffled through the glass. Drinkwine pulled back the sliding door and crossed the room, which was darkening with the end of the day, snapping on a lamp as he settled onto the bed and retrieved the phone. "Yes?"

The female voice on the other end spoke English with a strong Persian accent. "Detective Drinkwine?"

"Yes," he answered.

There was a moment of silence before she offered, "This is Atefeh Naji. I was told you wished to speak with me."

"Yes, thank you for calling," Drinkwine stalled as he searched his mind for association to the name. Then, remembering, "I understand you were the one who found the body?"

After a brief pause the voice came back, "Yes."

"I'd like to speak with you in person, if I may."

"Yes," the voice waivered slightly, "of course."

"Where are you?"

"Here, in the Science Center. This is where many of the researchers are housed." The voice had a pleasantly feminine ring to it. "Perhaps we could meet in the Sky Bar, it's on the top floor and is restricted."

"That would be fine. Would an hour from now work?" As Drinkwine spoke he absently slid the drawer of the nightstand out. Sitting there was a new copy of the Quran.

"I'll see you then. Oh," the voice halted, "how will I know you?"

Drinkwine was still staring at the book. He broke from his trance, "I'm an American, Miss Naji."

There was a moment of silence on the other end, followed by, "Oh." A second later, "I'll see you in an hour."

After hanging up the phone, Drinkwine lifted the Quran out of the drawer. Feeling the weight, he opened it, fanning the stiff, unread pages and perusing the foreign writing before setting it back from where he had taken it, sliding the drawer back into the nightstand.

He noticed the long ash of his Holland was close to crumbling under its weight. He looked around for an ashtray. Nothing. He tapped the ash off into his palm, dropping it into the trashcan, then laid back on the bed. On the television the muted hotel channel continued its presentation of lush hotel amenities; an attractive Arabic couple toasting in the hotel bar under a curved glass dome that provided a view of the nighttime star field. The closed captioning that ran across the bottom of the screen read in English: *"...or relax in the Science Center Sky Bar, sitting atop the twentieth floor, offering stunning daytime views of the plains of Mars and nighttime star gazing. The Sky Bar is a restricted establishment, ensuring an environment of exclusivity, comfort, and relaxation for our esteemed guests."* Drinkwine took another drag off his cigarillo, blowing the smoke out into the room, watching it swirl and dissipate in the stillness.

--Chapter 7

D RINKWINE TOOK THE ELEVATOR to the top floor of the Science Center, arriving at the Sky Bar. He entered the establishment, which was discretely dark, emphasizing the dramatic nighttime view afforded by the domed glass ceiling that ran the length of the room. The place was only sparsely seated. He spied a woman sitting at one of the sunken conversation pits. She was dark-skinned and dressed in the plain blue jumpsuit of the researchers, often worn in off hours out of ease of habit.

As he crossed the room Drinkwine noticed the Iranian flag patch on her right arm, affirming his initial assessment of her being Persian from the brief exchange on the phone. Her long black hair was pulled up efficiently into a tight bun at the back of her head. Feeling his approach, she turned just as he arrived at the table. Other than somewhat captivating eyes, she was nothing much to look at. She had no discernible feminine features in her figure. A stern face and thin lips that, upon polite smiling—as she was doing now—revealed horribly crooked teeth. He extended his hand, which she took with a firm grip. Being close to a woman, touching, only served to bring thoughts of his wife back to him for a fleeting second.

"Miss Naji, I'm Detective Drinkwine. Thank you for meeting."

"Of course. Please," she said, motioning for him to sit down. "Drinkwine, what an interesting name."

Drinkwine managed a smile.

"Of course, you must get that a lot." Her voice was soft.

Drinkwine pulled a small note pad from his pocket, a pen neatly clasped to it. "How long have you been on Mars?"

She looked off, searching her mind, then, "I arrived last February, the 22nd."

Drinkwine looked at her, a little embarrassed, "I'm sorry, that must've sounded like a formal investigative question. I was merely making conversation."

"Oh," she said, with girlish inflection.

The two of them laughed slightly, which eased the awkwardness.

"And you?" she inquired.

"I arrived this afternoon."

"Not a man to waste time, are you?"

"Well, after all, the body was discovered over six weeks ago," Drinkwine exclaimed, "so I feel drastically behind on the investigation."

The waiter approached and placed a coaster before Drinkwine. Tray in hand, he looked at the white man with half moon eyes, having to struggle to form the words in English, "What may I for you get?"

Without hesitation Drinkwine responded, "A bourbon, please."

The waiter and Naji exchanged glances. She intervened politely, "Detective, they don't serve alcohol here."

It took a moment for him to remember he was in an Islamic state. "Oh, pardon me, could I get a..." having to consider, then, surrendering, "a Ginger Ale, please?"

The waiter looked puzzled, turning to her for help. She translated the request in Farsi and he turned on his heel, moving off quietly across the carpeted lounge.

Drinkwine settled, "I forget," placing the pad on the table between them. "If you don't mind, may we begin?"

She settled into the plush sofa, taking a sip of her mint tea, setting the small glass on the table.

"If anything I ask upsets you, please, just say so."

She nodded, serious, hands clasped demurely in her lap.

"You discovered the body?"

"Yes," she began, regarding the questioning respectfully. "Well, technically. But there were others there immediately. I work with the water measure teams, we were on deployment in the riverbed."

"How many were there, on the team?"

"There would be myself, my supervisor, and four other researchers," she offered with an ease of deportment.

"Can you tell me exactly what you found?" Drinkwine asked.

"I noticed something odd among the dead vegetation that line the riverbed," she said, remembering.

"Dead vegetation?" Drinkwine inquired, unfamiliar with Mars.

"The clusters are remnants of early expeditions and experiments to green the planet. They're a serious nuisance, virtually everywhere. The seeds were unintentionally spread by the winds across Mars. They took root, flourished, and then died."

"Why did they die?"

"No known reason."

Drinkwine stopped writing. He looked like he had more questions about the botanical phenomenon.

"Detective," her voice carrying an enigmatic tone, "you'll find that this place has happenings according to its own weird."

"Yes, so I'm learning. You were saying?" Drinkwine prompted.

"Well, anyway, when I got closer I saw it was the hand and arm of a human, buried in the sand."

"Did you, or anyone on your team attempt to uncover it?"

"Certainly not, Detective. Perhaps it's our role as scientists," she offered, "but we immediately understood this was something very serious."

"And why was that,?" Drinkwine asked, jotting something down. Her blank face begged explanation. "This is just routine questioning," he reassured.

"Finding the decomposing remains of a body chained to vegetation and buried in a riverbed isn't exactly a common occurrence," she answered, a slight tone of offence in her voice. He felt her body tense. It was due the waiter arriving with his drink. He placed the glass in front of Drinkwine and disappeared again.

"Do you know who exhumed the body?" Drinkwine asked without looking up from his pad, knowing her dark eyes were on him.

"They dispatched several workers to dig it out of the sand," raising her glass to her thin lips, sipping thoughtfully at the hot mint tea.

He stopped his writing, "Did anyone in an official status observe this?"

"Official status?"

"The police."

"I don't believe so," absently pushing the mint leaves into the steaming water with the plastic stirrer.

"Do you remember anything about the body, how they uncovered it, how they handled it?" he asked, returning to his note pad.

Her eyes wandered the bar as she recalled the experience. "One of the workers vomited when they started digging out the sand around the body."

"Understandable," he said obtusely.

She lowered her gaze, "They handled it rather roughly, as if it were a piece of scrap meat." Voice softening, "I thought how sad, because somewhere that person once had parents, and if they could see…, well. Now…" her words stopped there. "I do remember," she continued, "they started to unravel the chain from around the arm. We told them that it was important to leave it as they found it. They seemed rather dumbstruck at the notion. After that they lent a little more care to the handling of it. Probably because they knew we were watching." She looked off, "It was so stiff." She rubbed her fingers, remembering. "They stumbled in the sand and dropped the body. One of the legs broke with a loud crack. It started to swing a bit. That got them to laughing for some reason," she spoke with a hint of dismay. "Then, they wrapped the body in plastic and placed it on the bed of their service rover, and headed back to the city. That was the last I saw of it." She was looking blankly at the table, unblinking.

"I regret having to make you remember this, it must have been unpleasant," he offered sincerely.

The words snapped her from her trance. "Oh, it wasn't seeing that, Detective," voice full of contemplation. "I mean, certainly, the brutality was unnerving, even if it was just something that happened between the workers."

The words struck Drinkwine. There was that presumption again; that this was merely a simple-minded squabble escalated by ignorance among some workers. Strange, coming from a seemingly compassionate and educated woman.

She continued, unaware, "It's just the thought," she paused, "that's where we all end up. No one is immune, Detective."

Drinkwine jotted down some notes before closing his pad, then raised his eyes to meet hers. In the darkness of the lounge, the star field brilliant above them, her large brown eyes pooled slightly. The bewilderment in her smooth brown face gave her a kind of attractive vulnerability. Drinkwine was unsure what to say or do, his professional callousness momentarily abated in the face of a woman suffering some quiet, private anguish that shadowed the theme of their unpleasant conversation.

To avoid having to console her, Drinkwine's gaze drifted the lounge uneasily. His eyes settled on a baby grand piano, the ebony instrument almost lost in the darkness. He rose, her eyes following him as he crossed to it. Pulling the bench back he settled in at the keyboard, gently running his large fingers over the keys, a film of dust covering them from lack of use.

After a moment of contemplation, as if summoning some distant memory, Drinkwine began to play Chopin's Prelude No. 4. He winched at his rusty awkwardness, embarrassed at numerous missed notes, but continued to play, the piece unfolding its haunting melancholia. The sparse notes sifted through the lounge, quieting a conversation at the other end of the bar. Several businessmen listened politely for a moment before resuming their talk.

Naji got up and, as if drawn to a mythical siren, crossed the room, settling at the piano, listening, studying his fingers in their unexpectedly delicate touch on the keys.

Drinkwine brought the sad piece to a finish, the final notes resonating. He sighed, running his hand affectionately across the smooth ivory keys.

She did not speak right away. When she did, she said simply, "That was beautiful."

Drinkwine, self-conscious, let out a little laugh.

"What is it?" She asked, curious as to what was so humorous.

"Nothing," he said. "It's just that I only know three pieces."

"Did you make that up?" she asked sincerely.

"I'm serious," Drinkwine answered, "That's all I know, just three pieces."

"No," she came back, "I mean, did you make up *that* piece of music?"

The smile left Drinkwine's face. He looked at her, perplexed, unsure what to say. "No," he began. "That was…" he stopped. He cupped his hands together in his lap, and uttered with a kind of sad bewilderment, "No, I didn't make that up."

The glass ceiling held a blanket of stars that spread out over the silence between them. Unsure how to interpret his sudden quiet, she looked out into the ink black night. "Look," she brightened, "the Earthrise."

Drinkwine looked out at where she was staring. "Pardon me?"

She pulled herself closer to him and pointed to the horizon. "See that faint blue planet, just now rising above the rock peak in the distance?"

Drinkwine followed the length of her slender arm into the eastern sky. Barely visible among the field of shimmering stars, having just crested the horizon, was a tiny, pale blue orb. It sparkled faintly, disappearing and reappearing in the immense distance.

"Do you see it?"

"Yes," Drinkwine responded, captivated.

"That's the Earth, Detective," she said, as if entertaining the whims of a young boy.

"How far away is it?" he asked.

"This time of year," she considered, "about one hundred fifty million kilometers."

He marveled at the sight. Earth—one hundred fifty million kilometers away—shown vaguely. Most everything he knew, or cared about, was back there, on that tiny soft blue orb easing its way into the Martian sky. Everything.

After a moment of contemplation, Drinkwine finished off the remainder of his Ginger Ale, the ice clinking the glass, wishing for something with some kick to it. "It's late, isn't it?" he said, inferring the interview, and the evening, was over.

†

Chapter 8

D RINKWINE WOKE WELL BEFORE the alarm went off. He dragged himself from the bed and pulled back the curtains, flooding the room with the dull light of the new Martian day just beginning. The whole of the city had been dusted with a thin veil of red. The sand, raised into the atmosphere the previous day by the winds, had fallen like a light snow during the night, blanketing the entire area. Far below, in the gray of predawn, an army of orange vested workers waded into the dusted red streets armed with large push brooms. With solemn strides, in slowly advancing line, they crept the avenue, pushing the carpet of red before them to deposit back into the desert somewhere—a never-ending ritual.

After a shower, shave and a coffee, Drinkwine pulled one of his linen suits from the closet. He'd brought five. They were almost identical save for some slight variation of color. The fine linen freshly laundered, he had hung them, evenly spaced, side-by-side.

As he dressed, Drinkwine looked down onto the street far below. The broom men were now nowhere to be seen. They'd done their task and had swept the whole of the avenue and sidewalks of the inconvenience of the ubiquitous sand. No doubt they would be back in the next morning cast, as the sands will have most assuredly returned. They will once again go about the duty of sweeping the red annoyance from view before the city awakes, before the shopkeepers and patrons arrived.

On one of the construction cranes among the skyscrapers, silhouetted against the dawn, Drinkwine watched a worker as he made the arduous climb up the steel ladder to his operating cabin. Far below, casting the long, slow shadows of morning, a parade of workers spilled out over into the city, funneling through the avenues, returning to their jobs in somber strides. They were like ghosts, without life, weighing out their days, resigned to defeat. They brought with them the metallic clamor of industry.

✝

Emerging from the Science Center into the strange, still warmth of morning, Drinkwine raised his arm to hail the lone yellow taxi trespassing the empty avenue. The electric/hydrogen cab swerved across three lanes and slowed to the curb. As Drinkwine climbed into the back seat he was overcome by the stench of perspiration and sun-baked vinyl, instantly immersed in an orgy of HiDef screens, all flickering with a confusion of adverts. The roof, the door panels, the seat back all bellowed in a mudding cacophony of commerce. The driver craned his neck over the bench seat in welcome. He was white and the skin of his face was scored with deep wrinkles born of the stresses of life and long exposure to the unrelenting sun. A badly preserved forty-five years of age perhaps.

Drinkwine discerned the driver's recognition of him as a fellow American and, therefore, most likely earnestly in hopes of conversation. "Science Center Transportation Depot," Drinkwine said curtly in hopes of aborting it. "Could you turn these off, please?" referring to the bombardment of advertisements.

The driver silenced the screens then punched the meter and steered the taxi onto the barren thoroughfare.

Drinkwine made quick study of the cabbie's I.D. card, noticing the driver was wearing the same shirt he'd worn the day the photo was taken. Beneath; Robert Haze. Drinkwine filed it away in the back of his head somewhere, a habit born from a lifetime of noticing minor, insignificant details. Robert Haze, an American. Most

40

certainly, Drinkwine thought with a kind of dread, he would speak English. And he did.

"I don't get many American fares," eyes studying Drinkwine in the mirror. "In fact, none at all. Name's Robert Haze." The hum of electricity followed, eyes trading glances between the avenue ahead and Drinkwine in the mirror. "A lot of fares call me Hazee. You know, cause of, what I mean, well, you know. But, 'Hazee?' Go figure."

Drinkwine didn't want to encourage talk and remained quiet. The tact didn't work.

"What line a work y'in?" Robert Haze asked.

"I'm sorry," Drinkwine snapped, "but I'm in a bit of a hurry."

Robert Haze's shoulders stiffened. He bit his lip. Then, "I come up here, to Mars," he offered, "cause there was nothin' in the way of work on Earth. Took every cent I had, and then some, mostly from family, to get here and buy the hack, the taxi, that is."

"I have a great deal on my mind, could we just..." but as Drinkwine searched for the appropriate word, Robert Haze continued.

"Things are okay, sure, not what I hoped, since the settlers aren't quite comin' in like planned yet. But you wait, you jus' wait, when the people start comin', everyone's gonna say; you's saw it, you's was smart, you done's good."

Staring out at the passing city, Drinkwine was becoming irritated by the ignorant babble, wanting to deny he shared a nationality with Robert Haze. This was his fellow American, his body odor the crowning achievement to his class. Drinkwine suddenly blurted out, "Could you just be quiet? Please?"

The warm Martian morning swirled the awkward quiet of the cab. Eyes loomed in the mirror. There was only the hum of the electric motor and the peal of tires against the pristine pavement to fill the silence.

After a moment the cabbie revealed his hurt. "I ain't mean nothin' by it, jus' tryin' ta make conversation."

After what seemed an eternity Drinkwne felt the cab slowing. It stopped at a non-descript building at the edge of the city, perched on the edge of the desert. The meter blinked 183.1. Drinkwine fished 200 Dirham from his pocket and set it on the pay tray that separated the front from the back of the cab, reaching for the door, not waiting for change.

The driver's words followed him, "I don't mean nothin' by it, it's jus' you bein' white and a American and all, like me, I thought, maybe we could'a talked..."

Drinkwine sprang for the sidewalk, eager to distance himself from the yellow taxi, from those insulted eyes, from the ignorance, but mostly from the guilt of shame for sharing a race and nationality with Robert Haze. He felt his lungs starved for air. He remembered the warnings. As the Ambassador had said; the atmosphere on Mars was as thin as the air on Earth at 3500 meters. He calmed and took measured breaths. The cab had already taken a wide arc of turn and was headed back into the city in search of fares that were not there. Soon, the streets would be flooded with fares. That's what everyone that had relocated to Mars was hoping for, especially since the newness and adventure of Mars had begun to wear on them. Soon. Everyone was hanging on that; soon.

†

Drinkwine was ushered through the small facility where Martian rovers were serviced and recharged. The shop was awash with vehicles in various stages of disassembly. The area reeked of hydraulic fluid and burnt motor oil.

Parked behind the building, which led directly onto the red sands of Mars, four well-used tractor tread rovers were plugged into recharging stations, trickling their way to full charge.

Kurian was there, wearing what looked to be his attempt at outdoor attire; white long-sleeved shirt and pants and a wide-brimmed sun hat. He was placing a bottle of water in the cab of one of the rovers. When he saw Drinkwine he greeted him eagerly, "Ah, find it alright?"

"Pardon me," Drinkwine said as he approached, seeing Kurian had already placed several personal items in the cab. "But I prefer to work on my own."

Kurian was stopped in his actions, turning to Drinkwine. "But," he seemed stunned, the idea of not accompanying the detective was a complete surprise. "Detective, the deserts of Mars... it is not only unwise, but I would be remiss as Ambassador, if a visiting official were to encounter any difficulty while in my charge."

"It was all in the letter," Drinkwine came back, avoiding eye contact. "You and your office are relieved of all responsibility. The department saw to that in the legal document that was forwarded on my account."

"Do you even know how to operate a rover?" Kurian asked with an assertion of self worth.

"I'm sure it can't be that difficult," as he looked into the cab at the dashboard. "Besides, there isn't too much to run into out there, is there?"

"Detective, you put me in a tight spot."

"It's the way I prefer to do things," Drinkwine said as politely as he could.

"But?" the Ambassador began.

"I prefer to work alone," Drinkwine stated flatly. "My methods require a great deal of patience and solitude. I'm afraid you'd be terribly bored." Drinkwine put a period on his last comment by taking Kurian's water bottle out of the cab and handing it to him.

"You'd best take that with you. The desert can be most unforgiving." Kurian was staring out at the desert as he said it. "Also, you need to be aware of the mid-day sunstrike."

At that moment Drinkwine slowed in his movements. His head went light. He reached out to brace himself against the rover.

"Are you alright?" Kurian studied Drinkwine. "It's the air, Detective. It takes some getting used to. You need to be more conservative in your actions."

Drinkwine took several deep breaths and stood erect. His mind returned to the last point of conversation. "Sunstrike?"

"Yes, the Myoko mirror," Kurian responded. "There is a flaw in its operation; a transitional period each day when the mirrors are readjusting for optimum efficiency. For a brief period the full intensity of the beam crosses the plains. You'll be out of range of the warning siren, so be aware."

"I'll consider myself warned," Drinkwine said, somewhat distracted as he went about preparations for the trek.

Kurian, sensing the detective wasn't appreciating the severity of the situation, said, "Detective, this is not a matter to be trifled with. It is quite dangerous. You will need to find cover."

Without looking at Kurian, "Were the coordinates put into the GPS?"

"Yes," he answered, slightly annoyed, "the trip will take you approximately two hours out and two hours back, pending any dust storms."

"What's the forecast for storms?"

"The dust storms, I'm afraid, are at the whim of the desert, Detective." Kurian, somewhat insulted at Drinkwine's resistance to letting him go along, then gestured to the desert, as if to say *good luck*. He turned and started off, calling back, "The sunstrike comes each day at approximately thirteen hundred hours."

After a quick study of the coupling for the charging line, Drinkwine detached it from the rover and got into the small, dual track vehicle. The dashboard was a simple array of instruments; land speed indicator; exterior temperature; battery charge. He took note of the hand throttle with settings for Slow, Medium, and Fast. Two levers controlled the tracks by means of steering brakes. The push button gearbox was comprised of merely Drive, Low, and Reverse. He dumped the rover into gear and gently throttled it forward. The treads chattered noisily over the small slab of concrete before dropping the vehicle off the edge and into the desert sprawl, the tracks churning up the soft red sand behind. Drinkwine steered for the horizon, reckoning by the GPS.

†

The first stop was the sprawl of semi-underground dorms where Michael Byrne resided when he wasn't working. A low-level grunt with no specific title, he had been relegated to the remote outpost where the workers were interred, far from view of the majestic towers they were building into the Martian skyline. As he approached, Drinkwine saw a chain link fence topped with razor wire, quartered by watchtowers. It looked like a prison. The flat roof of the listless dormitory was flush with the sand, the cells situated below ground to protect them from the howling winds and unrelenting sun. As he approached the gate, Drinkwine slowed the rover to a stop, lowering the window and presenting his badge. He was waved through the gate by the dark-skinned guard.

✝

Feet clomping the metal stairs that descended into the dimly lit labyrinth of narrow, submarine-like corridors lined with bunks, Drinkwine followed a guard as he weaved his way through the cramped space, ducking under a makeshift clothesline and around the protruding foot of a sleeping worker from the graveyard shift. The space was woefully depressing and smelled of a thousand perspirations, the air punctuated with a distant, unseen conversation and the irritatingly bad reception of a radio, the music distorted beyond recognition.

The guard stopped at a three-level bunk recessed into the wall, drawing back the top curtain to reveal a narrow bed, the sheets rumpled. He was uninterested in the detective's work. "This was Byrne's bunk. He hot-bedded with another worker."

Drinkwine knew the term. It described the practice of two people sharing one bunk according to their hours; while one is working, the other is sleeping—and vice versa. The detective took note of the sparse personal items that filled a tiny shelf built into the backside of the bunk wall; a toothbrush with frayed bristles; a squashed, near empty tube of toothpaste; a favorite coffee mug with a chip in it; a flashlight; and a faded, dog-eared comic book, the type without words for those who can't read. Drinkwine fanned the pages; muscular Middle Eastern super heroes in leotards and capes fighting dangerous villains, all of them ugly whites.

Removing a padlock, the guard opened a small metal locker that separated one bunk from the next. Inside were sloppily folded tee shirts, some trousers, worn socks, a thin jacket and a cap. Piled at the bottom were work clothes soiled with granite dust.

Drinkwine lifted a corner of the thin mattress. Wedged between the foam and the perforated steel baseboard was a pornographic magazine, as well thumbed as the comic book. He flipped the pages.

The photos were mostly of Middle Eastern men having abusive sex with white American women. In some photos three men took one woman, a penis in every orifice. The photo spreads all ended with the same scenario; subjugating ejaculation onto the woman's face. Drinkwine was unmoved. He'd seen everything… twice. He tossed the disturbing material back onto the steel frame and dropped the mattress over it. There was nothing of value here—in any sense of the word—that would suggest why Michael Byrne's head had been blown away. Drinkwine nodded and the guard let the curtain fall back to cover the pathetic enclave.

†

The rover churned up the soft sand in a disturbance of tracks, like a small craft adrift in an interminable expanse of undulating waves frozen in time. The stretches of smooth sand were broken by patches of hard-packed ground, covered with jagged rocks that battered the rover. With throttle fixed and course set, Drinkwine had resigned himself to the pitiful pace, frustrated by the almost imperceptible movement that, at times, had him believing the rover was standing still. In actuality it was the immensity of the dunes and the towering mountains in the distance, crowned with cliffs, that was distorting the progress. The speed indicator had held a constant thirty kilometers per hour since departing the depot. The monotonous rattle of the steel treads running over dry rollers drove Drinkwine's thoughts. They were concentrated on the sand; a serene, waterless ocean, the tranquility cleverly assuaging an ever-present threat of drowning. A drowning on dry land, he thought.

The GPS showed eight kilometers remained. With the rover set on its own whim, Drinkwine fished one of his precious Hollands from its pack. He lit it and let the sweet smoke flush the dryness of his mouth.

It was a relief to be out here, to be alone, despite the harshness and nothingness of it. Back there was the city, Jannah, the great experiment of colonizing Mars. Man was coaxing the first metropolis out of the sand. It was rising up in all its false promise.

The only disruption in the ceaseless desert was an occasional terraforming station, the towering smokestacks lording their presence over the barrenness. The unmanned factories spewed a concoction of chemicals in brackish plumes into the azure sky twenty-four hours a day, seven days a week, altering the makeup of the planet, bending nature with divine purpose.

The changes man had brought with their science and wisdom had wreaked havoc. The terraforming project—*atmosphering*, as it was called—was grossly behind schedule and horrifically over budget. Eighty years of imported science had dramatically altered the planet's weather patterns. The predictions of a mild year-round climate had proven horribly wrong. Over the decades the freezing cold had gradually been supplanted by livable warmth. However, the temperatures had continued to rise—and were still rising—due the unexpected proliferation of greenhouse gases, giving way to oppressive heat, broken occasionally by sudden, unpredictable cold spells. Off the tongues of those who had been here long enough the Mars year was described as, 'Sixteen months of wind, and eight months of hell.'

Regardless, man had come. And he showed no signs of leaving. The intruders, the conquerors had come from far away and were taking the planet by a slow and steady force. They dared to break a billion years of solitude and spoil the lifeless serenity with an explosion of industry. Man had arrived. They had turned their attention to exploiting everything the planet had to offer—and then some. Minerals, buried for an eternity, were being exhumed and used to conjure a new world.

The real estate brokers had arrived in earnest over the previous decade and were hard at work carving up the nothingness into plots to be sold. The heavy hitters had arrived with checkbooks to invest in the skyscrapers that would form the first Martian metropolis; Jannah. Drinkwine harbored disdain for the provocateurs that were slicing up the planet. Nothing was immune, and everything with a price. Where next, after Mars? What planet would succumb to man's bewildering appetite for avarice? How much wealth had been generated on Earth? On the Moon? They'd found inventive ways to put a price on the use of the oceans, on the air. In time they'd figure out a way to put a price on the sand, Drinkwine thought, as the gracefully undulating waves of red rose and fell beyond the windows of the steadily advancing rover.

Jannah. For years the marketing materials had been trumpeting the Carefree Life on Crime Free Mars. The campaigns were tantalizing, encouraging vast numbers of bewildered Earthlings to place deposits. Carefree life on crime free Mars. Then someone had gone and gotten himself murdered. Drinkwine surmised that the powerbrokers that were pouring billions into development were concerned about the negative press a homicide might have, threatening the outcome of the investments they'd undertaken. He could imagine the ad agencies, on high retainers, all waiting to see what impact this would have. All ready to reshape their campaigns and diffuse the controversy to keep the money flowing. That's really what this was all about. Money. Merely hiding itself behind the façade of a better life. In that scenario was the reality that people were watching him—the invisible personages behind the convoluted amalgamations of corporate entities. He knew that the outcome didn't matter to them, whether he found the killer or not. All that would matter in the end was if the unfortunate inconvenience of murder might taint Mars in the minds of potential settlers.

Drinkwine cynically surmised that somewhere an accountant was figuring the rate of depreciation that an unseemly homicide might have on the price tag of the luxury apartments eagerly awaiting residents. The paint wasn't even dry yet. The apartments smelled of new carpet and the large plate glass picture windows still had the decals on them. Drinkwine wondered, how much might a murder reduce the asking price?

†

Chapter 9

T HE CHIME OF THE GPS alerted Drinkwine that he had arrived at the site where the body had been found. The rover automatically steered itself to within ten meters of the actual pinpoint of the shallow grave and chugged to a stop. The sound of the rover's treads, which had been a constant drone since departing the transpo center two hours ago, suddenly ceased. When Drinkwine shut the rover's electric gyros off it gave way to perfect silence. He got out of the vehicle, emerging into the oppressive heat, and surveyed the area. It was eerily still. The quiet was so absolute that Drinkwine could hear his heart beating. The ride had aggravated his persistent tinnitus and his ears were buzzing with white noise. It actually masked the horrific isolation, the barrenness.

The pictures of Michael Byrne's body and its location were so well imprinted on Drinkwine's mind that he easily recognized the root cluster to which the body had been tethered. Someone had had the good sense to tie a strip of red plastic tape to the dead branches as marker. In the intervening weeks since the body had been discovered the winds had had their play, scattering any clues into the great expanse of desert, shaping and reshaping the surrounding area a dozen times over, mischievously pushing the great dunes of sand about in a teasing of burials and exhumations. The shallow grave was but a vague indention in the desert floor now, washed over many times by the trespassing winds, making it almost imperceptible.

It didn't really matter. Drinkwine had already surmised that the murder had taken place elsewhere and that the perpetrator—or perpetrators—had brought the body here, burying it in this grave of opportunity in hopes that the water that would eventually fill this basin to form the lakes of Mars would conceal the body in its depths. The water. Everyone was waiting for the water. The investors, the politicians, the builders, the landscapers, the engineers, even the murderer was waiting for the water.

Water, they were going to need a shitload of it to transform this Godforsaken place into anything remotely resembling the artists' renderings. An estimated twenty-two thousand cubic kilometers were what they figured would eventually be required to flood the plains and form the Great Lakes of Mars. Drinkwine had learned back on Earth that the powerbrokers were already deciding a price. If you had money and ego enough you could have the future Martian lakes named after you. Of course, who could say when the lakes would actually take shape. Like everything else here they were horrifically behind schedule.

Drinkwine had read that the forming of the lakes, which were to be derived from the ice that the Myoko mirror was freeing from its million-year hibernation at the pole, was some twenty to thirty years off—depending on whom you were listening to. Looking at the sweep of endless desert and the ancient, dried riverbed, Drinkwine thought how this entire area would one day be under several fathoms of water. Well, he chuckled to himself, not any time soon.

A good amount of that precious water would go to flowing fountains and blossoming flowers so that a prettiness could be brought to this place. But the more they promised to make it like home, the more they were serving to propagate the lingering, seldom mentioned homesickness. It was all so inane, but necessary, the ornamentation of life. Home... they kept saying. Home... he kept hearing. No, this was merely a place to wile away a life. If this place was the new promise for the settlers, how hopeless must their existences be on Earth to warrant the move?

Circling the area where the body had been exhumed, Drinkwine stared at the perfectly groomed waves of sand, the jagged black rocks, and the dead plants. They had witnessed it all. They'd seen the faces, the moving of the body, struggling under the weight of death, the shoveling of sand in around the corpse to conceal this ugly thing that had taken place. Though mathematically implausible, it was a well-known phenomenon that a dead body had the impression of weighing more than a living, breathing one. Drinkwine wondered, if the sand could talk, what would it tell him? He stared at the meandering silky dunes of red as if there were secrets there, which the sand was cruelly keeping from him.

Dropping to a crouch, Drinkwine ran his hand over the perfectly groomed ripples of sand. He scooped up a handful of the fine red grains and let them pass through his fingers like a sieve. Felt the warmth. He watched the sand spill onto itself, like that of an hourglass, the fine granules tumbling under their weight to form a perfect cylindrical pyramid. When the last of the grains had passed through his fingers in adolescent play, he swatted the red residue from his hands.

"Why did you get killed, Mr. Byrne?" Drinkwine spoke to himself, the words muffled by the surrounding sand.

Drinkwine studied the clumps of dead shrubs half-buried in the perfectly combed sand. The dead plants served as reminder to man's attempt to impose a foreign nature on this inhospitable place. For decades teams of arborists had been bringing seedlings up from Earth to instill some life on Mars. Some of the species had taken root, sprouted, but died mysteriously. Others had floundered only to flourish in groves where the winds had indiscriminately spread their seeds, confusing the arborists with their strange rhythms of life and death. He could make out the root the body had been chained to by the deep scars left by the murderers' binding.

Drinkwine could have guessed this excursion wouldn't produce anything of value. But it was necessary. A benign start to what was certain to be an ugly intrusion into the people's lives here. They had better things to do than to be bothered with a murder. But, if nothing more than to have been in the same space that the killer had been, that was a start from where the investigation would blossom into an unsightly rose of facts and figures, most assuredly producing an interesting cast of characters. Drinkwine understood all too well that he would not be getting a great deal of support. He would be on his own. And that was fine. He was certain that the murder had taken place elsewhere. This was merely a grave of opportunity to hide the crime. To hide away a murder. Was it one killer or two? Perhaps three? Without facts to support it, Drinkwine believed that there was one killer. Who was it? And why did they do it? What had the poor son of a bitch done to deserve getting killed? That was the question. Behind every murder there is a reason. However vague, however complicated, there was always a reason. Drinkwine ran the mantra through his mind, over and over again. What was the motive? The days and weeks ahead would slowly unravel the tapestry of friends and acquaintances that Byrne had. His dealings, his habits, his vices. Lives have a way of weaving a pattern that paints a thorough understanding of all they were.

Drinkwine pulled the voice recorder from his jacket and turned it on. He spoke into it. "The homicide almost assuredly took place somewhere else. The location where the body was found is merely a dumping zone. The seven weeks since its discovery has made any hope for clue recovery impossible. The winds have taken a very large broom over this area." He studied the barren desert that reached to the horizon in all directions. "The killer's intent was for the water that would eventually flood this area to conceal the body." Wiping the sweat from his brow. "If it's one killer, he, or she, has given Mars the mystery of its first murder. If there were accomplices, by now there most likely would've been some sort of tension or flair-up that would have produced a slip of the tongue, then, a crack in the façade. The plan, the great secret would have come undone. Such is the reality when the tides of men's blood is stirred within, that tempers of mistrust will eventually arise."

Surveying the area, Drinkwine continued, "The act of murder induces a powerful paranoia that splits even the most loyal partners. I don't like to guess, but if I were to, I would say there was one perpetrator. The investigation will have no tangible evidence emerging from the sand. The only fact is that whoever did this had access to a rover. So I now turn my attention to the relatively small number of people with that privilege, and to further reduce that to who was in possession of one during the period of time between seven and, given the estimate of decay of the body, nine weeks ago. Also, those who had access to the murder weapon." He snapped the recorder off.

Drinkwine thought to himself with morbid pragmatism; somewhere on Mars is the location where the murder took place. There will be Michael Byrne's DNA splattered about the whole of the area. After all, the spread of a Roches riot gun? All the cleaning in the world couldn't wipe that simple truth away. Given the severity of the wound, there will be a good deal of brain and fragments of skull—impossible to brush up every last bit. And, there will be the remnant overshoot of shot pellets, either imbedded in a structure or scattered about an outdoor location. Every murder leaves behind stubborn and beautifully incriminating evidence. Already Drinkwine's mind had assembled an overview that was so rudimentary it was almost embarrassing in its simplicity. The entry wound was at the back of the head. The angle was one of dominance, from above, at roughly 45 degrees. The victim was most likely knelt on the ground. The skin of the victim's wrists, what was left of it anyway, had no signs of being bound when alive. Only a relationship of familiarity, of trust, would allow for someone the opportunity to get that close to the victim without suspicion. What was that relationship? Friends? Acquaintances? Lovers? Let the great mystery begin, Drinkwine thought to himself.

During the course of this mental checklist Drinkwine had absently fished a Holland from the pack in his breast pocket and lit it. Staring at his shadow against the soft sand he discerned a shift in his outline, the surrounding area growing brighter. His shadow became more defined and then was abruptly washed out in a gathering glare. He checked his watch: 1:11. Then suddenly remembered; the sunstrike. Drinkwine headed for the only cover offered out here; the rover. It was just twenty-odd meters off, but as he strode for it the entire area was collected up into a sudden and intense increase in brightness, the desert seared to white as the misguided rays of sunlight from the Myoko mirror engulfed him. In his haste, Drinkwine was exerting himself. The thinness of the atmosphere wasn't enough to fully feed his lungs and he began to gasp. With his brain starved for oxygen he became lightheaded, each step measured out now with straining effort.

The harder Drinkwine strode the sand, the deeper his shoes sunk in, each movement met with a gasping for the putrid air. He heard Kurian's voice and the warning he'd given. He had shaken off the advice of the little brown man. Drinkwine now realized how foolish that was, for he was trapped in a massive, endless oven, being roasted alive.

By the time Drinkwine got to the rover and climbed in the entire area was battered with the blinding sunlight being reflected off the

Myoko mirror from four hundred kilometers out in space. Trails of sweat streaked Drinkwine's face as he gasped for air. The heat sucked the air out of the cab. He looked at the gauge for the outside temperature. It had been steady at 32 degrees Celsius all morning. Now, it climbed rapidly to 40, 45, tapping out at a blistering 53.9 degrees Celsius.

Drinkwine had to close his eyes against the piercing whiteness that consumed the desert with blistering fury; an oven turned up full. The concentration of reflected sunlight pounded the rover relentlessly, the body creaking as its metal shell expanded against the heat. Drinkwine, eyes closed to slits, removed his jacket and unbuttoned his shirt. His chest was matted with sweat. He sunk his face into his hands to shield his eyes against the intense glare. He was dripping sweat now. His mouth painfully dry.

Then, as quickly as the onslaught had hit, it abated. The white hotness subsided. The rover sighed with relief as the temperature dropped, the metal body groaning as it cooled and condensed, Drinkwine following the rapid progression of decline on the temperature gauge.

The shift from the inferno blast to the oppressive heat of the previous hours felt like a Godsend of cool. Drinkwine opened the door of the rover, the air rushing in to displace the staleness of the vacuum inside. He breathed it in as he fumbled for the liter bottle of water Kurian had placed in the rover. How stupid, he thought to himself, to not have anticipated this, to have not brought more water. How foolish. Next time. Next time he would be prepared. As Drinkwine stared out at the glare evaporating from the sky, returning it to a calm of pale blue, he was possessed by a new, unquestioning respect for this place. "Jesus fucking Christ," he uttered, sloshing the warm water around in his mouth.

Drinkwine took the beating as a harsh reminder to the lethal potential of the scientific mistake floating four hundred kilometers above; the great marvel of the Myoko orbiting mirror with its daily misdirected reflection of sunlight. It had spanked him good with a murderous wagging finger of warning. He drank more of the water, downing fully half a liter to quench the burning, dry thirst. Next time, water—plenty of water.

Smoothing the strands of his thinning hair across his scalp with water, Drinkwine punched in the command for the GPS to retrace the route the rover had come. The tired vehicle hummed to life in an awakening of electronics, cranking one bank of tread that spun it on its axis and started it back toward Jannah.

†

Far from where Drinkwine had suffered his first joust with this place, the gusting winds made their mad play in the private remoteness of the desert. Far removed from where the humans toiled, they swirled the sands into great funnels of red, spinning them in a drunken ballet across the barren plains. The sand, the sun, and the winds all conspired a wonderful chaos to disrupt the calm, raising great waves of dust to send across the plains in search of humans to annoy.

†

For the past hour the rattle of treads had acted like a metronome as the rover trekked the harsh, barren plains of rock and sand. Drinkwine had steered the vehicle off its original coordinates by five kilometers in order to break the monotony of the landscape already trespassed on the way out to the grave site. But there was little to distinguish this part of the desert from what he'd crossed earlier in the day. He was still acutely aware of the potential misstep in judgment concerning the severity of the sunstrike and the harsh reminder that, out here, water was to be valued above all else. Water and cover and smarts. Water and cover and smarts he drummed into his thoughts.

As the rover unraveled its course back to the center, navigating a barren stretch of hard-packed ground littered with rock, Drinkwine studied a flow of sand dunes in the distance. Standing out against the red was a breach of what looked to be bright white stone. Drinkwine tapped the left tread brake, feathering the rover onto a slightly altered

JEFF BUCHANAN

course that aimed it for the distant apparition. Detouring from the hard-pack surface the treads sank into the soft sand, churning the powdery red into a mist that rose and fell behind.

The sun was conspiring with the elements, creating a mirage that made it appear as though a layer of refreshing water had been spilled out over the planet's surface in the distance. The mirage spread its lie across the desert between Drinkwine and the apparition, the white patch hovering in the heat waves as the rover droned closer. Whatever it was, it was much larger than Drinkwine had first thought. He watched, waiting for it to evaporate like the damning rumor of water in the mirage. But as he approached, the white object stayed fast to the horizon, slowly taking shape as the distance was eclipsed. He eased back on the throttle to quarter setting, slowing the rover to a crawl, then stopped within close proximity to the mystery among the dunes.

The heat and thinness of the atmosphere were certainly at play again, confusing Drinkwine's head with nonsensical images. He wiped his eyes and tried to blink away the vision. His eyes had not betrayed him. There, before him, listing slightly in the rolling sand dunes, was a full-scale Mississippi paddlewheel steamboat. It glowed white against the sun with three decks that tiered to a rise of the wheelhouse, flanked by towering, flanged smoke stacks, all trimmed in red and gold. The large blades of the paddlewheel—cracked and peeling from constant abuse in the elements—were motionless, dug deep into the ocean of red.

Drinkwine hesitantly exited the rover, his feet sinking into the soft sand, spilling into his shoes. He surveyed the area in search of clues to this oddity as he tentatively approached the mammoth boat. As he drew closer, Drinkwine saw the ship's paint was not as pristine as first thought. From the distance it looked fresh and flawless. In reality it had suffered daily assaults from the desert. The once new teakwood deck planks and cabin doors had been routinely sandblasted, robbed of their polished sheen.

Certain the paddlewheel steamer was some strange illusion conjured by the thin air, Drinkwine timidly reached out to touch it, expecting it to vanish. His fingers butted against the hull. It didn't vanish. He ran his hand over the smooth, white finish. He took hold of one of the oxidized brass cleats and hoisted himself up onto the deck. His weight creaked the teakwood planking as he crossed the

56

main deck to the staircase. He stopped to peer into the open hatch of the engine room where a cast iron steam engine sat ready. It looked as if it had never turned, the crankcase, valve covers, and rungs of tubing virtually unstained by the misting oil of normal operation. It was spotless, save for the ever-present dusting of red sand left in the wake of passing storms.

Ascending the wide stairs to the second level, Drinkwine took hold of the darkly lacquered handrail. The upper deck afforded a generous view of the surrounding dunes. The boat was marooned in an endless sea of red swells. The rumor of water was still a good twenty years off by most estimates. "What on Earth, or Mars, rather," Drinkwine corrected, "is this doing here?"

As Atefeh Naji had so poignantly said, Mars had happenings according to its own weird. But this was man-made, Drinkwine thought to himself as he settled onto one of the ornate benches in the shade of the third deck. In no particular hurry he indulged another of his Hollands. Ahead of his allotment, he felt the solitude afforded by the desert, and the strange find of the boat, justified it. Drinkwine wondered what the story was behind the boat, for surely there would be a story. Why would anyone build a replica of a paddlewheel steamer? And why here, in the middle of the nothingness of the nothingness?

As he sat there studying the magnificent boat, Drinkwine felt a very subtle atmospheric drop in pressure, like those that precede a storm on the plains of West Texas. That unnerving gulp the atmosphere takes before blowing the hell out of everything, uprooting trees and tossing mobile homes. He drew thoughtfully on the cigarillo.

Then, out on the open expanse, Drinkwine saw a faint swirl of movement. He watched as a slight incarnation of wind roused a thin column of sand that disturbed the calm, twirling itself into a funnel that rose from the plain. The funnel waivered, swaying from side to side in drunken impropriety. He watched as the winds drew more sand into the tempest, stirring it to frenzy. He thought of the many threatening tumults the planet was warden to; one recent... man-made, this one... ancient.

The distant mass of swirling red dust quickly grew, rising like an incredible wave in absolute silence. It wasn't until the wave drew closer, sweeping in with surprising speed to blot out the sun and plummet the area into darkness, that Drinkwine comprehended the size of it. What had been thought a noiseless phenomenon suddenly revealed itself to be a mad, blinding wind with ferocious sound. That was when Drinkwine felt the first sting of a wind-driven grain of sand against his cheek. In surprisingly short order the calm had been incited to a rebellion of angered revolt.

Drinkwine dropped down the stairs and with surprising agility leaped off the bow, his shoes burying themselves for a second in the sand as he headed for the safety of the rover. Here he was, once again, seeking out cover in the rover. In mere seconds the entire area was engulfed in a violent sandstorm that rattled the boat, creaking its hull. Drinkwine had tossed the Holland and was now forging through the swirling, stinging morass of blinding sand. His face and arms and eyes were pelted. The desert had been put upon him yet again. He couldn't make out a thing in the madness. Reaching the rover, he felt blindly along the contours of the bodywork for the door handle. Fumbling, he managed to open it and clamor inside, struggling with the wind for possession of the door, pulling it shut against the ripping menace of the winds.

The rover's windows were quickly blanketed with red, the sand pummeling the vehicle in violent play. Drinkwine sunk his face into his arms out of fear the windows would shatter under the force, covering his ears against the deafening metallic drumming. The violent hammering of sand was punctuated by the discordant thump of small rocks that bounced themselves off the rover's body and ricocheted out into the blind abyss.

The abuse continued for several minutes, Drinkwine befuddled by the aggressive nature of Mars, before he felt a lessening up of the violent forces that had held the rover at a constant angle. As the vehicle settled against the diminishing wind, the pounding subsided, eventually granting visibility out the windows.

The sky was still clearing as Drinkwine forced the door of the rover open against the sand that had been piled against it by the virulent winds. The dark curtain of sand had passed and was eloping across the desert to wreak havoc elsewhere, leaving in its wake an absolute calm adorned with an azure blue sky overhead. As if a traveler in time, Drinkwine stepped into a completely different environment than the one he had escaped just moments ago. The dunes had been reshaped and combed to perfect smoothness with virgin ripples of delicately groomed sand. The rover sat, buried up to its main tread rollers in the ocean of red.

As he brushed the sand from his hair and whacked the dust from his sleeves, Drinkwine saw that the winds had draped the steamship in a quilt of red, making its appearance among the dunes an even stranger oddity than it already was. Drinkwine stared with bewilderment at the retreating nuisance of wind and sand that lorded over this place.

Gathering up a handful of the red grains, studying them with careful deliberation, he could scarce believe that this soft stuff was the fuel that was coerced into those battering storms that tore and ripped and gouged at all that stood in their path. Drinkwine considered the planet's steady repelling of man's attempts to tame her.

After emptying his shoes of sand, Drinkwine climbed back into the rover and turned the main switch on, putting the vehicle into gear. Electric motor straining, the rover labored to turn its treads against the sand, digging through the immaculate smoothness, gradually extricating itself with relief as it climbed out of the shallow grave.

†

The rover churned out its monotonous drone of rattling tread as it skirted the desert landscape, headed back to the steeples of industry presently coming into view in the distance. Drinkwine's nerves had been rattled by the display of the irascible temperament of Mars. One, the grand fuck up of the Myoko mirror; man-made. The other, merely one of the natural, vicious occurrences of Mars. They seemed to be competing for shows of brutality. It was all an example as to the undoing of one's wits that this planet was known for. Drinkwine's ability to compartmentalize his thoughts had been interfered with by a very real threat against his life. Survival. Man's basic instinct. He had been sidetracked from the business at hand by the collective hostility of the planet. He gathered himself as the rover droned him back to Jannah. Oddly, after the peril doled out by the two ordeals, there was a kind of relief upon sight of the city.

Obscured through the quivering waves of heat rising off the surface of Mars, the distant steeples of Jannah came into view. They repeatedly appeared and disappeared in the wafting, unseen currents of air, the majestic towers of smooth metal—the color of gun barrels—glistening in the afternoon sun. With each passing day they rose a little more into the pale, thin sky.

✝

After returning the rover to the depot and setting it to charge, Drinkwine had made for the Science Center, eager to get into clean clothes and rinse away the sand that was scratching his eyes and itching his scalp. As he made his way down the pattern of carpet in the 14th floor corridor, seeking solace in the privacy of his room, he saw someone sitting on the couch in the hall adjacent his room. It was a woman. She had long black hair. She straightened upon sight of him. As he got closer he realized it was Atefeh Naji. She had gone to some effort to make herself up, wearing a beautiful manteau, as if trying to make up for the workman-like impression she had left in their initial meeting and remind him she was a woman. Drinkwine wondered what was on her mind. As he approached, her eyes registered shock at the sight of him; beaten and thoroughly dusted with red sand.

"My word," rising, "where have you been?"

"I went out to see the site where the body was discovered. I got caught in a sandstorm."

"You were out there alone?" her words wearing surprise. "That's dangerous. Even when you're prepared and familiar with Mars."

"Yes," he responded, painful reminder to his foolishness. "I'll take better precautions in the future." He patted some of the red dust off his sleeve. "What might I do for you Miss Naji?"

"Detective," she said, dispensing with niceties. "I remembered something that might be helpful."

Despite suffering the day of abuse from the elements—wanting to get into a shower to rinse off the wrath of the desert—Drinkwine was eager for any information that might aid the investigation. "And what was that?" he asked, waiting for her to speak.

She cocked her head slightly, as if she were expecting a more cordial response. "I'd prefer to talk in a more private situation," she said through lips she'd managed to enhance with some color— referring to the public nature of the hall.

"Well, shall we meet in the bar after I clean up?" running a hand over his mussed hair in less than subtle hint. "I've been out all day in the desert."

She stared at him. "Detective, to be a woman, unescorted, at a bar—it wouldn't be...," she searched for the word, "... proper."

She wanted to be in his room.

"Yes, yes of course." Drinkwine ran his palm over the metallic I.D. plate and the dead bolt drew back. He pushed the door open, then courteously made a welcoming gesture.

She entered the room to see one of the walls was seeded with pictures and maps and diagrams, held up with push pins, outlining a threadbare investigation comprised of cartoonish renderings of the city and an X indicating where the body had been found. It was pathetically sparse.

"Please, sit down," Drinkwine offered, assuming she would sit in the chair. He was surprised when she settled on the edge of the bed. As he emptied his pockets onto the desktop he accidentally spilled sand onto the floor. They exchanged looks. He shook his head. "It gets into everything."

She shrugged her shoulders, having gotten used to the nuisance some time ago.

"So, what did you remember?"

"Well, one of the workers they sent to dig up the body, recognized the victim by his I.D. card." She troubled to remember as best she could. "He said something to the effect of playing cards, gambling I suppose, and that, 'his cheating must have caught up with him.' Referring to Mr. Byrne."

Drinkwine let the words sink in. "That could be helpful, thank you."

A silence filled the space between them. She seemed eager for more of a response. "I don't know if it's relevant, but you'd said, 'anything I may remember.'"

"It's all helpful, especially in these early stages." Drinkwine was eager to get out of his red-misted linen suit and wash the desert from his body. "Thank you." He said it with the intent of her excusing herself.

"I was wondering, Detective," her voice less self-assured, "if you would like to have dinner together?"

Drinkwine studied her. He wouldn't have thought her hair was that long or thick given the workman-like way it had been pulled back when they first met. She'd done her best to present herself this go-round. "I have to clean up, then I need to go out to the mining operation to interview the victim's supervisor." He saw her disappointment. He tried to soften it. "Thank you, perhaps another time. Now, I need to get cleaned up."

The room was being swallowed by the failing light that came with the end of the day. Her face, framed by silky strands of hair, was strangely attractive in the gathering darkness. He snapped on a lamp.

"Would you at least indulge me in a drink before you go?" She said it without any hint of a smile, then pretended it was for his own good. "I'm sure you could use it. The sun and the elements, they tend to take it out of you."

He'd been six weeks in transit on the main ship, with scarce little interaction with others. Now, here was a woman to talk with. He acquiesced. "Yes, that would be fine. It'll have to be brief," he offered. "Shall I meet you up in the Sky Bar?"

"Detective, may I wait for you here? As I said, it's unseemly for a woman to wait in a bar by herself."

Drinkwine considered. "Certainly, but if you don't mind, I do need to wash up before we go."

"Thank you, Detective," she said, the words wearing a kind of soft relief.

Drinkwine peeled the soiled linen jacket from his tired frame, spilling more sand onto the carpet and revealing the leather shoulder holster, his sidearm tucked into the worn sheath. As he swatted the glaze of sand from the linen suit her eyes went large at sight of the menacing weapon.

"I've never seen a handgun before," she said absently, more enthralled than uneasy, "not in person."

He unsnapped the straps and removed the holster, wrapping the harness loops around the weapon before setting the lethal bundle on top of the chest of drawers.

Intrigued, she asked tenuously, "May I hold it?"

"It's loaded," Drinkwine came back, "better not."

The notion that the gun was loaded only roused her interest. She seemed to regard him with more respect. "Have you ever shot anyone?" she asked, her face carrying that disturbing curiosity people have about cops and handguns.

"I'm afraid you're romanticizing what I do," Drinkwine stated flatly. "I've only discharged my weapon at the firing range." He unbuttoned the sleeves of his sweat-stained shirt as he retrieved a fresh one from the closet. "I just ask a lot of questions."

She appeared unconvinced.

"If you'll excuse me," he said as he went into the bathroom, closing the door behind.

Once behind the closed door of the bathroom Drinkwine re-ran everything she'd said through his mind, understanding she had designs on the evening. He began to unbutton the string of buttons that ran down the front of his shirt. In the mirror he saw where red dust had patterned his shirt through the opening of his jacket. He shook his head in dismay at the thought of having to launder the suit after just one wearing. As he blinked away the scratch of sand in his eyes he spun the tap and felt the water as it slowly came up to heat, then plugged the sink and let it begin filling.

Using one of the fresh white towels soaked with hot water, Drinkwine did a preliminary wipe of his forehead, temples and cheeks, ridding his eyes of the stinging grains of sand. When he withdrew the towel he saw it was stained with a residue of red.

Atefeh sat on the bed, listening to the sound of splashing water on the other side of the bathroom door. She was looking at the holstered gun on the chest of drawers. She heard the shuffle of movement as Drinkwine removed his shirt. The tonal sounds of the water were changing as the basin filled. The sound washed out the quiet of the room. Entranced by the gun, she scooted to the edge of the bed and reached out to touch it.

She could hear Drinkwine splashing his face and washing his torso, the sound spilling into the room through the crack at the bottom of the door, accompanying the shadowed movement. Atefeh unsnapped the safety strap and carefully slid the weapon out of its holster. She felt the weight of it in her delicate, dark hands; studied the polished steel. Her fingers absently caressed the control panel, accidently snapping the weapon on... it illumed with readiness. The unintended activation startled her; she held a loaded gun in her hands.

As the sink sloshed behind the bathroom door, Atefeh lifted the gun to study it more closely, marveling at the smooth feel of the machined metal. A disturbing detachment came over her and she raised the gun to her lips, closing her eyes and taking the barrel in her small mouth. Running her tongue over the cool, smooth metal, her finger lightly flirted with the trigger mechanism. She trembled at the promise of easy death as a tear slipped from her closed eye and streaked her cheek.

The strange moment of disconnect was interrupted by the sound of the faucet being snapped off. Atefeh opened her eyes and withdrew the gun from her mouth. After returning from someplace else to exhale, she turned the weapon off, wiping the residue of saliva off the barrel before sliding it back into the leather holster. As she settled back onto the edge of the bed she wiped the tear away just as Drinkwine opened the bathroom door. Dressed in a fresh shirt, drying his face, he studied her for a moment, aware that something of the many oddities of human nature had just transpired. He tried to decipher her enigmatic expression, which gave up nothing of her little secret. Drinkwine let it go, but he knew, something profoundly odd had just taken place. Happenings according to its own weird, he thought to himself.

†

The Sky Bar was shrouded in the final twilight of the waning Martian day. The star field above had not fully revealed itself. Drinkwine and Atefeh were seated at one of the polished tables. She had an iced lemon flavored fizzy water in front of her.

Drinkwine, dehydrated from his trek into the Martian outback, traded between taking gulps from a bottle of water and an ice-filled glass of Ginger Ale, longing for something hard to mix with it.

Atefeh seemed to be acutely aware of her surroundings, her movements, studying the way her hands fondled the glass of her drink, admiring the shape of things on the table. It was as if the earlier, momentary detour into flirting with death had stirred a profound appreciation for the simplest of things.

Drinkwine watched her, wondering, not knowing, where this odd beguilement in her character had come from.

"I saw something today," Drinkwine broke her from her quiet introspection. "Something that, well, I shouldn't say it doesn't make sense, because obviously it makes sense to someone."

"You're learning," she smiled, adding, "as I said, happenings according to its own weird," the words holding more about herself, than the planet.

"About fifty kilometers due west of here," he paused to thirstily down more water, "in the middle of nowhere, I came upon a paddlewheel steamboat, just sitting there in the sand." Drinkwine spun the ice cubes in his glass. "It looks fully functional, with an engine room, everything."

"It is," she responded, running a finger thoughtfully around the edge of her glass. "A wealthy Chinese investor who was building several of the skyscrapers commissioned it."

"What for?" Drinkwine, genuinely intrigued.

"Well, evidently he was enamored of the great American river boats of way back when." She stared out at the gathering darkness. "He surmised that once Mars was colonized, there would be need for amusement, attractions. With the Great Lakes that would be formed from the melting of the polar ice caps, he decided to build the paddlewheel steamship so that people could go for nostalgic lake excursions." Atefeh's voice softened. She ran her finger through the condensation sweating her glass. Then, with tender sentiment, "He had a wife."

Drinkwine studied her. In the darkness she traded between appearing homely and strangely pretty.

"He loved her a great deal," her words revealing envy. "When it was finished, he named the boat after her. Isn't that sweet, Detective?" She was still looking off, somewhat dreamily. "He named the boat after her."

Atefeh raised her drink but stopped with it halfway to her mouth, thinking. "But, the waters were slow in coming. So the boat sat. A decade passed, and the water still hadn't come. Then his wife became ill. She was sick for about a year. Then she died. She died before the waters arrived to lift the boat."

Atefeh sifted through the continuity of events in her mind. "After that, after she died, they say he lost all interest in his business concerns and eventually they all failed. He was evicted from the penthouse in the very skyscraper he had built. With nowhere else to go, he took up living on the ship. The story goes that he died there, in one of the cabins, penniless, having not spoken to another person in more than a year." Atefeh was longingly adrift in the romantic notion, despite the heart-wrenching aspect of it. "He died of a broken heart, Detective."

"And the water still hasn't come," Drinkwine responded cynically, as he downed the last of his Ginger Ale, crunching the ice in his teeth.

"Do you find that at all sad, Detective?" she asked, hoping for some sentimentality to justify her own.

After a moment Drinkwine answered her with another question. "How far behind schedule are the lakes?"

She shrugged. "That depends on whose projections you wish to consider. There's been twenty years of litigation over the delays. Thankfully, my work is just to measure the water when it comes, not make predictions of when."

Drinkwine looked at her sitting there, her face shrouded in a growing melancholy against the dimming away of daylight beyond the glass ceiling. "We all have our jobs to do," he said, rising from the couch. "Thank you."

She seemed startled at the suggestion of good night. "Do you need to go?" she spoke before thinking.

"I'd love to stay and talk, but I've work to do, Miss Naji," Drinkwine said dryly.

"Please," she came back, "Atefeh."

He hesitated for a moment before saying, "Atefeh." He saw the faint shine of pride in her face.

"What's next? For the investigation?" She inquired.

Drinkwine signed the tab. "I need to go out to the mining operation to speak with the victim's supervisor."

Her eyes grew wide, "You're going out to 'The Hole,' at this hour?"

"It's the shift Byrne was working," Drinkwine answered, matter-of-fact.

"Be careful, Detective."

From her tone Drinkwine could only surmise what might be waiting for him out there, on the edge of the night. He nodded goodnight and turned for the door.

She ran her finger around the edge of her glass as she watched him go, thoughts flushing her mind.

†

—————————————————————Chapter 10

T HE ROVER TRAVERSED THE night, grinding along a deeply
rutted service road punctuated with drifts of wind-driven sand
that slithered across the tarmac like diaphanous snakes,
illumed momentarily by the dull reach of headlights as they slinked
off into the dark. Drinkwine squinted into the mad parade of blinding
headlights that belonged to the massive Mars Movers approaching on
the adjacent lane. They came upon him in the darkness at speed,
rumbling the ground, announcing their presence with bullying blasts
from their air horns. The big trucks didn't flinch on the narrow road
and sped past, boisterously passing within inches, the concussion of
turbulence slamming the diminutive rover. He watched each vehicle
in turn as it whipped past and disappeared into the blackness of the
rearview mirror, headed elsewhere to some urgent task of industry in
the night.

After the stampede of the metallic pachyderms had passed,
Drinkwine saw an ominous green glow against the night sky. As he
drew closer he saw it was the ambience of mercury vapor work lights
illuminating a massive operation spread out over a wide swath of the
Martian landscape.

Rising above the clamor of the rover's treads the discordant sounds of heavy machinery and the violent clang of iron gave scope to the operation, still some distance off. A perpetual cloud of dust rose a hundred meters into the night sky like some strange dome shrouding the strip mine, illumed by the ghostly work lights, their generators starved for air, straining against the thin atmosphere.

The eternal peace and quiet of the planet had not prepared it for the arrival of the humans. Mars had stood sentinel, majestic, for millions of years. Now, industry demanded a disruption of the solitude. With great facility the humans were cutting deep into the Martian surface, displacing billions of cubic feet of ore to be smelted into buildings and cars and things. Things.

Drinkwine drove the rover up as near to the open strip mine as possible. When he emerged from the vehicle his ears were assaulted by the noise. The air wafted with a haze of granite dust and the pungent scent of overheated hydraulic fluid. As he walked for the perimeter of the great hole the ground shook with the dull jolt of a deeply planted explosive somewhere off in the blackness, set to loosen the hard rock far beneath the surface. The shockwave rippled out underfoot.

He arrived at the edge of the man-made gorge being carved out of the Martian landscape in a great caldron of hard industry. From deep within stirred a tempest of arc welding and pneumatic drills. The gaping hole was giving up the essential ore to build the distant metropolis skyward.

Down below, the workers, bound together in a brotherhood of gray rock dust, thrashed their tools against the imposing walls of blunted and jagged, blanched granite. They'd long since tired of swearing at the reluctant rock and quieted their anger with the monotonous, ceaseless work. Now, there was only the rock, the endless rock.

It was said a worker toiling away with discipline and the reward of overtime could amass a small nest egg. It was said. So they came. They came not with fanciful dreams but rather, with simple hopes of securing a livelihood. The bunkhouses where they were interred were not far off from where they toiled away the hours in The Hole, and resonated with the sound of the great hammers. It was said the workers hear the metallic clank of the hammering long after they've repaired to their domiciles, taking the droning pounding to their beds where it drove away any dreams that might come. The bunkhouses were erected in the vacant gouges of excavation to protect them from the ever-present, ever-blowing wind. The sun-scorched rock held the heat of day long after night had come. The whole of the area was polluted by the dreamless sleep of gift-less labor. This landscape pounded men's hearts in a slow wearing down of dreams. These people had exhausted their capacity for sorrow, faces long since surrendered to solemnity. The soulless hammering was eating their brains away from the inside out. If you had a strong back there was medical help and a host of pharmaceuticals to keep you alive and working. So long as you could lift and strain and pull and obey they would keep you going. And so they went, on and on.

Drinkwine approached an aged worker, leaning his tired weight against a cane as he peered down longingly into The Hole. He supposed him to be a retired worker, past all usefulness, forlorn for the thankless tasks he could no longer perform. Drinkwine imagined that he came to this place each night to gaze into the pit and remember; because a man longs for purpose, however menial, however pointless.

"Pardon me," Drinkwine spoke, but the man didn't budge. He tried again, shouting, "Excuse me!"

The man slowly turned, staring at Drinkwine through milky cataracts.

"Where is the foreman?" Drinkwine yelled over the incessant clang of steel and the thrashing of rock.

The old man took account of Drinkwine, a fellow white, curiously drawing his gaze over the fine suit, the expensive shoes. After a moment of deliberation he pointed into the gaping wound of industry to a small work shed at the center of the chaos. With the same emotionless countenance, he pointed to a ramp of dirt that descended into the massive excavation. Drinkwine left the old man to his business of pondering the machinations of the mining operation, forlorn and envious for the hard and hated work he could no longer do.

Descending the dirt ramp into the quarry, Drinkwine shone like some arrogant apparition, arriving in the depths of the dusty dig in his tailored linen suit. He was the only shimmer of color amidst the gray of the surrounding walls of stone. By the time he reached the bottom of the ramp his trouser hem and shoes were patterned with dust. Drinkwine stamped his shoes to rid them of the soot.

Silhouetted in the erratically dancing white hot light of an arc welder, immune to the crack of high amperage, a cluster of men were tasked with bracing the weight of a heavy crane arm as welding rod pooled to mend a crack in the fatigued structure. Through intermittent flashes of arc, which painted veins of hot blue that lingered on the optic nerve, Drinkwine discerned one, then another, and another huddled around the blinding arcing, turn to look at him. The ominous figures were like hulking apes around a campfire.

Searching the area, Drinkwine glanced through the oscillating machine arms that clattered and stamped against the rock, seeking a path to the corrugated steel shack. Down here, the workers—all of them American—spoke in raised voices, their ears having long since suffered varying degrees of hearing loss. They went quiet one by one as Drinkwine strode past. The laborers, these endeavoring men and women, seemed uniform in their disapproval of him, as if some scheming messenger had run ahead to alert them of a disruption to their lives. Rumor preceded him. They were wary. They had all heard that someone had arrived from Earth to piece together the murder. He would be asking questions, shining a light on them, the workers, exacerbating already strained relations with upper management. After all, this was their hard-earned opportunity of employment. They feared whatever it was this man was bringing down to them might well upset that. They didn't know how, or why. But they wished he would go away and not disturb the frail routine of their livelihood with this thing that must be solved. Michael Byrne didn't figure into the equation any longer. He was just some thing that was no more. No one really cared. He was merely a nuisance now. They all wished to be done with this, for the murder to be swept away along with the rock dust. They wished for this stranger to go away as well and leave them to their routines.

As he neared the work shed, ears bombarded by the clamoring of heavy machines boring into the granite, he saw a man wearing a yellow hard hat standing out front, making notations on a clipboard. The man traded glances between his writing and Drinkwine's approach with a knowing, irritated look. Just as Drinkwine was about to yell the man interrupted with a shake of the head, pointing to his ear, indicating speech was futile and motioned for him to come inside the shed. Drinkwine followed.

The door of the shed banged closed, cutting the decibels of the laboring work outside significantly. The man was white, an American. He hung the clipboard on a hook in the wall and tossed his hard hat on the desk. The light of an overhead work lamp gave Drinkwine a clear view. The foreman looked to be late thirties, but it was hard to tell. Years of hard manual labor tire a man well before his time. He was handsome, despite his face having been put back together a few times. Possibly work accidents or, more likely, barroom brawls. Drinkwine presented his badge, "I'm Detective Drinkwine."

Upon hearing the name the foreman smiled, with that familiar expression of disbelief. "Seriously?"

Drinkwine just nodded.

"I wondered when you would come," he muttered. "I'm Jack Bishop," he offered, straightforward. "I'm the foreman of the graveyard shift. I was Michael's immediate supervisor. I assume you have questions," scratching his head, "I'm not sure I have answers."

"You mean you may not want to give them to me?" Drinkwine inferred.

"That's not what I meant." Bishop mulled things over in his head. He was tired. "Look, I'll tell you what I know, it just may not be a lot, or helpful," he said as he settled into the swivel chair at his desk. "By the way, the company has already spooked the hell out of the workers."

The statement caught Drinkwine off-guard, "What do you mean?"

Bishop, relaxing his edge a bit, motioned for him to sit in the other swivel chair. Drinkwine settled into it, squeaking the dry springs.

"They said someone was coming. To ask questions," Bishop spoke without loyalty.

Drinkwine sensed Bishop's resentment toward the conglomerate he worked for.

"They told them they'd be docked for the time they were being interviewed."

Drinkwine nodded. "So," he started, "what *can* you tell me?"

"About the deceased?" rubbing a grain of sand from his eye he pulled back a drawer and produced a time sheet. "I went back and looked at the logs, figuring someone would eventually come and ask." He ran his finger over the card. "Last time Byrne worked in The Hole was eight weeks ago. He went missing. No one seemed to know, or care about what happened to him."

"Why was that?"

"Byrne wasn't what you'd call a gifted worker, Detective." Bishop weighed out the ramifications of what he was about to say. "And he was an idiot." Once he said it, more poured forth. "He was lazy and incompetent. That probably makes me a suspect now, huh? So, he was useless and I wanted him gone. Doesn't mean I wanted him dead."

"I appreciate your candor, Mr. Bishop," Drinkwine said sincerely. "It's a rare commodity."

"So, you've discovered that already have you?" Bishop offered, warming to Drinkwine. "I know he owed people money."

"What for?" Drinkwine, stone-faced.

"Who knows?" Bishop answered with bewilderment. "Playing cards, bootleg skag, naked girly pictures, shit... naked *boy* pictures. Everyone has their perversions. Take your pick." Bishop stared out the window. "He wasn't liked."

"Any idea who he owed money to?" Drinkwine waited to jot down names.

"If I'd asked a few weeks ago, maybe I could've learned something," Bishop tapped a pencil against the desk. "But no one's talking now. Ever since the company announced the docking of pay for the interviews, everyone's gone quiet. You see, to them," indicating the workers toiling in the pit outside, "all this murder represents is a potential loss of income. So, you're not going to get much help." He studied Drinkwine, the suit, the shoes. "Detective... Drinkwine, did you say?"

Drinkwine nodded.

Bishop smiled, humored. "You may find that trying to get answers out of these people is going to be as hard as getting the ore out of this hell hole." There was a palpable respect between the two men for some reason. "Who killed him? Who knows? Why does one person get killed and not another?" Bishop looked out the little glass window at the mining operation, the shadows of workers distorted against the rock face by the powerful work lights. "They don't want to talk to you, Detective."

"I'm not going to go away," Drinkwine, resolute.

"I know," Bishop said, swiveling the chair. "That's what concerns me."

Drinkwine stopped writing and looked at him, searching for deeper meaning, "Concern, for the investigation?"

"Concern for your well-being." Bishop stopped swiveling. "You're an oddity, Detective. Surely you know this. You're not one of *them*, yet you're not one of *us*, not really. You're a white with a brown's education and privilege. You're an unknown entity. You bring with you an unknown circumstance. These people don't know what to make of you. Except that, in their eyes, they fear this whole thing could blow up into something bigger. To them, you're a threat to their jobs."

The words caused Drinkwine to cock his head slightly.

"That's right, Detective," Bishop continued. "This shithole of existence, this morbid, endless digging into Mars is all they have. Most of them lied about their nationality, their past, their education, even their religious beliefs just to get the damn job. You're shining a light on them, making them real. And a lot of them don't want that, because if this grows, if this thing becomes a regular topic on the news and it gets out how many of them are here illegally, they'll be deported—what other option would the government have?"

The two men regarded one another.

"I understand you have a job to do," Bishop continued, "but these people, they just want to be left alone, to remain in the shadows." He looked intently at Drinkwine. "And just think, these are the lucky ones. Do you realize what these people went through to get here?"

Drinkwine looked up from his notepad.

"Yes, Detective, to get here, to get to this," as he swept his arm to suggest the great nothingness. "How bad were their lives on Earth, and the Moon, that this, this," he emphasized with disgust, "was worth it? And as pitiful as it may seem, they fear losing it. They would be happy if this whole thing just went away, so that that spotlight of a badge and the righteousness of the law would stop shining on them and just let them dig the rock out of this fucking place."

"Whether they want to talk to me or not doesn't really matter," Drinkwine sighed. "They will talk to me. They have to. It's the law."

"On Earth, Detective," Bishop reminded with more sympathy than malice, "on Earth."

The two men sat quietly for a moment, Bishop subconsciously tapping his pencil against the desk in time to a pneumatic jackhammer chipping into rock somewhere out there among the mining operation.

"Right now," the life-tired foreman continued, "all they see is some needless toiling that threatens them."

"'Needless toiling,'" Drinkwine repeated, "a man was killed."

"Yes, someone was killed," Bishop responded, exhausted. "Maybe they had it coming. You ever think of that? What if all your questions and righteousness just turns up some sordid behavior that resulted in exactly what the man deserved? Either way, do you really think any of them give a high fuck about someone who had the good fortune to get murdered?"

A distant siren bellowed through the night above the churning noise of the mine. A moment later another of the underground concussions of a distant charge of dynamite passed beneath the work shed in a tremulous wave.

"You may think I'm being an ass," Bishop offered. "Actually, I kinda' like you for some reason. I don't know, maybe it's the name," eyeing the fine linen, "or the suit." He rubbed his eyes, tired, "Maybe it's because we're not that far apart."

Drinkwine stopped writing. "Excuse me?"

"Don't be so shocked. You and I are resented for our position," he said, staring at Drinkwine. "I'm a foreman, you're a man of the law. We have educations, we represent authority. We have to walk the line between all these things we've been handed, our stations in life, if you will."

Drinkwine closed his notepad, experience telling him the conversation having turned to philosophy that the useful information to be had was at an end. He nodded slightly in agreement as to the sad reality of what Bishop had said. He gathered himself and rose out of the chair. Bishop followed suit, rising to show him to the door.

Before he opened the door, Bishop tilted his head toward Drinkwine's chest. "That badge under your jacket, the questions you bring, your arrival, it's everything they feared was coming." Bishop continued, "But I'm afraid all you've done here tonight is put a face to that fear."

Bishop opened the door, letting the noise from the ceaseless grind of work fill the work shed. "Don't be ruinous, Detective," he advised in parting with an unintentional foreboding as to what may lay ahead for him.

As Drinkwine emerged from the shed into the noise of the mining operation he could feel the fall of eyes on him. As he crossed the frenetic work area, seeking out anyone who might give him a moment, Drinkwine became aware of the precarious ballet of creaking cranes overhead; a confusion of industry without any oversight for safety, the danger heightened by the turmoil of shadows struck by blinding work lights in the blackness. He felt the thinness of the atmosphere exerting its strangling effect on him and had to slow his stride in order to appear stolid.

Each attempt to approach groups of workers was met with a scattering. They disappeared like scared rats into hidden coves and behind racks of piping, slithered behind wheels of cable and scrambled over mounds of rock. The thin air prevented Drinkwine from giving chase. He understood their reaction, knew it was futile to try and garner any useful information from them. They wouldn't speak to him. He decided this was enough for now, let them see the stranger that had come. Perhaps it would diffuse their preconceived animosities. Besides, they would all be summoned to an interview, for which they must attend. Fuck them and their concern over their docked pay. Fuck them, Drinkwine said to himself. Nothing more of the night could be done, so he retraced his path to the dirt ramp that led out of this.

Drinkwine laboriously ascended from The Hole, leaving behind the monotonous clamor of the machines. As he approached his rover he saw that the windshield had been smashed—a spider web of fractures spreading across the width of the glass.

Nearby, huddled together, a group of dust-covered workers smiled with twisted pride and bold challenge at their malevolence. Drinkwine looked into the threatening faces—all of them American. They had the ignorant, violent indifference of wild animals in their eyes. These were his fellow Americans, he thought to himself. He resented them their ignorance. Yeah, fuck them, he declared in unspoken consultation with himself.

Helpless against them in their numbers, Drinkwine climbed into the rover. When he shut the door behind him to lock out their stares the force shuddered through the fractured glass in a rippling,

76

crunching wave. As the rover pulled away in a rattling of tread an empty bottle sailed through the Martian night and smashed against the roof. A rise and fall of laughter pierced the night, acquainted with some profanities thrown out in English that chased after the rover. How ironic, the first people he'd encountered here who had English as their first language had used it in such viciousness. Drinkwine pushed the rover to speed, repeatedly looking in the rearview mirror at the receding threat, the insidious laughter sliding further and further into the darkness behind.

†

Drinkwine had stopped the rover on a crest of dune. It was quiet and still and dark here under the perfect black canopy of night. He was loitering, enjoying another one of his Hollands. Yes, he was devouring them at an alarming rate, but he justified it against the stresses of threat and the ugliness he'd just encountered. Surrounded by blackness he felt suspended in space. The only thing corrupting the perfectly inked landscape was the sparkling city of Jannah, far off in the distance. Through the cracked webbing of the smashed windshield the city was an island adrift, sparkling jewel-like against the Martian night, appearing like a child's play toy.

To the east, he saw the tiny blue orb of Earth beginning its slow rise into the night sky. Before him was the city. Behind, the malice of dangerous men. And out there, far away, was home.

Eventually the Holland had been smoked down as far as it could go. Drinkwine crushed it out, then reluctantly turned the rover toward the sparkling gold and blue lights of the city and made his way, without great purpose, toward the remote outpost of life.

As the rover descended the dune, headlights illuminating the sand and rock ahead, Drinkwine thought of the covering of night, the anonymous black, where lay the germ of ill thought among men. Night gave measure to their disturbing contemplations, their obscene desires, their animal brutality. Night was the time for crimes, where cruel notions festered.

Drinkwine recalled a beautiful spring day at university when they were studying the inordinate percentage of crimes carried out at night as opposed to the number that unfolded during daylight hours. He remembered being seated next to a row of windows opened to the warm blossoming of nature and thought how the somber theme of that lecture unfolded with odd contradiction against the smells of spring. Blackness. Mars had it in abundance.

†

Tiredly making his way to his room, Drinkwine brushed the irritating sand from his scalp, wiped the grains of sand from his eyes. It was late. The day, and the night had been trying. He wiped the dusted lens of his glasses against the sleeve of his linen suit, leaving a faint residue of red. Running his palm over the I.D. sensor the bolt slid back.

As he opened the door the light of the hall spilled into the room, the narrow slash falling across the bed. Drinkwine stopped. The covers were drawn up over a body. As his eyes adjusted to the darkness he saw it was Atefeh, asleep in the bed. Her clothes were draped neatly over a chair. In her sleep she wheezed slightly. Her mouth was open and a small trail of saliva streaked her chin. Her hopeful intent of a romantic liaison had been dashed by the lateness of his arrival.

Careful not to make a sound, Drinkwine backed out of the room, quietly closing the door behind without disturbing her uneven breaths. Standing in the hall, Drinkwine longed deeply and tiredly for the comfort of the bed, where, presently lay an unwanted seduction. Uncertain what to do, Drinkwine reclined on the sad couch in the corridor. Head falling back in exhaustion, he let out a sigh. He closed his eyes and easily drifted off to sleep.

†

_____Chapter 11

T HE MARTIAN DAWN WAS introducing the first hints of light to the corridor in long, gold shafts. Tweaked uncomfortably on the small couch, Drinkwine had his red-stained linen jacket drawn over him like a blanket. He woke to the sound of the door bolt being drawn back. He watched as Atefeh, slightly disheveled, dressed in the clothes of the previous night, came out of his room. She froze when she saw him there on the couch. Their eyes met. Her blank face gathered into that scorn of a woman whose bold advances have been rebuffed. In a confusion of anger and humiliation, without a word, she hurried off down the corridor, wanting only to be gone. Drinkwine thought to himself; Hell hath no fury like a woman not propositioned.

Drinkwine took stock of his pathetic situation. His face hung with exhaustion. His suit and shoes were filthed with the sludge of The Hole. He had not slept much at all, cramped by the couch into an unnatural bend, for which he would pay the price for several days. Rising with difficulty, the stiffness permeating his entire body, he looked out the fourteenth floor window at the creeping dawn. Down below, in their morning ritual, the broom men waded into the fresh carpet of sand that had draped the streets during the night.

†

The shower ran hot, steaming the bathroom mirror. Drinkwine was letting the water run over his tired body, creaked from cramped sleep. He turned off the water and dried himself. As he wiped the condensation from the mirror he ran a cotton-swabbed stick in his ear. It came out covered with red residue. When he caught sight of himself in the reflection through the dense steam he was stopped in his actions. Drinkwine thought he was looking at some old person who had entered the bathroom uninvited. He studied the tired, aged face staring back at him, wondering who this old man was that he was responsible for shaving every morning.

†

The marble floor that led to Kurian's office in the embassy building echoed Drinkwine's footsteps as he strode the austere corridor. The fountain that adorned the lobby had yet to be plumbed, so it sat idle, the curvaceous jugs the joyous stone statues hoisted heartily overhead, tilted to relieve them of their contents, poured nothing but emptiness for the time being.

When he arrived at the open door of the office the two Middle Eastern female secretaries standing there looked surprised, their girlish laughter abating upon sight of him. Drinkwine wasn't sure if it was his presence as a white, or merely anyone, as the embassy had little to no business to occupy itself, and therefore visitors were uncommon. If it was his color, their reactions were understandable, their apprehensions presaged by decades of violent erosion of civility in America. He was quick to put them at ease with, "Good morning, I'm Detective Drinkwine, here to see Ambassador Kurian."

†

Drinkwine was escorted into Kurian's office by one of the women who obediently stopped at the door, gesturing for him to enter.

Kurian looked up from reading on his thin, translucent blue glass reader, the text of a document written in Urdu visible in reverse. He was dressed in another of his perfectly tailored silk suits, this one a matching paisley pattern of green and orange slacks and jacket with a brass button vest that augmented alligator shoes. "Well, good morning Detective. Sleep well?"

The comment inadvertently felt like some inside joke, as if the Ambassador was in collusion on the previous evening's failed sexual interlude. Drinkwine stared at Kurian, looking for any hint of knowledge about the embarrassingly awkward encounter with Atefeh. No, there was no way. He was just being paranoid.

"Fine, thank you." Drinkwine settled into one of the plush chairs before Kurian's large oak desk. Hardwood desks were a sign of status, having to be brought up from Earth at great expense due to their weight and size. "Do you have the list of names I requested?"

Kurian peeled a single sheet of paper from his polished desk and handed it over. "Yes, these are the names of all the people who would have had clearance to reserve a rover during the stated period," Kurian continued, "as well as those who have access to the buildings where the weapons are under lock and key."

Studying the list, Drinkwine asked, "And, the interviews?"

"All arranged," Kurian answered politely, "scheduled for today and the day after tomorrow. We've put you in one of the offices here. Your first appointment is at 9:30," the Ambassador said as he glanced at the large gold watch on his thin wrist.

Drinkwine checked his own watch; a shopworn timepiece without prominence or pretense. "I'd like to see the secure room where the guns are kept."

Kurian responded with a dutiful nod of the head, but not without revealing a hint of inconvenience. With an exaggerated gesture he turned his reading device off and scraped his large leather chair back from the desk.

†

The attending security officer used one of a dozen keys on his belt ring to unlock the metal gun locker. When he opened the cabinet Drinkwine saw the six pre-shaped enclaves that harbored five Roches riot guns. One of the docks was empty.

"How many people have keys to this cabinet?" Drinkwine asked.

The officer seemed reticent to impart the information, before offering in broken English, "Myself, and four other officers."

"I'd like to speak with them," Drinkwine said as he studied the cabinet. "Also, I'll need to see the logs."

The officer's brow furrowed, "Excuse me?"

"The gun logs," Drinkwine repeated. "The paperwork for who took charge of which weapon, when." He saw the confusion in the officer's face. "Certainly, being an arm of government, you have administrative protocol for these weapons."

After Kurian translated Drinkwine's words the officer and he had a brief discussion in Farsi. The Ambassador addressed Drinkwine, "He says that the only time the logs were noted was upon delivery."

"And when was that?" Drinkwine asked, anticipating an answer to support his failing impression of the organizational competency here.

After another brief exchange in Farsi, Kurian turned to Drinkwine. "Sometime in February."

Drinkwine looked at the two men in turn. "Do they realize, that if the weapons aren't maintained and serviced regularly they're useless? Or worse, they'll blow up in your hand."

Kurian took this as accusation against his people. "Detective, we are a peaceful society. The only reason we even have the weapons is because of an archaic law on the books which, strangely enough," with a flippant wave of his small hand, "is a remnant of American Imperialism, that declared each colony have them." Then, with caustic tone, "Rest assured, that ruling is being appealed. Until then, we have abided the law and have fulfilled the requirements."

Drinkwine's eyes were a more emphatic dressing down than anything he could have drummed up in words. By routine, yet assuming the answer, he asked, "Did any of his officers think to dust the cabinet for prints?"

After another exchange in Farsi, that seemed to go on longer than warranted, Kurian translated, "No. They weren't aware they were supposed to."

"Was that really all he said?" Drinkwine asked, "It appeared like he said a great deal more."

Kurian just stood there, his lips pursed, eyelids fluttering nervously with repeated, uncomfortable blinks.

Drinkwine considered, then motioned that the officer was free to close the cabinet, which he did with more force than necessary, the rattle of the metal resonating defiantly through the empty offices.

The attending officer was dismissed and eagerly made his way down the corridor of the building, as if some urgent task was awaiting him. Unlikely. Drinkwine took up at the large plate glass window that had a view of the desert.

Kurian stood nearby, attentive, poised with bent arm, another of his monogrammed white handkerchiefs clutched to his chest, waiting for Drinkwine to speak.

"So," Drinkwine began, "we have a murderer out there, in possession of a weapon."

"Come now, Detective," Kurian responded in disbelief, "do you really think the person would be so stupid as to not have disposed of it by now?"

"What would make you assume that?" Drinkwine said, staring out across the desert.

"That would certainly be my inclination," Kurian said glibly.

"Yes, 'your inclination,'" Drinkwine uttered. "Unfortunately we don't know *their* inclination." Drinkwine absently ran his finger along the windowsill, leaving a small trail in the thin film of red dust that had managed to seep in around the seals of the windowpanes. "A Roches riot gun with as many as a dozen charges still in it. I need to assume it's still in the murderer's hands," he came back as he wiped the dust off his finger. "I'd be foolish to think otherwise."

Kurian was staring at the back of Drinkwine's head. "I suppose, given your position, you need always to assume the worst in men."

The Ambassador was pitying him now. Drinkwine didn't respond, choosing instead to gaze out at the plains of Mars.

†

The first round of interviews went exactly as Drinkwine expected they would; a pointless parade of well-schooled researchers, scientists, and various employees with clearances who—in various languages translated by Kurian—all uttered an endless litany of, "I don't recall," "I'm not sure," "I wasn't there," and more than one fuming at the thought of a white man asking them accusatory questions and exclaiming, insulted, "Am I a suspect!?"

In turn, each interviewee printed their name and office affiliation on the official interview form and signed it in affirmation that what they were saying was the truth, the whole truth, and nothing but the truth. As each interviewee rose from the questioning chair, eager to be done with the intrusive and insulting ordeal, Drinkwine would make notations on character traits and disposition in the margins of the paperwork that might come into play later. One never knew. Then he would sign on the line at the bottom as proof that the person had complied with the request of the Office of the Ambassador as regards to the ugly matter of murder.

After the final morning interview, before breaking for lunch, as Drinkwine made notes alongside the last interviewee's name, a siren rang through the concrete canyons of Jannah with a haunting wail, reminiscent of the air raid sirens on Earth. Drinkwine looked to Kurian for explanation.

Checking his gold watch, Kurian said matter-of-fact, "The sunstrike," before returning to his various Ambassadorial duties.

Drinkwine rose to look out the window at the city as the warning siren continued its disturbing howl. He watched as the few pedestrians that were on the walkways quickly scattered, taking refuge inside buildings. The cars on the avenue accelerated with purpose and disappeared into underground garages, leaving the streets eerily empty. The workers combing the high rises took cover in the appointed safety shelters. In a matter of moments the entire city of Jannah had been dipped into a funerary atmosphere.

As the siren continued its painful bellow, Drinkwine watched the skies transcend various shades of blue to increasing intensities of brightness.

Without taking his eyes from his screen text, Kurian reached with practiced ease for a wall switch that altered the sheath of chemically treated material imbedded in the windows, electronically tinting them with dark fields of neutral-density filter to ward off the coming glare. The room was simultaneously cooled with a heightened blast of air conditioning, the temperature plummeting as the outside world swelled to baking, the two environments counterbalancing one another to accommodate the radical shift.

Watching the transformation, Drinkwine was enthralled by the power the Myoko mirror was able to deliver from its silent orbit four hundred kilometers above. He pressed his hand against the windowpane to feel the immense heat that was pounding the city, radiating off the towering skyscrapers. The building creaked, expanding against the sudden rise in temperature. Even with the neutral density filters in place the view beyond the window was obscured in a haze of blistering glare. Drinkwine squinted into it.

Through it all the siren continued its haunting cry, baying like some wounded animal in the distance, caught in the jaws of a predator. Then, as quickly as the blinding white and blistering heat had taken the city, it subsided. The siren stopped, the vestiges of its cry fading off. In moments the sky was returned to its previous pale blue as the outside temperature fell back to its pre-assault level. Drinkwine watched as the pedestrians resumed their routines and cars took up in their various ventures down the thoroughfares of Jannah as if nothing unusual had transpired. Drinkwine ruminated on what Atefeh had so rightly proffered; Mars had happenings according to its own weird. Yes, absolutely goddamned right, he thought to himself; happenings according to its own weird.

What Drinkwine found most perplexing was how unaffected Kurian was by the whole affair. During the entire ordeal he had steadfastly made notes in his official journal, unperturbed by the rage pounding the city. Perhaps his months and years here, enduring the daily hits, had calloused him. What else had he been calloused to, Drinkwine thought to himself.

"Detective," Kurian broke the quiet of the large office. "There is a gathering tonight, if you wish, at the Ambassador's Mansion. Nothing too formal, just a get together." Kurian continued tapping away on the keys of his translucent computer glass. "There will be people there who would like to meet the man who has come up from Earth to conduct a formal investigation."

†

Chapter 12

I N THE PRIVACY OF his room Drinkwine studied the growing wall
of investigation. A large poster board had been procured and was
pinned together in a map of notes and photos and facts—of which
there were few. A piece of string connected the pushpins in a tapestry
of speculation. Though impressive in its detail and execution, it
offered precious little in terms of genuine value. He'd been here
before; the inevitable lull preceding the windfall of leads. Still, it
frustrated him to have so little to go on.

Looking out from the fourteenth floor at the budding city beyond,
Drinkwine was painfully aware that down there, among the
pedestrians, the cranes, and the smiles, was a killer. A knock at the
door pulled him from his thoughts.

Drinkwine opened the door to a porter standing there with one of
his linen suits, freshly laundered, draped over his small arms. After
an exchange of niceties in their respective languages the porter gently
handed over the suit, excusing himself with a bow and retracing his
path down the hall with quiet strides.

After closing the door Drinkwine crossed to the closet, ripping the
plastic off the hanger. As he hung the laundered garment up he
noticed that the hem of each trouser was stained with a faint,
stubborn imprint of red, the Martian sand having imbedded itself
deep in the threads of the fine linen.

†

The formerly attired doorman escorted Drinkwine, fastidious in another of his perfect white linen suits, up the grand staircase of the Ambassador's Mansion. He was being led toward the din of a social gathering; sparse tinkling of glasses accompanying a soft cacophony of conversations in foreign tongues.

The doorman led Drinkwine into a large sitting room. At the far end—seated around the stone hearth of a fireplace that held a perfectly built fire—were a dozen women with long, passive expressions. They were mostly Middle Eastern and Asian, dressed elegantly in expensive gowns. They had been sitting quietly, sipping at their fine crystal glasses of expensive fizzy water until Drinkwine entered. His arrival got several of them to whispering into one another's ears. The doorman retreated without a word. Not sure where to stand or what to do, Drinkwine felt uneasy, his gaze drifting about the ornate room. He realized that what at first had appeared to be a blazing fire in the stone fireplace was in fact a plasma screen carrying a 3-D image of perfectly licking flames. Happenings according to its own weird.

After a moment Kurian appeared, entering the sitting room through a heavy oak door that was flush with the wall, almost like a hidden passage. He immediately spotted Drinkwine and made directly for him. He was wearing yet another audacious silk suit, this one brilliant purple, immaculately accessorized right down to the purple silk handkerchief folded with perfect triangles in his breast pocket. "Detective, so good to see you, thank you for coming."

Kurian linked his arm through Drinkwine's and led him, without acknowledging any of the women, toward the oak door and the room beyond. "This is an opportunity for you to meet some of the influential people here, an opportunity to ingratiate yourself to them." And on that, Kurian pushed through the flush oak door.

The small sitting room on the other side of the wall from where the women waited was constructed of fine wood and set with plush leather couches where men of Middle Eastern, Asian, and Russian blood were gathered in circles of discussion. The room lifted and fell with occasional laughter in response to various humors. What Drinkwine found interesting was the presence of alcohol and tobacco. Each man held a glass and had a lit cigar in his hands. They blew smoke into the stale air from their circles of conversation that mingled with the clinking of ice. Several of the guests turned at his arrival.

Here were the power players that were settling Mars, dressed in fine tunics, thobes, and tailored suits, with their expensive watches and jewelry. The room reeked of wealth. Drinkwine was acutely aware that these were the very men who were benefitting handsomely from the gruesome, backbreaking work of the mining operations. They were a far cry from The Hole, far removed from the numbing tendencies of the jackhammers that were dredging the ore out of the planet—far from the stench of hydraulic fluid and the raising of granite dust that was paying for all this.

Drinkwine immediately spied the bar where a lavish array of exclusive whiskeys, bourbons, and Scotches were lined up, tempting his severely dry palate. He was mesmerized, looking at each label in turn, absently licking his lips like a man who has been lost in the desert and is now spying water. Placed as proud centerpieces along the bar, lit by the sharp beams of small spotlights, were bottles of Dalmore, Macallen, Mortlach, and a Glenfiddich, all of which Drinkwine had only seen in photos. Here they were. He knew the bottle of Glenfiddich, the finest of Scotches, had a price in the neighborhood of a quarter of a million dollars in US currency on Earth.

Observant enough to see Drinkwine's awe, Kurian was quick to pacify, "What will you have, Detective?"

"Scotch," he blurted out a little too eagerly. "The Glenfiddich," he followed, absent his usual careful deliberation of response.

Kurian spoke to the bartender in Farsi. He turned back to Drinkwine, "How do you take it?"

"Neat," Drinkwine responded, close to salivating.

Kurian smiled slyly, having discovered the detective's soft spot, then translated to the bartender who retrieved the ornate bottle. Drinkwine watched as the luscious liquid was carefully poured to fill a glass, which was then presented to him. He raised the glass to his lips and savored the first sip of alcohol he'd had in seven weeks. He gave himself this little indulgence, letting down the stern, principled demeanor in favor of experiencing perhaps the universe's finest Scotch. He felt he owed himself this much. And if they were pouring, he wouldn't deny them their hospitality.

Kurian took special pleasure in watching Drinkwine's appreciation. He let him have a moment before asking, "Cigar?"

Drinkwine was still savoring that first sip of the Glenfiddich, letting it wallow in his mouth and tingle his tongue. His expression said it all.

Kurian laughed out loud, opening a fine wood case on the bar filled with perfect rows of Gurkha Black Dragons.

Drinkwine knew Kurian was trying to butter him up. How stupid did he think he was? Regardless, he plucked one of the cigars from the box. From out of nowhere a pretty young Iranian girl appeared wearing a tight Turkmeni dress, holding an ornate gold-plated wand in her bejeweled fingers that had a perpetual flame burning at the end. She demurely presented the lighter. As Drinkwine ceremoniously puffed the expensive cigar to life he realized that the holder of the lavish lighter was in fact, a boy. Happenings according to its own weird, he thought to himself as the tobacco glowed and the cigar took.

The smooth tobacco mixed with the fine Scotch in an elixir of excess. Drinkwine told himself he would regain his professional composure and ethics after this momentary detour into extravagance. Certainly he deserved that much, didn't he?

The room was clouded with a dense atmosphere of expensive, exhaled smoke from the lips of the urbane men, all with deep ties and influence over the vigorous and prodigious transformation of Mars. Under a vibrant cacophony of dialects, superficial arguments over business and politics were punctuated with laughter—the room intoxicated with an underpinning of the mad grab for wealth.

After all, this was the American Old West during the heady time of the Gold Rush. And who made money during the Gold Rush? Drinkwine thought to himself cynically; the men who sold the shovels. Well, these men here, in their silk dishdashas and tailored threads, puffing out thousand-dollar clouds of pale blue smoke between their pontifications, were the sellers of shovels on a grand scale.

Drinkwine was fully aware of the inquisitive looks he was receiving; all begging introduction. The men regarded him like some circus act—or perhaps one of their caged rare animals—with a curious air of novelty to it all; a white man, an educated white policeman, from America, here, conducting an investigation.

Moreover, Drinkwine discerned simmering reservations. It was to be expected, after all, these were the men tied to heavy investments, to which the future of their fortunes may well rest in what would transpire here with him and his findings over the coming weeks. He could feel their uneasiness, their questions, their less-than-sincere efforts—under the guise of friendly banter—to get acquainted with the man who had come to delve into their private society. Drinkwine ascertained correctly that these were the men who, behind closed doors, had impressed upon Kurian to do all that was possible to pacify him and cater to his whims to help soften any findings that threatened their interests. As a result, Kurian was exhibiting a joy in having found what he believed to be some corruptibility in the detective's weakness for good liquor.

Over the course of the following hour, reluctantly, Drinkwine was led about the room like a quaffed poodle, Kurian eagerly spiriting introductions with so-and-so, and so-and-so, who worked for such-and-such; and here was Mr. Sedeghi, head of Bank of Iran—and Mr. Wong, with the Chinese Embassy—oh, and Mr. Moisiev, with the Russian Heavy Industries Company, Zardk. Even for a man of Drinkwine's capacity for the intake and retention of a great amount of information it was all a bit of a blur.

Through it all, the yapping mouth of Kurian enthusiastically spewing bits of verbal garbage. For an Ambassador he was a little too impressed by the power and wealth in the room, always a hold of Drinkwine's arm, in between the empty introductions leading him to the next frivolity with a clandestine lean into him with whispered gossip about the pending, costly divorces and the various mistresses ensconced in the Tower Suites; the height of status among apartment buildings reserved for mistresses. The gossip provided Drinkwine with a more in-depth reveal of the little brown man divulging it, than the trite information could ever provide about the men in question.

Beleaguered, Drinkwine found himself dragged into various clusters of conversation where the men haughtily tossed out opinions about the state of things, such as how settling Mars would be the greatest achievement of man. They proselytized how new alloys would allow for yet taller skyscrapers and increased speeds of travel. How it's a pity that a beautiful place like Tuscany had to be decimated with an H-Bomb, when in fact it was but a small minority of Italians that were rebelling against the country's acquisition by

China.

Drinkwine listened to the various diatribes, wishing he had the balls to tell them all how full of shit they were, and how crappy the quality was of the build of their precious skyscrapers. But instead he just smiled and let them talk. It was best when you were in a room of men with erroneously inflated egos. The mere fact that these men had conjured great fortunes out of their respective industries predisposed them to arrogance and a distasteful sense of entitlement that could never be reasoned with. Also, these men, these scheming men, were not accustomed to having their ideas and opinions questioned, certainly not by a white.

In passing there was strangely candid talk of Drinkwine being an American, which ushered in a comment by an acerbic Arab, "America was great once, yes, but that was a very long time ago."

"It's a wasteland now," an overweight Iranian offered, fingers turning an expensive cigar around in his mouth as he spoke, the tip soiled by his prodigiously wet lips.

The comment sparked another, a Japanese man, to say, "Yes, but let's not bite the hand that feeds. Think of the labor force that America's decline has provided for us here. Wonderfully low wages and the abolition of meddling unions."

The Arab stroked his eyebrow, "Ah, but the Americans seem grateful."

"Yes, well," Kurian contributed, "a tin plate serves some as equally as fine china."

"True, true," came out of a Saudi in thoughtful repose. His nodding introducing a small circle of heads bobbing in agreement.

What Drinkwine found most fascinating was that none of the gathered men seemed to think that their words would offend him as an American, as a white. They were too obtuse. Then the topic turned, as it always did, to his name.

"Drinkwine, such an odd name."

"Drinkwine, is that actually a family name?"

To which Drinkwine waded through his tired responses.

As the evening wore on and the novelty of Drinkwine was diffused, some of the men ventured to ask about the investigation. They were seeking answers to assuage their concerns—not for justice, but for their investments. After all, nothing quite derails the value of real estate quite like a murder. Drinkwine wanted to tell them to get used to it, that there were going to be plenty more in the years ahead. He deeply wished to say that this was merely a formality, the busting of Mars' immaculate cherry with the harsh reality of its first cold-blooded murder. But Drinkwine was too polite for that.

"Surely, Detective," began one rant, "you don't believe this thing that has happened has any larger bearing than that of some argument among the lowers?"

To which Drinkwine could only benignly respond, "Well, we'll have to wait and see what surfaces."

"Detective, I've read your book."

It was a powerfully-built Russian. He looked like a boxer in a nice suit. His nose had been broken somewhere along the path to his wealth, probably early on in rough and illegal dealings slugging his way out of the Moscow ghetto. Finely tailored clothes could never fully hide a man's roots if he was from the streets. Drinkwine wondered what line of work he was in. Probably heavy construction, where it was rumored the most brutal threats and exacting bribes won the more lucrative contracts. The Russians seemed to have a knack for that.

"You suggest that man has evolved past basic primal instinct, beyond acting on impulse," the Russian's words were muddled by what appeared to be a limitation in the movement of his jaw. "Violence playing out only with reason?"

Drinkwine felt the eyes of the circle fall on him. "That would be over simplifying the science. But yes, in general, when it comes to homicide, I believe man has arrived at a place where technocracy has altered certain patterns. There must be some gain to be had to warrant it."

"Descartes' 'rational man?'" an East Indian man suggested.

The astute observation impressed Drinkwine. The Indian gentleman quieted any further comment with a sip of his bourbon.

"My friend," a small Iranian began.

But Drinkwine clung to; *my friend*. Why do they say that when you've only just met?

"Are you saying that gone are the random and senseless killings that plagued your country at the end?"

"My country is still intact," Drinkwine patiently responded. "But if you're referring to the recent civil war, that would be politically motivated... again, reason."

"Ah, but a shadow of its former glory," a handsome, square-jawed Saudi mused.

The Russian, who had not taken his eyes off of Drinkwine, then spoke, his deep voice softening, "A lot of savvy American businessmen profited nicely from that demise." He said it with disturbing praise. "They saw the end coming and parceled out the vast open plains for foreign countries to dump their refuse. Brilliant."

Drinkwine studied the cold calculation in the big Russian's eyes. He appeared to be taunting him. "I suppose, if you want to call turning a beautiful country into a dumping ground 'brilliant.'"

"They made billions," the Russian proclaimed, deeply envious.

"Well," Drinkwine came back, "trading money to destroy nature might be perceived by some as short-sighted."

The Russian just smiled as he sipped his Vodka, his eyes taking inventory of Drinkwine's responses.

What an ass, Drinkwine thought, as he tipped his Glenfiddich back.

"The ways of America, with its wars and its international meddling, would eventually come to no good, everyone knew this," a rotund, high-voiced Pakistani proffered. "They were still depending on their facility at making war to usher them into the 22nd Century, trying to conquer and reshape the Earth with brute force, with violence. Didn't they realize those wars cost money to fight?"

"Now, the fountain pen does that," a Japanese man uttered, smirking as he stared into the stirring of ice in his glass.

"The fountain pen has its own degree of brutality," Drinkwine came back, which quieted the circle as each man drank and smoked, nodding in agreement.

☦

Having escaped the room of foreign tongues and exhausting pomposity, Drinkwine explored the mansion, coming upon a beautifully appointed study, walled with cherry wood bookcases reminiscent of an old English manner. He eagerly perused the

93

JEFF BUCHANAN

impressive collection of leather-bound literary classics lining the shelves, which reached to the ceiling. He was surprised to see a very old volume of *Moby Dick*, the title embossed in lacily scrawled gold leaf down the spine. He reached for it, hungry to see Melville's words on fine paper, only to discover that the book was in fact part of a large plastic façade. Bewildered, Drinkwine realized there wasn't an actual page of text in the entire study.

Leaving the fake books behind, yet wanting to avoid the trying triviality of the conversations in the other room, Drinkwine found refuge on the large stone terrace. What he first believed to be a view of the night sky turned out in fact to be an artificial dome; a miniature scale planetarium with stars projected as a slowly rotating field to mimic the night firmament of Mars. The counterfeit sky was an appropriate coupling to the falsehood of the study, replete with an occasional shooting star. The terrace wall overlooked an artificial jungle of dense plastic foliage; a phony tropical forest to accent the lie of night sky. The setting even had artificial fireflies and a soundtrack of jungle noises to sweep people to some other place— anywhere but here.

Drinkwine surmised the Martian landscape was too unpredictable to chance the annoyance of wind-driven sand blotting out the scenery and hammering attending dignitaries. This was, after all, the Ambassador's Mansion. This was ground zero for the selling of lies and securing of bribes. They dare not risk the undoing of deals on account of some unbecoming weather. Instead, a smart construct of artificial, comfortable environment to seduce and secure the contracts that would make Mars habitable.

Before coming out here Drinkwine had secured a fresh glass of Glenfiddich and snagged another Black Dragon. The smokes and booze he had consumed thus far were the equivalent to perhaps a quarter of his yearly salary. Though the Scotch went down nicely, and the smoke followed it sublimely, Drinkwine wondered, even if he could afford it, given the great strife afflicting the various worlds, would he be able to stomach the guilt that comes with this degree of excess and indulgence for very long? He settled at the terrace wall and closed his eyes as he savored the Scotch and dragged on the cigar.

Audible through the open French doors, behind the sheer drapes wafting in the breeze of the air conditioning, Drinkwine could hear

94

bits and pieces of conversation inside, where men drank expensive black market booze and drew on smuggled cigars. He heard a voice in Farsi say, "Drinkwine, yes, the Detective. He's an American, but still, a very nice fellow." Drinkwine laughed to himself. Another man spoke in Urdu—Drinkwine struggling to translate—"Is Drinkwine really his name, or is that some nom de plume to conceal his true identity?" Drinkwine was immune to the comments from too many years of dealing with it. He heard someone mention the title of his book, *The Alchemy of Murder*, suggesting that it must be enjoying a reprise in sales due the snippets on the news about the murder. This invited another guest to speculate as to what too much news coverage might do to the reputation of Mars. "Yes, this man Drinkwine. He solved the Moon's first murder," which was followed by a flurry of exchanges; "Hadn't there always been murders on the Moon?" "Certainly nothing unusual about that." "No, no, no," a voice fired back, "this Drinkwine solved the Moon's very first murder." Which was followed by, "Well, I don't know anything about that." Another offered, "A well-spoken man, nonetheless."

'A well-spoken man,' Drinkwine thought to himself, humored. You never heard them say how well-spoken an Arab, or a Pakistani was. How many times had he been complimented as to his impressive deportment and breadth of vocabulary; 'Doesn't he have a broad vocabulary for a white?' Always followed by; 'Despite being an American.'

Drinkwine had been promising himself for some time now to tackle the task of learning Farsi or Chinese to better ingratiate himself. It was all part of the great shift, the lines of status that had been drawn and redrawn in the Martian sand. If you planned to have a livelihood, English wasn't the language to have sole custodianship of. Drinkwine had been spared the indignity of poverty because of his chosen field. There was plenty of work for one trained in the art of forensics, regardless of their color or religion. As his chief had once said, 'Crime is a growth industry.'

To help dilute the rash of rude comments Drinkwine took a sip of the Glenfiddich. He thought about his life, how he came to be here; a white man on Mars, drinking expensive booze and smoking a fine cigar. He had been born the final lineage to a once prominent, white family dealing with rapidly declining wealth—which had been burdened further by the exorbitant cost of a formal education for their youngest. Advice had been offered from a number of well-meaning aunts and uncles as to the importance of upholding the family name despite the dour circumstances. It had been decided that young Drinkwine should attend Harvard in order to secure a decent means for himself, as his inheritance had been steadily and systematically siphoned off by the immediate needs of the family and their acquired standard of living.

The great institutions of learning across the country had become the exclusive proprietorship of those with the means to afford it—mostly foreigners. Eventually, due the shifting dynamics of economic inequality, the doors of education closed to the majority of Americans. Drinkwine had the distinction of being the last Caucasian to have graduated Harvard. He was easy to find in the graduating class picture; the lone white face and fair hair in a sea of brown and yellow and black.

In the end, the family was dismayed when their only son chose the unlikely career path of criminal pathologist and forensics, as opposed to a degree in business or law, which was their preference. One particularly outraged aunt had accused young Drinkwine of spite. Drinkwine hadn't taken up his field to spite anyone. He simply was fascinated with the dead. They were no longer alive. They didn't suggest life paths. They didn't meddle in other's affairs.

None of it really mattered. The family was eventually evicted from their sprawling estate when years of debt—afforded by the leniency of the last remaining American financial institution—was called back by the new foreign owners. Some seven generations of Drinkwines was, in essence, wiped out with the stroke of a pen. An inordinate number of relations chose to take their own lives rather than succumb to lives of poverty, the inevitable consequence of those who only spoke English. When Drinkwine accepted his diploma there were no family members to witness it, those who had survived all blown to various corners of the nation and unaware of their nephew's achievement. How odd, now here he was, on Mars, smoking a Gurkha and getting to the bottom of a third glass of Glenfiddich.

In the years since entering the field Drinkwine had come to relish his work. People always asked about how horrid it must be to deal with the dead. It didn't bother him at all. In fact, he preferred the dead to many of the living, partly because the dead don't talk.

They've said all they're going to say and patiently wait out the long hours of toil and study, never complaining about the prodding and poking. They are tirelessly agreeable and conveniently still. They demand no responses to their ideas and thoughts, expect no niceties, and harbor no ill will toward any misstep of manners. They are, quite perfectly, dead.

Memories of his old school days came back to him, perhaps stirred by the solitude of being out here, alone, segregated from the voices in the other room. As a young student Drinkwine had suffered through the indignities of being the only white in school. His skin had predisposed him to isolation. As a result he had only his schoolwork to occupy him. There were none of the nostalgic college high jinks or mischief for him. No, those frivolities had been reserved for the other boys and girls whose family's wealth had already secured for them bright futures. Their schooling was merely a formality, a time to enjoy some of the fruits of carefree youth before they would be handed companies to run. Drinkwine had been, without question, the poorest student in his school. White and poor; two heavy social strikes against him.

His fellow students had made derogatory comments about the financial limitations of solving crimes. That seemed to be their focus; how much money there was to be made. They couldn't fathom why a man would want to limit himself fiscally with the task of solving crimes when it paid so pitifully. All Drinkwine could do with the memories was chuckle about the absurdity of it all as he tilted back the Glenfiddich. The coursing of the fine liquor down his throat dissuaded any serious concern he had about these men, or anyone for that matter, and their views of him, or America, or the work he was carrying out. Yes, he thought, the dead are so much more pleasant.

The moment of quiet contemplation was intruded upon by Kurian, "Ah, Detective, you have found the balcony." The Ambassador took up next to Drinkwine at the terrace wall. "I come out here quite often to think," he said, listening to the soft rush of a simulated stream, closing his eyes and breathing in deeply of the processed air.

Turning to look at Kurian standing there in his purple suit and pointed suede shoes—eyes closed dreamily, doing that little boyish thing of rocking himself up onto the balls of his feet—Drinkwine wondered exactly what it might be that Kurian thought about on the occasions when he repaired to this plastic sanctuary. He allowed him to wallow in his splendor for just a moment before bringing him back to Mars.

"Ambassador," his tone rife with reality. "You know, I will need to question some of these people."

Kurian slowly dropped down from his toes onto his flat feet. His eyes labored open, the weight of what had just been said stirring him uncomfortably. "Detective, must you?"

Drinkwine saw the first crack in the seemingly unflappable courtesy of Kurian, the Ambassador suddenly aware that his little ruse of indulgence hadn't quite taken.

"Detective," Kurian began, his voice unsettled. "These are developers, dignitaries, heads of very important financial institutions, what would they have to do with a murder?"

Over the clink of glasses and the muffled sounds of hypocrisy unfolding inside, Drinkwine responded, "I'm conducting an investigation. I'm trying to find out why someone was killed."

"Why a *worker* was killed," Kurian emphasized, "a worker." He blinked his eyes in agitation. "What has that to do with these men here?"

"For all I know the man was killed because he was going to file a labor dispute, or blow the whistle on a hazardous work environment."

"'Blow the...,' do you mean to suggest, in your parlance," the Ambassador said deprecatingly, "that there might be dubious activity going on?"

"I need to look at all the possibilities." Drinkwine steady, calm.

"I can assure you, those people are not about to make waves. They are quite content to have found jobs." The Ambassador seemed piqued at the mere suggestion. "They would never be so stupid as to do anything to upset that."

Drinkwine didn't answer, letting Kurian stew.

"Detective Drinkwine, I beg of you, don't call these people in. They are engaged in a great many deals. This type of...," fumbling, "... unsavory questioning is an affront to their character, it could jeopardize some of those dealings. Do you appreciate the gravity of this? The amount of money concerned?"

"So then," Drinkwine came back, "how much is a man's life worth?"

Kurian dropped the hand clutching his silk handkerchief to the terrace wall. "Please don't be naïve."

"I need to consider all the angles." With a tired wisdom, "You can't build a society and not expect there to be crime, whether that be among workers, or the leaders."

"Detective, I can assure you, the majority... nay, all of the crimes being perpetrated on Mars have been, and are going to be, the doing of the workers; the whites and the blacks. Surely you know this." Kurian saw Drinkwine's reaction. "It isn't a racist statement. It is proven fact, Detective." Kurian was adamant, "They are prone to deviant behavior,"

"You're so convinced it was a worker."

Kurian looked at him oddly, "Come now, surely you don't suppose..."

"I don't 'suppose' anything," Drinkwine fired back. "I work in facts."

"Then... yes, I believe it was between workers. And I say," handkerchief waving frivolously, "let the workers have their crime," adding shamelessly, "just keep it in the camps, away from the decents."

"And what do you intend to do with the workers after the buildings have all gone up? When the thoroughfares have all been built?" Drinkwine asked point blank.

"You lead me, once again, to arguments that serve no purpose. The important thing is that for the time being there are things to be built, and that is creating jobs." Kurian had stiffened significantly, his slight physique tense. "Do you have some manifest desire to undo the good we've offered these people?" Kurian put forth as a rhetorical question. "Detective, believe it or not, I am trying to assist you. But you must understand that these people here, in that room, are accustomed to a certain amount of respect. To be questioned by a white will never go over well."

Silence between them.

Kurian regained some of his professional decorum. "Why don't we leave this evening for leisure. Give them their Scotch and brandy. We can make this all up in very short order."

Drinkwine was reticent.

Kurian sought a path to soften things. "Tell you what, tomorrow there is an event, which many of the men here, and more, will be attending," Kurian offered in truce. "It's quite monumental, you may actually enjoy it. We're releasing one million Monarch Butterflies into the Martian atmosphere."

Drinkwine considered, trading looks between Kurian and where the voices of men droned on behind the long, draping curtains. "And you'll help pave the way to those people?" Drinkwine asked.

Kurian smiled in subtle victory, raising his handkerchief up against his chest, regaining that conceited stance. "Yes, certainly," relieved, "certainly Detective. So then, until tomorrow?" he asked, hesitantly.

A pause fell between them. Drinkwine mulled it over as the soundtrack of the stream filtered through the artificial night.

Kurian used the pause to excuse himself before another joust of words arrived to undo the moment.

As the Ambassador's footsteps faded off, Drinkwine turned back to the plastic forest and the pre-recorded jungle sounds. He tipped the flaking gray ash of his Gurkha Black Dragon over the edge of the terrace wall, watching a thousand dollars worth of burnt and flaked tobacco fall into the blackness beyond.

†

Night had poured an immaculate blackness out over the Martian landscape. The winds had ceased their virulent whims and repaired for the night to their secret enclaves, leaving unseen in the darkness the perfectly groomed dunes of red sand they had labored over during the course of the day. Out on the plains, mountains of layered shale reached into the night sky, painted in soft gray. The majestic peaks had been here eons before their imported metal brethren polluted the landscape. The stillness placed a false aura of calm over the night that would surely be erased in the coming day with an inevitable rising of winds.

†

Chapter 13

T HE SQUARE IN FRONT of the financial center had been set with several rows of white wooden folding chairs, neatly spaced to face a portable podium. Luckily the Monarch release had been scheduled for early morning to reduce the chances the Martian winds would make a play at upsetting the festivities.

Haunting the shadows of one of the skyscraper's mammoth columns, Drinkwine observed from the distance as a parade of dignitaries waffled through their overlong speeches, painfully thanking a plethora of anonymous people by name. Each speaker in turn took up the mantle, boring the gathered yet further, with virtually everyone attending wanting an end to it, eager to get on with the great spectacle. Mothers and fathers had begun to lose control of their children who had become bored and ornery from the tedium. Dressed in their little jackets and ties they wanted only for the grass, to play, to be children, their simple desires slapped down with the back of a hand and quashed with harsh whispers of threat.

Behind the small stage, several dozen perforated metal boxes had been placed. They held one million Monarch Butterflies that were to be released into the Martian atmosphere. The release of foreign species into the still forming atmosphere (like that of the previous decades' efforts to seed the planet with greenery) was always a gamble. No one could predict how these fanciful events would play out. That didn't prevent the powers that be of making a big show of it with these boring exercises of pomp. As the last of the speakers sent their garbled, amplified words out over the gathered with occasional pops of feedback, one million Monarch Butterflies waited in perforated steel boxes, unaware they were to be set free in a strange place.

Kurian had been first at the microphone over an hour ago to make the initial introductions, and now, after a host of people had been erroneously imbued with some sense of importance and delivered their banal speeches, he returned to wrap things up. Taking the podium, Kurian encouraged ovation among the weary crowd with animated clapping. There was a polite smattering of applause in response, followed by an embarrassing shriek of feedback as Kurian leaned into the microphone, which elicited the biggest reaction thus far from the audience—albeit laughter.

"We thank you, Mr. Asah, for your generous help in bringing this monumental occasion to fruition."

Kurian was enjoying the moment of attention just a little too much. Drinkwine smirked, wondering if this would turn into another monumental fuck-up, like so many other endeavors that had thus far been undertaken here.

"We also would like to thank the 1st Martian Bank Real Estate Development Fund," Kurian continued, "for their contribution to this worthy cause." The Ambassador had to once again prod the audience to show their appreciation by clapping his little, manicured hands together in front of the microphone. It was all so embarrassingly ridiculous.

"And now," Kurian teased with dramatic pause, "the moment you've all been waiting for."

Yes, Drinkwine considered, the moment we've all just been dying for—literally.

"Gentlemen," Kurian uttered with a graceful drop of the arm to cue the handlers. The perforated steel boxes were unlatched and the hinged doors swung open. To the appreciative *oohs* and *aahs* of the gathered, one million colorful Monarchs were freed from entrapment in a beautiful confusion of fluttering color, forming a circling mass of delicately flapping wings that blotted out the sun and set the entire area into a brilliant commotion of dancing shadows. The handlers tapped the metal boxes to spook all the Monarchs from their confinement, until all the boxes were empty.

When Drinkwine saw the crowd immediately rising from their

seats and dispersing, he crushed out the cigarillo he had been clandestinely smoking and made for Kurian. The ambassador was spewing out his pleasantries to some of the attending guests.

"Ambassador," Drinkwine intervened, "you said you would make some introductions."

Kurian raised a finger as if to say wait, turning to address one of the guests.

Drinkwine kept pace with him as he sidled through the crowd. "Ambassador," patience wearing thin.

"Mr. Drinkwine, if you can just give me a moment," Kurian threw over his shoulder as he waded deeper into the crowd, shaking hands and bowing to the cluster of people offering their thanks and appreciation.

"It's Detective Drinkwine," he corrected loudly enough to be heard by those around them.

Kurian was unsettled by the outburst, stopping to lean into Drinkwine and whispering, "This isn't a good time. Let's not mar this joyous occasion with such ugliness, please."

"When *would* be a good time, Ambassador?" He saw Kurian's anxious face. "Ambassador, I'm going to speak to these people, either with your help or without it. It's your call." And on that Drinkwine left a ruffled Kurian to his duties of Ambassadorship, stalking off with angered, impatient strides.

Kurian watched him go, his face awash with concern and uncertainty. He regained his composure and went back to the task of the shaking of hands and spouting of pleasantries.

†

The Martian sky had begun its nightly ritual blush to dusk. Once again the muezzin's call to prayer filled the concrete canyons of Jannah, the pre-recorded tape echoing hauntingly with a hissing of white noise and distortion that lent a charming, somewhat humorous sentimentality to it all. The streets were soon empty of inhabitants, all finding their way to places of prayer. From the vantage point of his room, at this time of evening, the city was a towering garden of tall cranes silhouetted against the fading sky. Motionless, the cranes had been silenced with the end of the workday. The crews, the men and women who were raising these steel and concrete giants out of the sand and nothingness, had been shuttled back to their quarters. Drinkwine ruminated that the laborers, who ceaselessly toiled to fabricate the great wonders, would never be allowed inside the luxurious structures once they were completed. Many of the lowly workers could scarce comprehend the notion of people wealthy enough to afford such lavish living spaces.

With the lace of his untied shoe in his fingers, Drinkwine had been sitting on the edge of his bed for a full minute, lost in trance. He was staring, puzzled and saddened, at a Monarch butterfly squashed into the sole of his shoe. His eyes traced the beautiful and colorful intricacies of design in its delicate, crushed wings.

His befuddlement over the squashed Monarch was usurped by something on the muted TV screen; a clip of him entering the embassy. Drinkwine read the creeping closed captioning in English as the female Pakistani newscaster spoke in silence, her words translated in black and white type: "… police have not ruled out suicide. However, officials declined comment pending further investigation into the death." Drinkwine soiled yet another face towel with red as he wiped his neck and forehead, shaking his head in disbelief.

†

In the darkness of the room Drinkwine lay awake in the bed. It was late. He tried to not think about the scratch of a grain of sand that was irritating his left eye. He had been to the bathroom twice already to try and flush it out, but to no avail. The more he tried to ignore it, the more aggravating the scratching became. He was too exhausted to get up yet again and try to excavate the grain, but too bothered to allow sleep in. The sand, it got into everything.

†

The Myoko mirror sat silent in its perpetual orbit high above Mars. The gargantuan framework held a surface of Mylar panels that reflected sunlight toward the planet below. From afar it was a technical marvel. Upon closer inspection, it was clear the satellite had suffered its abuses over the years, taking a beating from passing meteors so miniscule as to be almost invisible to the naked eye, yet carrying enough velocity to have pierced the Mylar panels, leaving behind millions of tiny holes that let the sunlight pass through, giving it the appearance of a giant sieve. Entire sections of panels had been knocked askew, tethered only by their electrical wiring, buffeted by the invisible currents of space. The complex of supporting alloy framework had been rippled and dented over years of ceaseless celestial hammering.

There were more devastating examples of larger meteors that had smashed into the Myoko during its decades of service, leaving gaping holes large enough to drive a rover through. The once perfect mirror was pockmarked with thousands of such fractures, the result of being estranged in space, without ward, without protection, for all these years. The satellite suffered it all without complaint, continuing its quiet servitude that was reshaping the planet below into something the cosmos had never intended.

†

When Drinkwine arrived for the second day of interviews Kurian's manner had been affected. He wasn't his usual, forced buoyant self and instead tried to pretend to be busy with articles of papers on his desk to avoid eye contact.

"Good morning," Drinkwine addressed Kurian jubilantly, just to antagonize him. The Ambassador glanced up just long enough to nod and force a perfunctory smile. Drinkwine presumed that the powers above Kurian had expressed concern about the visibility of the investigation, having made its way onto the news. Drinkwine could almost feel the lingering warmth of the phone where Kurian's hand had held it as he was admonished by those invisible personages who were most certainly growing anxious over the matter.

"Is everything alright?" Drinkwine inquired.

"Yes, yes, why shouldn't it be?" Kurian came back too quickly to be sincere.

Drinkwine could feel the Ambassador's uneasiness. "What's bothering you?"

Kurian took a breath, "I trust we can do our best to keep this investigation as discrete as possible."

On that, Drinkwine knew the Ambassador had taken a scolding from someone. "It's a murder investigation, Ambassador," Drinkwine said firmly, "it's not a very pleasant thing. I'm being as discrete as I can be."

"I understand," Kurian said, shuffling in his large chair, his reflection spread over the polished surface of the desk. "It's just, I ask that you try and be sensitive as to what a lot of unnecessary press might do to the perception of the colony, a new and critical colony to the future of Mars, and the cosmos," Kurian's voice growing desperate. "A great many people have an investment in the future of this planet. I'm not just talking of investors, but families, children, this is their future home."

Drinkwine studied Kurian hard, trying to decipher the source of this new angst. "If I'm ruffling feathers, those with the ruffled feathers can talk directly to me." He waited for explanation.

"Well," Kurian had to force out. "Yes, there are those who are concerned that this whole…" careful of his choice of words, "situation, not escalate." Kurian was holding one of his fine pens in his delicate fingers, uneasy under Drinkwine's intense stare.

"I've a job to do…"

"…yes, I understand…" Kurian came back, nervously twirling the pen.

"A man has been killed," Drinkwine said calmly.

Kurian dropped the pen, his face raged with red, and blurted out in a fit of anger, "He was just a worker!"

The words hung accusingly in the air. The quiet that settled over the room was rife with revelation. Drinkwine studied Kurian's heightened breathing. He could see Kurian already regretting the irretrievable impropriety of his words.

On that, Drinkwine calmly switched his brief to the other hand, then turned and crossed the office to the door. With one final look back, smiling, enjoying the vague victory, he headed down the hall. Kurian listened as his footsteps strode the polished marble floor leading to the interview room.

†

The second day of interviews was unfolding with the same tediousness as the first go round. Drinkwine was a study in patience as a steady stream of people were paraded through the spare office in the embassy. Nothing of interest, not even the hint of suspicion with any of them. A good many of the workers, those who couldn't read, were unaware a body had even been found and were confused as to what this was all about. Several complained openly about lost wages resulting from the time away from The Hole.

As the day dragged on the interviews transitioned to a higher level of education and position; engineers, managers, accountants. Presently seated opposite, a high-level researcher was expounding on his duties as a climate custodian, excitedly going into great detail about how they measure the temperature and track changes. Drinkwine glanced at the interview registration form, his eyes working to bring the name into focus: Jafar Barr, age 34. Pakistani. Languages; Urdu, Farsi, English.

"I enjoy my work," Jafar droned on, speaking in heavily accented English, "it may seem odd, but I'm happy."

He seemed pleasant enough. Certainly was enthused about his work. Drinkwine had already grown disinterested. There is usually some thread of uneasiness, some residue slip of the tongue with the guilty. That wasn't present here. He was one of the researchers who had access to a rover and had actually secured one around the estimated time frame of the killing. He'd used it to travel to a remote research station.

"What do you do with your free time, Mr. Barr?" Drinkwine asked. "Any hobbies?"

"I like music," Jafar responded, becoming even more effusive, bouncing his shoulders excitedly, "I collect vintage vinyl records."

"Vinyl records?" Drinkwine repeated, but the words seemed to come from someone else.

"Yes, I have a very extensive collection, some two hundred old discs. I play them, on turntables I rebuilt myself," he said proudly. "Vinyl records replicate the music with a quality of audio unmatched by modern digital components. You have to be careful how you handle them, and how you place them on the turntable. It's fascinating, magical really, how the needle draws the music out of the grooves." Jafar waxed philosophical, "Music performed by artists who are all dead now."

Drinkwine wasn't sure if it was the monotony, or merely the man's persona—which was erudite, yet terribly boring—but his mind seemed detached from his head. It was as if his brain had found escape through his ears and was now floating about the room, teetering on a fog of jumbled thoughts. The periphery of his eyes was pulsating with an out of focus rim that appeared to be closing down. He wondered if he was getting sick. After all, most of the dishes served here, with their spicy ingredients, didn't always agree with his stomach.

Snapped from his wandering, Drinkwine suddenly realized that the current subject had been waffling on about his records. He hadn't heard a word. Drinkwine was finding it difficult to maintain his train of thought. He blinked away disconcerting blotches of what appeared to be neon lights shimmering in his lower field of vision. It scared him. He thought for a moment, *Is this what a stroke feels like?* The flickering neon globs were spreading further across his sight.

Jafar stopped talking and lost his smile when Drinkwine teetered slightly in the chair, his elbow sliding off the armrest, snapping him sharply to attention.

"Are you okay?" Jafar asked.

Drinkwine thought perhaps he was going to be sick. His professional composure was evaporating. All he wanted was to lay down.

"Yes, fine, fine," Drinkwine answered, wiping perspiration from his forehead. Suddenly the room went topsy-turvy with the glare of the fluorescent ceiling lights dancing perpendicularly through his line of sight in a gathering fog, then, all went to blackness. Through it all Drinkwine heard Jafar's voice asking repeatedly, "Are you okay?

Are you okay?"

†

The next thing that registered in Drinkwine's head, after what seemed like a long, deep sleep, was the bright yellow paint of the ceiling, an overhead light fixture silhouetting several figures standing over him, speaking in detached voices.

"Mr. Drinkwine, Mr. Drinkwine, can you hear me?"

Drinkwine didn't recognize the voice, or voices, as there seemed to be several chiming in with the calling of his name to try and retrieve him from the edge of unconsciousness. It was all he could do to nod his head and try to form words, but they didn't come. He attempted to sit up but the yellow ceiling spun, dipping off once again to blackness against the chiming chorus of, "Mr. Drinkwine?... Mr. Drinkwine?"

†

When he came to, Drinkwine found himself on the long leather couch in Kurian's office, a moist towel across his forehead. As he blinked himself to consciousness one of Kurian's secretaries came into focus, sitting alongside, gently holding his hand in her dark, lithe fingers with their elaborately painted nails. "There you are." She smiled, relieved.

"What happened, where...?" were Drinkwine's first, confused words.

"It's alright, you fainted," she offered with soft reassurance.

"It's not uncommon," a harsh voice pounded out from the other side of the room, hurting Drinkwine's forehead. A heavyset, dark-skinned man with matted patches of sweat in the underarms of his dress shirt was winding up a stethoscope, which he crammed into a little black bag. "You haven't acclimated to the thin air yet."

"Where…" he repeated as he tried to sit up too quickly, a sharp pain in the head stopping him.

"You mustn't try to get up," the secretary said as she helped support his weight, settling him back onto the couch.

"You're in Ambassador Kurian's office," the doctor said with an air of detachment as he looked at his watch, pulling on his jacket. "Do you remember? You were conducting interviews. You fainted. It's the thin air."

"It happens to most," the softer voice soothed. "It catches up."

As the room settled for him, Drinkwine came to his thoughts again. "Yes, yes, I remember."

"They brought you here," she explained as she handed him a glass of water.

"Drink plenty of water," the doctor barked more than advised.

The secretary smiled at the doctor's harshness, "It helps."

He took the glass and drank, more to appease her kind demeanor than obey the doctor's orders. "Thank you."

"Good day Detective," the doctor tossed into the air on his way out of the office, not bothering to look back. "Plenty of fluids." A door banged somewhere, relieving the room of the man's perspiration.

Drinkwine came around a bit, the room sharper. He immediately felt for his gun, making sure it was there. It was. "What happened to the subjects?"

"The subjects?" the secretary inquired.

"The people I was interviewing?"

"Well, let's see, you almost made it through all of them," presenting the stack of signed releases. "Only the last two were not seen," setting the forms down on the table.

Of all things, Drinkwine thought of her slender fingers, how they had been holding his hand and were now resting on the stack of forms. He wished there was cause for her to resume her nurturing touch.

†

Alone in his room, Drinkwine sat quietly on the edge of the bed, his hands clasped together in thought. The fainting spell had spooked him. For one brief moment, as his body was failing him during the interview, he thought he was having a heart attack. He had feared, what if this is the way his life ended, here, in this Godforsaken place? The thought made him feel horribly alone. The idea that he could pass, and *she* would not know of it for some time. Worse, that she may not be all that moved by it.

Drinkwine was perplexed by the race of emotions. Surely the air was still toying with him, confusing his brain with its thinness. He got up and urgently pulled on his linen jacket, intent on getting out into the desert, into the nothingness, to breathe, to be alone.

†

Drinkwine welcomed the familiar clang and rattle of the rover's treads, the churn of sand behind, as they were all tools that would get him to that remote place of peace and solitude, the only place on Mars that had given him some thread of solace.

Peering out at the passing terrain, Drinkwine studied the horizon, which was once again pouring its lie of water out over the desert in shimmering mirage. A man, thirsty and light of head, could be easily coaxed into chasing that promise of water. What a cruel place, he thought. The ocean of sand possessed quiet tides capable of pulling a man out into the great, suffocating abyss. The malevolent sands were loitering out here in the nothingness, conspiring with the winds in plans for indiscriminant and unbiased, brutal beatings, assault against the greedy conquerors that had come. The planet was doing everything it could to repel these people. He was with Mars on this one.

Drinkwine stared, distrusting, at the desert. He was leery of the unnerving calm. It was said that more than one resident had gone mad with the winds and the ever-present red sand that washed over every inch of everything with a dusting of rebellion. He wiped his perspiring brow with one of his perfect white handkerchiefs. When he removed it he saw a smear of red.

Breaking the stillness, a narrow funnel of sand was roused from the desert floor by the distant winds. Without a sound, it wavered drunkenly, back and forth, stumbling over the emptiness in a misbehaving of balance. Drinkwine watched the dance of the solitary funnel with trepidation, as he knew this was how innocently the pounding storms began. He was relieved when, having found no partner, the swirling column dissipated, spinning itself to nothingness. The sands, the malevolent sands, he thought to himself.

Drinkwine justified yet another of his Hollands, addictively savoring the cigarillo as the steady progress of the rover brought him to the familiar location. He felt a sentimental twinge at sight of the marooned paddlewheel steamer, listing in the motionless ocean of dunes.

The clanging treads were silenced as Drinkwine stopped the rover to gaze at the beautiful boat. It seemed to have acquired an even more regal quality since he first saw it. It appeared to be bravely weathering the storms out here in the middle of the desert, proud of its whimsical nature, which contradicted the obsessive concerns of commerce brewing back there, across the nothingness in Jannah.

Drinkwine approached the paddlewheel steamer. With each step his shoes sank into the soft red sand. He arrived at the bow. There, just below the gunwale, painted in the lacy scrawl of another era was the sun-faded name, Yuki, flaking off in brittle wisps of gold paint. "Yuki," he said to himself. So that was her name; the wife of the sad Chinaman—source of his heartbreak. Drinkwine reached out to gently touch the wafer-thin borders of the gold leaf letters that had been peeled back from the hull by the unrelenting sun. Despite his tender touch the delicate, translucent letters flaked off and floated away.

Pulling himself aboard, Drinkwine wandered the deck. For years it had taken repeated, harsh beatings from the marauding storms. The whipping sands had dulled its shine, but it was still beautiful, Drinkwine thought. A light breeze swept through the boat, creaking doors and unlatched windows, turning the boat into a symphony of soft clanging. It seemed to be grieving its sad fate, its loss of purpose. By the time the waters arrived there would be nothing left of her, Drinkwine considered, as he ran his hand over the smooth teak railing and oxidized brass fixtures.

The tiny cabins of the second floor were looked in one by one as

Drinkwine made his way down the length of the ship. Atefeh had said the Chinese businessman had died here, on the boat, in one of the rooms. As he drew open a door, there on the floor in the lonely cabin, were remnants of the Chinaman's last days; a rumpled gray wool blanket and an empty tin of food, with the spoon still in it. They were in front of a small, makeshift shrine set atop decorative lace, dusted with red sand. A square of tiny bamboo sticks framed a weathered photograph of a woman. Drinkwine respectfully left the picture where it was and squinted to try and get a better look. The photo was too faded to make her out, save for the long, silky black hair. Drinkwine wanted to believe there was great beauty there, enough to warrant this; a grand spectacle of love, wasting away out here in the harsh abuses of the emptiness. He considered the labor, the time, and the money that had gone into this vessel, undertaken out of undying devotion for a woman. To think, she died as they both waited for the water to raise the boat from her moorings of sand.

Drinkwine felt a strange union of pain with the Chinaman. How small and insignificant the world becomes when you lose someone, when the one you love is gone. No measure of logic, no rational thought, no consultations with history can convince a person that they will get past the loneliness, the heartache. When you're in it, there's no reasoning in the universe that can settle a forlorn mind. The odd ways of the heart, they also had happenings according to their own weird. It all felt so unfair and cruel. As proof, here it sat, one man's monument to the calamities of love.

Reaching out, Drinkwine touched the teakwood railing with a gentleness that betrayed him. "If I'd built her a boat," he uttered softly, "would she have stayed?" The words were swept up in a passing breeze that gently rocked the succession of unlatched shutters the length of the boat before dissipating into the desert.

Sitting there aboard the marooned paddlewheel steamer, Drinkwine looked out at the interminable desert. The water. Everyone was waiting for the water; the businessmen—to protect their investments; the pilgrims—to justify the move; the murderer—to conceal his deed. But saddest of all was the Chinaman's boat. Drinkwine suddenly yearned to see just how far the waters were from reaching her.

He slammed the door of the rover and set the coordinates for the blue patch on the GPS. The rover cranked to life and craned around in a semi-circle, the treads churning a circle of berm in the red sand before setting off, steadfast, into the abyss.

†

After twenty kilometers of the mechanical clang of treads across dry rollers, Drinkwine saw the calm, mirror surface of water stretched out across the valley ahead. It glistened in a proud display of life. Drinkwine actually allowed himself a moment to be surprised and thought to himself, *Damn, they're doing it. They're really doing it.*

The euphoria was quickly subdued as the rover approached the stubbornly creeping edge of the forming lake and Drinkwine was overcome by a horrid stench. Bringing the rover to a stop, Drinkwine got out and made careful steps in the muddy periphery to where the water's edge was lapping with lazy deliberation. He looked down to see the slush had already discolored his shoes. The water was perhaps only 200mm deep and covered the area in a motionless, milky sheet. He watched as the lip of the water's edge lapped an ebb and flow of almost imperceptible movement. The ancient water, unleashed from a million years of captivity in the ice by the orbiting Myoko mirror, was flowing in, slowly, without concern of time. How long would it take, Drinkwine wondered, at this rate, to fill the vast basin? He, like all those presently on Mars, might be long dead and buried by the time the lakes had reached maturity.

He didn't linger long. The sentimental feeling he had experienced cresting the rise that gave him view of the basin had been dashed by the stench of the water and the shallowness of its depth. Drinkwine referenced the GPS to plot the most direct route back to Jannah. It quickly mapped the most unobstructed path and the rover clanged forward.

†

After just a few kilometers of deep sand the rover crested a ridge that presented a view of a sprawling mesa. Drinkwine slammed the rover to a stop. He had wondered from time to time about all the industry that had been at work here for the past hundred years, preparing the red planet for settlement. He assumed it had produced a good deal of remnant waste and defunct machinery. Now he knew. Though he wasn't ready for what he saw. Before him, stretching to the horizon, filling the mesa with a palette of rust, was a junkyard of tired and spent machines, a burial ground for worn-out and obsolete technology.

The spent machines had been deposited here, far from view of the city, in a valley of forgotten invention. Old rovers, decrepit cranes, seized-up generators, broken jackhammers and busted hydraulic winches shared equally their useless value. The machinery had been systematically dumped here without being drained of their oils and hydraulic fluid. It was leaking out, coalescing in thick ponds of grotesque, swirling black and purple sludge that seeped into the once pristine desert. The red sands were absorbing the steaming marsh like some large blotter. Mountains of batteries oozed their lifeblood in an acrid leaking of poison. The discolored puddles created a stench that burnt the nostrils and watered the eyes.

Drinkwine pulled his handkerchief from his jacket pocket and covered his mouth and nose to try and ward off the sting and offending smell. He thought, this was but one yard. There were dozens, perhaps hundreds of others. As Drinkwine surveyed the rusted wreckage, he thought of how the machines being employed now to build the metropolis skyward would eventually be relegated to this place. Few people gave thought as to how the great buildings were created. So long as the granite was smooth, the glass clean, the air cooled, they really had no reason to concern themselves with how it came to be and where the tools of industry that created it ended up. Besides, Mars was huge, enormous. Certainly, they argued, there was abundant land to store the byproducts of progress. Certainly.

Inspired by some thought that had arrived in the solitude, Drinkwine retrieved his voice recorder and snapped it on. "April 23rd. The interviews provided virtually no leads, no suspects to focus on. I am still very much adrift in the investigation, with designs on..." He stopped, seeing the red record light was not illuminated. He hit the

115

button several times but it produced no response. When he pried the backing plate off there was a small cascade of sand. The red menace had managed to work its way into the device and suffocated its workings, rendering it useless. Bemused, Drinkwine pondered the malfunctioned recorder and the far reaches of the rusting junkyard. A shroud of dense gray cloud was sweeping the horizon, illumed deep within by menacing bolts of lightning. Drinkwine understood the planet's fury, for he felt something of the same searing frustration.

Setting the recorder on the passenger seat he resumed the trek. Resting his hands on the steering brakes he let his mind wander back into the hidden rhythms of the churning treads and surrendered to the long, lonely drive that lay ahead. He stared with jaundiced eye at the unnerving monotony of bleak ranges, with bleakness beyond. And beyond that, ranges bleaker still. The rover continued its clang and shudder of vibration as its treads churned the sand, headed back to Jannah.

†

The Martian day was drawing to a close and Drinkwine still had a sizable expanse of inhospitable terrain to cross, so he crushed out yet another Holland and lit up a fresh one—his tenth of the day—and promised himself he'd get back on track with restrained smoking starting tomorrow. Yes, definitely, he would curb his smoking habit starting tomorrow.

On the travel between the rusted yard of forgotten machinery and this point, Drinkwine had encountered, about an hour earlier, a sprawling dump. It combed the desert with its own dunes of filth, the tossed away garbage of the glass and steel city. Miles of it, smelling up the Martian atmosphere with a revolting stench.

He had also encountered the endless line of tanker trucks waiting to take their turn at dumping their loads of human waste. Hundreds of trucks waited patiently to open their tank valves and drop the untreated waste over the stretch of sand set aside as a kind of toilet, letting the sand absorb it all and smother out the smell. Drinkwine had wondered just what the hell they were doing with all the shit, as

Jannah had no working sewage. Now, he knew. Like everything else here it was merely being flushed down the great commode of the Martian outback.

†

Once again the rover was parked atop one of the dunes, granting an impressive view. The distant mountains were brushed with shades of purple as evening arrived. Drinkwine had not stuck to his promise to get back to a reasonable number of smokes in a day, presently drawing on yet another Holland. To be up here, away from the city, was his only escape, the sole respite from the frustration of the investigation. Dwarfed among the plains, the lights of Jannah were just beginning to shimmer against the onset of dusk, a glistening gem, he thought to himself.

He tried to busy his mind with thoughts about the murder but nothing came. Instead, just a lot of loose facts and dates and names floating about unconnected to one another with no hint of importance or relevance. Unsolved cases, they were almost a proverb on Earth. He'd even suffered several of his own. They don't sit well with cops. They never have. Black marks on a man's conscience, perhaps invisible to the outside world, but very much a real, often deep and festering wound of discontent for the owner of such failings.

But this was different; the red planet's first murder. Drinkwine felt perturbed at the notion that if he failed to come up with a suspect and unravel the complexities of the motive, he might set a trend of passivity toward these sorts of serious crimes in the future. Now that would be a difficult albatross to wear about his neck, he thought.

Sucking the last bit of smoke from the thin cigar, Drinkwine watched the ash burn right up to the filter before crushing it out in the sand he'd drawn up into his palm. With a long sigh he pulled himself behind the controls of the rover and reluctantly headed down into the valley, to that glistening gem of a city he so despised, but to which there was no alternative.

†

After returning the rover to the depot, Drinkwine made for the street and flagged down one of the few working yellow taxis. The evening call of the muezzin had begun its haunting pour into the empty streets of Jannah. Plopping into the backseat he realized it was his buddy, Robert Haze, the talker. Evidently Haze carried grudges. His eyes loomed large in the rearview mirror, seething with contempt. Not a word as he waited for orders.

"Science Center." Drinkwine, still getting settled, barely got it out of his mouth before Haze, vindictive, gunned the rig forward, sending him recoiling into the sun-baked, smelly vinyl seat.

As the electric taxi purred onto the avenue, Drinkwine looked out at the barren six lanes of immaculately poured concrete that split the city. The city planners had great expectations. For now though, the taxi, Haze's taxi, was one of just a smattering of cars humming along the thoroughfare in blissful denial. Drinkwine emptied the offending red sand that had collected inside the hems of his linen slacks, spilling it out onto the floor of Haze's precious taxi. The evening air was unusually warm. Drinkwine lowered the window and let it swirl through the cab, stirring the awkward silence.

Streetlamps dotted the avenue in a corridor of halos, illuminating the ever-falling mists of red. The sweepers would have it all brushed away before the rise of the sun tomorrow. Haze, strobed by passing streetlamps, swiped the windshield wipers to brush a thin layer of dust from the windscreen, leaving arcing trails across the glass.

Dwarfed by the towering skyscrapers, a lone pedestrian was on the sidewalk. As they neared, Drinkwine saw it was a slender woman dressed in a beautiful silk saris that perfectly outlined the contours of her body beneath. She was in no particular hurry, floating along in a playfully inebriated stride. She seemed to be welcoming the unapologetic caresses of the evening breeze. The taxi whirred past and left the woman to her private pleasures in the strange night warmth of Mars. Happenings according to its own weird.

†

Drinkwine brushed the ubiquitous dusting of sand from his scalp and off his suit as he strode the pattern of hall carpet that led to his room. His suit, only just laundered, was already in need of another going over after just one wearing.

The more this place made havoc of his clothes, arguing for adaptation of a more appropriate, workman-like dress code, the more determined he was to continue wearing the fine linen. It was the last refuge of his dignity. He couldn't let that be taken. Drinkwine shook his head at the absurdity of it all. Waving his palm over the I.D. window the door of his room opened.

Stepping inside, Drinkwine thought he'd entered the wrong room. The walls were bare, his collage of investigation; the photos, the maps, the handwritten notes... all gone.

He frantically opened the drawers of the dresser to see they were empty. The bathroom had no trace that he'd been there; the towels all neatly hung, no trace of the persistent red menace. The closet was empty of his linen suits. "What the hell?" Drinkwine said out loud. "What the hell!?"

Feeling the presence of someone, Drinkwine turned to see Kurian's driver standing in the open door.

"Detective Drinkwine," he began, but Drinkwine interrupted.

"Where are my things?" He asked angrily, pointing at the wall, "Where's all my work? That's official business!"

"Please," the driver offered humbly, "I am to collect you."

"What do you mean, 'collect me?'" livid.

"It will all be explained, I assure you." He then motioned for Drinkwine to follow him, "Please."

†

Sitting in the backseat of the limo, Drinkwine stewed. His face had a shade of red to it that matched the surface of Mars. When the vehicle slowed and swung into a wide circular driveway, he looked out to see where he was being taken.

The drive, lined by towering plastic palm trees, curved its way to the front of a luxury hotel on the edge of the city. It was lit up with an inordinate amount of candlepower, making its gold trim sparkle in a vulgar show of excess.

The limo slowed to a stop at the base of a grand staircase lined with red carpet, anchored with polished gold straps. A lone doorman descended the stairs with a flurry of overeager movement to open the rear door. He waited patiently and without words for the befuddled detective to emerge. The little brown doorman led Drinkwine by virtue of a pointed finger, as if instructing him how to move his feet across the carpet and ascend the steps, his only sounds a kind of guttural grunt as he ushered Drinkwine up the stairs and into the lavish lobby.

Their feet strode the marble floor, the sound resonating up through the lobby into the impressive steel beams and glass high overhead. Not a soul about. They breezed down the corridor, which was lined with high-end shops all closed and dark. However, no doors had been locked. No metal screens to protect the precious merchandise inside; gold and silver watches, pens, and jewelry, the finest of the finest, all within easy arms' reach of unscrupulous hands. Being predominantly Muslim, Jannah observed the punishment of removing the hands of those accused of stealing. The harshness of Sharia law appeared to be working. Not a thing had been disturbed.

Among the goods were designer goggles and sequined facemasks intended for stylish wearing to filter the air and keep the stinging grains of sand out of the well-to-do's eyes. It was survival chic, lavish excess to make the realities of inconvenience here somehow acceptable; a grand mall of flamboyant overindulgence. An air conditioned monstrosity of designer labels waiting for the wealthy to come and shop away their boredom. And what if they don't come? Drinkwine thought to himself. Just exactly who the hell needs a damn designer handbag here anyway?

As the glass and chrome lift silently ascended to the upper floors, Drinkwine, escorted by the little brown doorman—forever smiling despite not one word between them—looked out as the city fell away beneath them. The lift chimed with each passing floor, coming to a stop at the penthouse. The doors slid open to an opulent hallway. The doorman, with the smile still plastered on his face, motioned for Drinkwine to follow, again pointing at the carpet as if coaching the detective in the fine art of how to walk, prodding him along. There was a lot of gold; the light fixtures, the picture frames, the ornate door handles, the plates that held the beautifully inscribed door numbers—all polished to perfection.

Arriving at a double door, the little brown man—reflection distorted in the gold plate—swung them open with grandiose gesture. Drinkwine hesitated before tentatively stepping into the lavish expanse of the penthouse suite. Thick shag carpeting was groomed in waves toward a large plate glass window that had a commanding view of the desert to which the hotel butted, presently appearing as a black ocean with a canopy of stars. The room was obviously intended for visiting royalty.

The little brown man beckoned for Drinkwine to follow him on a tour of the large suite. Stepping into the bedroom, Drinkwine was surprised at how small the king size bed looked in the space. The doorman was eager to pull back the closet door and reveal the linen suits, immaculately laundered and neatly hung. All of Drinkwine's personal items had been carefully set on the desk or folded and placed in the drawers of the dresser. His toiletries were arranged in a semicircle around the gold leaf sink.

The doorman was most eager to show him the adjoining suite where an entire wall had been enlisted to hold the investigative patchwork of photographs, maps, and copious notes. A proper corkboard had been hung to better accommodate the use of the pushpins that held it all together.

Drinkwine scrutinized it, tracing the handwriting, the gathered notes and their corresponding placement. Everything was exactly as he had left it. Though he had no reason to be upset, he chose to remain so at the impropriety of their trespassing.

"It's all there and accounted for Detective, I can assure you." It was Kurian. He'd just entered, dressed in one of his paisley silk suits, the pant legs tucked into soft suede gray boots, delightedly pleased with himself for this new accommodation for the visiting cop.

"I wished you'd have asked me first," Drinkwine said with indignation.

Kurian was quick to defend. "It was handled personally by my own secretaries and with the utmost discretion as to the contents. Is it not exactly as you left it?"

After a brief hesitation, Drinkwine admitted, "Yes. But, still." He felt foolish for having been so irate. "But why did you feel compelled to move me?"

"Oh, come now," Kurian said as he crossed to the window. "The Science Center is quite nice, but please, there's really no comparison," his voice full of pretentiousness. "You'll be a great deal more comfortable here. And not to worry," manicured fingers splayed, excitedly rocking up onto the balls of his feet, quite pleased with himself, "my office is taking care of everything."

As he stared at Kurian, Drinkwine—presently displaying a deceptive calm—amused himself with the shameless and unscrupulous attempt to soften him by ensconcing him in luxury, intended to wear down his unrelenting duty to protocol.

The Ambassador took his time crossing the room to the large picture window, gazing out into the night, the city lights sparkling. He clasped his hands before him and let out a contented sigh. "We're doing it, Detective."

"And what is that?" Drinkwine said, not wanting to encourage.

"We're colonizing Mars." Kurian was unusually cheery. "Do you realize, out there, on the edge of the desert, we're creating a resort that will have four kilometers of beachfront, with artificial waves. It will hold every bit of beauty as anything nature has created on Earth." He paused. "Actually," considering, "better... because the sand will have underground cooling to prevent the beachgoers from burning their feet. Splendid, just splendid," Kurian let out excitedly, accompanied by an exuberant clapping of his hands.

"If you take on the desert," Drinkwine began as he fished a grain of sand out of his eye, "you will lose. Didn't we learn that on Earth?"

Kurian's face shifted into one of those exasperated looks he had been frequenting as of late and dropped from his tippy toe stance to the flats of his feet. "For someone with such a whimsical name, you certainly know how to put a stick in it."

The telling silence between them was broken by a strong gust of wind that brushed the glass for a fleeting moment, as if agreeing with Drinkwine's accusation.

"May I show you something?" Kurian asked.

†

The gold accented double door was opened to reveal an immense banquette room on the ground level of the grand hotel. It was empty, accentuating the enormity. The flower patterned carpet, smelling of newness and thoroughly un-trodden, stretched out before Drinkwine and Kurian as they entered—the chandeliers, high overhead, snapping on in succession all the way across the large room, illuminating the empty opulence.

"They'll be coming from all countries, with all kinds of backgrounds, all sorts of stories, all types of business," Kurian expounded, arms spread in a gesture of bold statement. "They're going to use this room for presentations, Detective." Kurian was walking deeper into the open space. "Seminars about health, food, real estate, jobs, family, leisure—yes, plenty of leisure. They're coming, Detective."

"The immigrants?" Drinkwine said.

Kurian hesitated for a moment. "Settlers," he corrected, "settlers." He took on that pose of his, with the handkerchief clutched against the chest. "They're coming, Detective, with hopes, with dreams. Many are going to pass through this very room for processing on their way to new lives on Mars. A shame for those dreams to be dimmed by the ugliness of this unfortunate thing that has happened."

Drinkwine was amused by the lack of subtlety. "Why are you showing me this?"

"So you can perhaps better appreciate the breadth of what we're doing on Mars," Kurian said with conviction.

Drinkwine was tired. He needed a shower. "I'm well aware of how unsavory this business of murder is for you," he paused, "you've made that resolutely clear," watching Kurian for his response.

The two men were silent, the only sound the soft hum of large ventilation shafts moving treated air around the ballroom.

Seeing that the newest gambit wasn't working to unscrew Drinkwine one bit, Kurian ventured, "It's a shame, all this work and not a single lead, not one suspect," the Ambassador condescended. Kurian continued his stride toward the center of the vacant ballroom. "You know, with the stroke of a pen the whole matter could be easily taken care of. You could conclude your business with an understandable result of no suspects." His voice softened, "And you could return home with a sizable bonus for the inconvenience." The air conditioner blew cold. "After all, the majority of murders go unsolved on Earth, it's nothing unusual." Kurian went after Drinkwine's distaste of the planet. "You could be done with it, Detective. Just think, you could get off this 'dreadful planet.' You could go home."

Drinkwine looked at him. "Would that suit your people?"

Kurian tried to pretend he didn't know what Drinkwine was getting at. "My people? You mean the settlers?"

Tired of the game. "Those you're working for. The people who orchestrated my move here."

"I don't know what you're talking about. It was my idea to move you." Kurian didn't look comfortable with the lie.

"Look," Drinkwine said, patience tried, "I understand you have a job to do. But I've got a job to do as well. I intend to do it."

"In time," Kurian began, "this incident will be regarded as just some isolated matter, and forgotten. Why tarnish the colony for the tens, nay, the hundreds of thousands, eventually the millions of settlers who are making plans, right now, as we speak, to come. Why upset their dreams? What good can come of casting a pallor over their future home?"

"Stroke of a pen, huh?" Drinkwine repeated.

"Yes, Detective," Kurian was suddenly hopeful he was making an impression.

"An 'isolated matter,'" Drinkwine, repeating Kurian's assessment. "Ambassador, unfortunately, as we found on Earth, as we discovered on the Moon, and as I am certain you will see with Mars, this murder will not prove to be some isolated novelty. It's merely the first."

"Oh, come now," Kurian dismissed, showing his perfect white teeth. "We're not barbarians."

"Yes," Drinkwine said with deliberation, "of course not."

The two men stood, dwarfed by the cavernous ballroom, as empty and bleak as the desert outside.

"Thank you, for trying to make my stay more pleasant," Drinkwine said as he started for the door.

"Mr…, pardon me, Detective Drinkwine."

Drinkwine stopped and turned to face him.

"My office would like to host you this evening at The Star," Kurian offered meekly, "Jannah's most exclusive restaurant. My driver will fetch you."

Drinkwine had learned not to argue. Better to take the meal. It was sure to be good. Besides, there was certain to be some point to it, even if Kurian wasn't about to impart any information presently. He nodded, then tiredly sauntered off, leaving Kurian to his budding apprehension in the empty expanse of the ballroom.

✝

The penthouse bathroom was palatial—painfully so. Drinkwine's every move in the shower echoing the lonesomeness against the tile and glass.

He dressed in one of his freshly laundered linen suits, choosing the one that had the least offensive reddish stains imbedded in the hems. Looking at himself in the mirror he filled a glass from the tap and drank. He stopped. Holding the glass closer he observed tiny particles of red sand swirling in a little tornado of water at the bottom. It was everywhere, he thought to himself. Everywhere.

✝

Waiters fluttered about the candlelit restaurant with silent, efficient purpose. They outnumbered the patrons. The moment a water glass was sipped, a waiter invisibly swept in to refill it. The soft clink of silverware and quiet conversations filled the room. The establishment was luxurious beyond imagination. Gold draped everything. The music was a politically correct composition derived from multiple Middle Eastern styles, a popular trend on Mars to pacify the wide breadth of tribal lines in residence.

The maître d' led Drinkwine through the restaurant, weaving between tables, the detective's presence tying a string of knots in conversations as he passed. Thankfully the education and class of the room saved Drinkwine from his usual prejudices. Those here were certainly aware of who he was, and why he had come. Still, there were glances held too long, accompanied by murmurings that most certainly concerned him.

The maître d' seated him at a small table near the kitchen door through which the staff was continually banging in and out. With each swing of the door came brief glimpses of the kitchen, the clang of pans, and the heightened voices of the crew.

Once seated, Drinkwine felt the eyes of diners on him. He was the only white person, save the two dishwashers in the kitchen, visible intermittently in the swinging of the kitchen door; sweating profusely, enveloped in clouds of steam ushering from the machine they worked. Drinkwine was a pariah here. As he took the menu from the maître d', he wondered what power plays were going on behind this little display of favor, buttering him up yet further. Fine, he'd play their game. Along the way he'd enjoy the food.

These well-dressed men and women—and worse, their children—all possessed a disturbing sense of entitlement. Either by their own devices, or perhaps the good fortune of their bloodlines, they commanded enormous wealth. Drinkwine wondered how much worth was here, in this room, at this moment. After all, these were yet more of the brokers behind the real estate deals and heavy industry unfolding across the plains of Mars.

The restaurant was windowless. There were no reminders of the endless, ceaseless desert that loomed just beyond the artificial clay walls. The lace, the velvet curtains, and the paintings had all been brought across space to replicate their familiar corner of the world back on Earth. The menu, the smells of the food, all worked to put them back there, if just for a little while. Drinkwine wondered that if in trying to make this place so much like home, were they in fact merely luring themselves into further longing?

As he perused the menu Drinkwine caught scattered bits and pieces of conversation. His rudimentary grasp of Farsi and Urdu allowed him to discern a woman's voice whispering to those at her table, "I hear he speaks quite well... for an American." Followed by the prerequisite exclamation, "Is Drinkwine his real name?" *Yes*, he thought to himself, bored with it all to the point of madness; *my damn name really is Drinkwine.*

A wave of exalted sighs swept the restaurant, accompanying a soft parade of waiters. As they weaved between the tables the guests broke out into spontaneous applause. The silver serving dish being carried by the lead waiter was elaborately laden with a prepared peacock, the head and torso cooked to glistening brown, its colorful, perfectly preserved plumage trailing behind, draped across the arms of two busboys.

The waiter placed the bird on a table before an older, obviously quite wealthy Middle Eastern man, and a beautiful, young, dark-skinned woman. She blushed, demurely cupping her tiny, heavily jeweled hands over her mouth in astonishment. The attending waiters deliberately draped the plumage to spill onto the floor in a supreme show of privilege. Guests at surrounding tables raised glasses in toast to the spectacle. Her sugar daddy enjoyed the vulgar display of wealth immensely. He was wearing a wedding band. She was not. No one thought anything of it. The couple settled into whispered conversation as the woman started in timidly with her knife and fork. His lips against his young mistress' tiny ear, she blushed at whatever it was he was pressing into her head as the restaurant slowly resumed its din of quiet conversations.

Drinkwine had read somewhere that only twelve of the birds had been brought up from Earth—thus far. One of them was presently adorning the table where its cooked body was being delicately poked at. Its price? Enough to purchase a small house on Earth. Drinkwine considered the lithe physique of the mistress, knowing full well she wouldn't be able to make a dent in the amount of rarefied meat before her. His capacity for disbelief was drawing shallow. How many more oddities did Mars have for him? What was next?

Drinkwine's dinner of chicken, creamed spinach and cauliflower with basmati rice, yogurt and garlic Nan had been enjoyed. He was following it with a coffee. He had watched the excitement over the rare peacock meal wane over the last hour. The couple had retired into little nothings of intimate whispers. The waiters, with silent efficiency, adeptly cleared the dishes without disturbing the amorous mood of the table.

The waiters passed within a breadth of Drinkwine, carrying the remains of the peacock. It hardly looked touched, with but a few bites taken out of the cooked, fleshy torso. The long, colorful plumage trailed behind, the beautiful feathers wafting softly in the turbulence of the waiter's stride.

As Drinkwine sipped his coffee he saw the maître 'd making his way toward him, a small gold tray in his hand. Sitting on top, folded in half, was a note of fine paper. So here it comes, he thought. The maître 'd made straight for Drinkwine, stopping to bow and extend the tray, eyes discretely fixed on the floor. Drinkwine took the note, waiting for him to turn before opening it. In a much too perfect hand the note read simply:

> *Detective Drinkwine, Would you please be so kind,*
> *and discrete, as to meet me at the aquarium facility.*
> *No. 4, the Asah Building.*
>
> *A.H.*

He had been waiting for something like this. Drinkwine knew the lavish dinner would not be entertained without some kind of reciprocal business—perhaps just a vague threat, or worries about investment, all having to do with the potential catastrophe of a tainted reputation for Mars. Strange, no one ever mentioned the victim. There was no apparent concern about finding the killer, probably because there wasn't any profit in it. Using only initials to sign the note was an unnecessary act, as the sender would of course wish to remain anonymous.

Drinkwine took his time finishing his coffee. It was his own, personal display of power, to keep the writer of that note waiting. The coffee subsequently acquired a slightly richer flavor. He understood now that this establishment had been chosen in order to put him in close proximity to the aquarium, which was the next building over.

A waiter emerged from the kitchen, setting the door to swinging. In the intermittent glimpses, Drinkwine saw the chef and his staff watch as the relatively untouched peacock was deposited into the trash. The door swung closed to shut out their befuddlement.

Drinkwine shook his head at the absurdity of it all. And so, with the last sip of the refined coffee staining the elegant cup with a tiny ring, he resigned himself to go meet this Mr. A.H.

†

The front door of the Asah building, number 4, had been left open. There was no one about. Drinkwine entered and stood in the dark lobby. At the end of one of the corridors a door was ajar. He surmised this was for him, as it fit the scenario of foreboding that the meeting was supposed to be creating. It wasn't. Still, he ventured to see where this would lead. For some odd reason he wasn't concerned for his welfare. Perhaps it was feeling like there wasn't a great deal to be giving up if someone wanted to play dirty. Besides, he had his service weapon tucked into the shoulder holster. Like a shot of whiskey, being in possession of a lethal sidearm grants its carrier a decent amount of confidence—perhaps erroneously. But phony tough was better than nothing.

When he reached the door and looked inside he was met with the reveal of an enormous warehouse, filled with large aquariums. They were stacked to the ceiling and held an exotic array of fish and sea creatures. The only illumination was from the lights in the tanks, swimming the room in oscillating webs of turquoise. Sharks, squid, and manta rays silently swam the lengths of their tanks over and over, swerving adeptly when they arrived at the glass walled confinement of their cramped environments to start again in the other direction. The only sound was that of the aeration pumps that were raising symphonies of bubbles that broke the surface, escaping into the stale air of the warehouse in a soft chorus of gurgling.

Drinkwine entered and slowly made his way down one of the tall corridors created by the stacked aquariums, his shoes striding the wet, raised wood planking.

"Thank you for coming," a voice ushered out from somewhere.

Drinkwine searched out the source but saw no one.

"How was your dinner?" The voice used slow deliberation in order to enunciate the English, no doubt a second, or third, or fourth language.

"Very pleasant. Thank you." Drinkwine saw a thin, dark brown man in a white thwab in the adjacent aisle, distorted through the glass and water of the aquariums. As Drinkwine made steps toward the mysterious Mr. A.H., he in turn kept equal steps to stay ahead and avoid a face-to-face encounter. So the man didn't wish to be identified. He'd creatively drummed up a dramatic setting to make a point. That was fine, Drinkwine thought, so long as he got to the point quickly. Which he did.

"Is there much of a living in solving deaths, Detective Drinkwine?" Mr. A.H. asked with a touch of disingenuousness.

"Are you really that interested to know?" Drinkwine came back.

Mr. A.H. let out a hoarse laugh. "Perhaps not. Forgive me. Money. It's where my mind is most of the time," Mr. A.H. said as his feet creaked the wood planking, running a finger along the glass of one of the large tanks. Two hammerhead sharks kept constant vigil in a graceful display of movement. "You have a task to perform here, we're all very grateful. However, we too have tasks. Ours are the tasks of investment, of business, of managing wealth—of which I can assure you, a vast amount has been brought up to Mars, and a vast amount more is en route." Mr. A.H.'s bearded face was distorted, elongated in the thick glass.

Drinkwine thought of Kurian, and wondered what kind of a chiding he'd taken from these people for not doing his job of curtailing the investigation. So, they'd stepped up their soft drumming of warning. Drinkwine wondered what Mr. A.H.'s approach would be, as he was obviously here to try and knock some corporate sense into him. "You're interested only with monetary concerns," Drinkwine responded, "I'm interested only in judicial."

"Can you imagine," Mr. A.H. continued, "how far some men will go to protect their fiscal concerns? It would sober even the most callous."

Drinkwine wasn't fazed. "All I can do with that is file it away with all the other vague threats that have come my way since I've been here."

"Heavens," Mr. A.H. exclaimed in surprise, "I don't make threats. We're just having a pleasant conversation, you and I."

The gurgling of the tanks resonated through the warehouse.

"Have you an affinity for the ocean, Detective?"

Drinkwine purposely didn't answer, keeping pace with Mr. A.H. as he continued along the wall of glass tanks in the next corridor.

"All life evolved from the ocean." Mr. A.H. was attempting to be philosophical, but it was obvious he had other, more important things on his mind.

Drinkwine let Mr. A.H. stew for a moment rather than ask him exactly what it was he wanted to say. "Yes, Man crawled out of the sludge of the ocean a long time ago on Earth." Drinkwine smirked, "too bad there isn't an ocean on Mars."

"Oh, but there's going to be," Mr. A.H. burst with exuberance. "We're going to make one. And we're going to stock it with these glorious fish you see here, with life, Detective Drinkwine, life. We begin with the Great Lakes of Mars. This facility is one of many. And that's just for the waters. We have outdoor holding areas with countless species of animals that will be let loose upon Mars, to breed, to populate the planet with the glory of God. Just think; giraffes, lamas, antelopes, all freely roaming Mars."

Drinkwine wondered how many tiers of characters like this he may have to wade through, with their various attempts to elaborately cloak exactly what it was they were trying to say. It was entertaining, nonetheless. "The Godding of Mars?" he let out with a touch of cynicism.

"Pardon?" Mr. A.H. retorted, unsure what he'd heard.

"Like playing God," Drinkwine stated reproachfully.

"God?" Mr. A.H. had to mull it over, "Hardly." Then, pleased with the notion, "Noah, perhaps." He studied Drinkwine through the bubbling waters as a school of colorful mandarin dragonet fish swam between them. "But we will bring only the most beautiful, the most majestic of species. We will leave behind all the poisonous, the violent, the ugly." Mr. A.H. peered at Drinkwine through the thick glass, saw the question, the disdain in his face. "I won't be made to feel guilty for affording this place of privilege, which allows us the opportunity to create Mars exactly as we wish. We will create a paradise here."

Each time Drinkwine thought he would get a clear look at the mysterious Mr. A.H. through the glass, some large spectacle of fish would intervene, as if on some agreed upon cue of collusion to keep him a mystery.

"Did you ever think that perhaps there's a balance of nature that needs to exist," Drinkwine offered; "The good, the bad... and the ugly?"

"Are you suggesting it's wrong to be in a position to choose," Mr. A.H. asked.

"Thankfully, it's not for me to say," Drinkwine came back.

"Ah," Mr. A.H. smiled, "but by saying that, you make your point."

"This planet was here for millions of years before humans arrived," Drinkwine lamented. "And it will live on millions of years after he's gone."

"Come now," Mr. A.H. studied Drinkwine through a flurry of fish, "don't be so cynical. You Americans were once such an optimistic people. Now it's our turn. There is great beauty and a great amount of prosperity to be had here."

"Yeah," Drinkwine uttered deprecatingly, "so I read in the brochures."

"If there is profit to be made with a place, then why not?" Mr. A.H. stated emphatically, pressing his palm against a tank as an eel slithered past, brushing the glass with its body. "It is the way man has always operated."

"That doesn't mean it's right," Drinkwine responded.

"Mars has changed all of that, Detective," Mr. A.H. inferred, his tone now somber. "It is yet to be determined what is right and what is wrong. Don't ever forget that."

Mr. A.H. curiously watched Drinkwine as he peered into one of the big aquariums. He was entranced by a large manta ray that came up to the glass before making a darting turn and slipping through the water.

"Are you a romantic, Detective?"

He was still watching the manta ray as it disappeared into darkness. "Don't try to flatter me." Drinkwine took in the room, "How many fish have you already lost over the years, dying in these tanks as you wait for the water?"

The comment bore into Mr. A.H. He stared, unblinking. "Every society has its teething, Detective. We're learning. Yes, we've had our mishaps. But we will get there. A paradise, without want, without unpleasantness."

"Every page of history is wrought with some unpleasantness."

"You're speaking of the Earth, of the Moon," Mr. A.H. defended, "where the bad elements were allowed to fester, without proper restraint." He stopped to peer into a large aquarium where a shark patrolled with vigilance. Admiring the menacing creature he fell into a trance, "We will manage things much more cleanly this go round."

"Do you really think you can get it right? Do you really think you can reshape a million years of evolution?"

"Oh yes," Mr. A.H. smiled, "the gardens are coming, you can be assured of that."

After a long moment watching the shark, he spoke. "Strange, with a name like Drinkwine, I would have expected there to be some aspect of whimsy in you, Detective. I see I was wrong."

Mr. A.H. abruptly pushed through a back exit and was gone, the heavy steel door slamming behind. Drinkwine didn't bother to go after him. What was the point?

†

When Drinkwine entered the lobby of the luxury hotel it was eerily quiet and hauntingly empty, given the hour. He strolled through the opulence and into the lift that ascended to the penthouse suite.

Moving down the long hallway of the top floor, past door after door of unoccupied rooms, Drinkwine discerned the sole sign of life other than himself; the sound of a vacuum cleaner. At the far end of the corridor a maid—white, hunched over with an aged physique well advanced of her years—was rocking the humming machine back and forth across the carpet in tireless, relentless sweeps to extract the ever-present nuisance of the red sand.

†

Settling onto the bed, Drinkwine kicked his shoes off, the upturned loafers depositing their requisite sand onto the carpet. Granted, given the evening's locations, it was a great deal less than the normal allotment—but bothersome nonetheless.

Lying back on the bedspread, Drinkwine studied the ornate ceiling of the room. He reached over and turned out the light. The exterior lights of the building, far below, cast lightly dancing shadows of palm branches, brushed by the wind, their distorted movement stretching up the vast height of the hotel. In the semidarkness he could see the corkboard in the other room, holding the pathetic progress of the investigation. A new scribble here and there, but nothing of any significance. He closed his eyes. Far off, muffled through the walls, the sound of the vacuum cleaner continued its oscillations, back and forth over the carpet.

†

In the middle of the night Drinkwine was awakened by the distant peal of tires. The sound would fade to the distance, only to return again and again. He rose and crossed to the big picture window, drawing back the heavy drapes. Out on the newly constructed stretches of freeway that would eventually link Jannah to the future cities of Mars, the Zenon headlights of four cars could be seen fishtailing across the empty lanes. Above the madness of revving engines and screeching tires could be heard the excited shrieks of youth, engaged in the killing of boredom.

With the water park unfinished and the schools yet to be opened, the sons and daughters of wealth had little to occupy their whims. Immune to conviction by the vague threat of authority, under cover of night, they took to the unused freeway on the edge of the city in expensive autos to get their kicks. Here, the skidding of tires granted an entertainment of speed and daring in fishtails and drifting, accompanied by the excited screams of adolescent girls. The young men, empowered by the machines, displayed their budding alpha tendencies in the strange mechanical mating ritual. One of the cars got away from its driver, rolling and twisting violently in clouds of dust, illumed green in the mercury vapor street lamps. The totaled auto was abandoned as the youths, unscathed and laughing riotously, made for their accomplices' cars, jumping in to continue the parade of daring. All those dark youths, Drinkwine observed, dancing nightly, so close to death.

†

Chapter 14

T HE BREAKFAST ROOM WAS empty. Fifty lonely tables all perfectly set with dainty cups and saucers and fine silver on white tablecloths. Only one was occupied. Alone in the cavernous room, Drinkwine's isolation was sorely emphasized by each echoed clang of his fork against his plate, resonating through the emptiness. The remnants of a slightly underdone egg and thin, crisp pieces of toast lavished with marmalade were strewn on the plate. The orange juice was instant, with a promise from the server that in time it would be fresh squeezed; just as soon as the trees took. Yeah, good luck, Drinkwine thought. When he lifted his spoon from the neatly pressed tablecloth to stir his coffee, he saw its faint outline in a misting of red against the white.

His attention was drawn to the whining of a vacuum cleaner as it plied the hall carpet, sporadically coughing on grains of sand. Drinkwine watched as an aged maid—dressed in a drab blue work dress with black, flat-soled shoes, her body bent feebly over her work—was momentarily framed in the open doors of the breakfast room as she passed, her face pinched in consternation over the annoying sand. After she passed, he watched the extension cord as it bounced and fell in jerks and tugs against her slow progress, the droning hum of the vacuum fading off. Drinkwine was sadly amused at the thought of what lay ahead for these people, futilely trying to suck up every offending grain of sand that found its way into the opulence. There was enough here to keep these women, and their offspring's offspring busy for the rest of their lives.

Beyond the glass was the desolate surface of Mars. The sands were still for the moment, the winds having not yet risen. In short order the temperature would rise, stirring the atmosphere and disrupting the calm. Drinkwine tried to gather his thoughts but they were drowned out by the music being pumped into the room. He was sick of the heat, the sand, the food, the restless winds, and this fucking music. It was a politically correct mix of traditional eastern styles rendered in a techno disco vibe with pop vocals blurting mundane lyrics of dancing the night away in an endless party of life. Certainly, he thought to himself, there were other things to sing about.

Ignoring the music, Drinkwine sipped at his coffee, staring out at the dunes, thinking how tranquil they looked. In years to come, the area would most likely be covered with dwellings. This place would be home to millions.

After checking the time he downed the last of his coffee. He had an appointment, summoned again via an anonymous note. Yet another of Mars' developers wished to bend his ear. When he settled the cup on the saucer the clank resonated through the room. He took a sip of water. As he did so he saw grains of sand settling back to the bottom of the glass. It was everywhere.

†

Rising with phantom irregularity to the surrounding landscape, the triangular design of the massive steel structure rose some one hundred meters at its highest point, tapering down to a mere ten at the opposite end. The slanting wedge of the roof hummed with an array of giant air conditioners that cooled the building's interior with industrial strength.

Drinkwine dragged himself through the rising heat of mid-morning to the mysterious meeting inside the building at the edge of the city. It was situated among half built amusement rides and an unfinished waterslide—the fiberglass channels dry and baking under the Martian sun. Drinkwine thought to himself what a sad sight a dry water park was. That was one of the uses the precious water would be put to here; a waterslide, for the indulgent splash of leisure.

Passing through the opaque glass doors, Drinkwine was immediately plunged into the chilled atmosphere inside. The building hummed with the constant stir of air conditioners and the excited shrieks of daring as skiers and snowboarders raced down the artificial ski slope that contoured the design of the building. Falling from above was a constant flurry of fake snow. Above it all was more of the ubiquitous music, piped in over the house stereo system. So, Mars had snow, Drinkwine considered as he waited for the mysterious person to present himself.

Nearby, seated in the concession area with a dark-skinned wife and a brood of pudgy dark-skinned children—all consuming ice cream—was a heavy Middle Eastern man who, upon sight of the detective, immediately got out of his chair and made straight for him. Drinkwine figured him for Pakistani. The sleeves of his pressed white shirt were rolled up and the buttons were undone, revealing several gold chains about his neck. His stomach hung over his belt, which he pulled up on to raise his pants three times in the short few steps between them.

The man's fingers had an array of rings, which Drinkwine saw as his hand came forward to shake in introduction. "Ah, Detective Drinkwine, pleasure, pleasure," he said as he took Drinkwine by the arm and led him to a less populated area of the wood planked patio. "Drinkwine, what a name, lovely name," as he drew him further away from the fun and sport of the ski slope, the cries of joy echoing through the vastness. "Thank you for meeting me here. Though not perhaps most conducive to business," referring to the interior ski slope building, "it *is* conducive to keeping children occupied, yes?" The one-sided banter unfolded with the speed of someone jacked up on cocaine. But his English was good. "Do you have children, my friend?"

There it was again, the empty throw away of, *my friend.*

"No, I don't have children, Mr....?"

"Not important. Though, being a Detective, if you really need to know my name it will be easy enough to come by in certain circles."

They were at a remote part of the building, where the steel walls caught the echo of the skiers, the scratch and tear of skis. "Hmm, unusual for a white to not have children," the man said, using his hand to wipe his mouth of ice cream as he threw the empty container into a trash can.

Drinkwine had long since been calloused to the off-handed comments related to his color.

"Children—they're the future—the future of Mars. We're carving out a wonderful one for them here," he spoke, looking at his children. "And just think, soon there'll be the first birth. Imagine, a whole new generation conceived and born here, colonizing Mars. The arrival of settlers is one thing, a glorious thing, but a truly indigenous populace is something else altogether."

"Are you saying there hasn't been a baby born on Mars yet?" Drinkwine asked, with a tinge of disbelief.

"Oh, there's probably been one among the workers," he answered with a disparaging wave of the hand, the words uttered with distaste, as if the mere impurity of it crossing the lips would offend, "who knows? But they would've gotten rid of it out of fear of deportment. I mean a proper birth, of proper blood."

The man was unwittingly spewing disgust, a slip of vulgarity now in every word.

"What can I do for you?" Drinkwine asked, eager to be done with him.

"Do for me?" the man responded, "perhaps better put as to what I can do for you."

"Am I to guess what that means?" Drinkwine proffered.

"Has the bloom gone off the bud of this investigation, Detective?" Although he presented it under the guise of genuine curiosity, the question was ripe with a kind of vague victory.

"Why would you ask that?"

"Some time now spent, a lot of inquiries, and, what do you have?"

Drinkwine studied the man for a long moment. "I'm curious, are you concerned for your children's welfare here?"

A laugh through the bounce of jowls, "Whatever are you getting at?"

"Your children... living on Mars. Don't you want to ensure they'll be safe? With law and order, the practice of justice?"

"Mr. Drinkwine…"

"Detective."

"Excuse me, Detective Drinkwine, I am merely a contractor, an investor. I am here to pave the way, quite literally, for the future generations of Mars. I will leave the future inhabitants of Mars with all the fruits of a wonderful world."

"So, you won't be staying?"

"I have work to do here, I am the purveyor of dreams. Once that work is done, I will go home. As you will go home when your work is done."

"So you don't fancy yourself a future resident of Mars?" Drinkwine said with unmistakable sarcasm.

"Do I detect some disingenuousness?"

"I don't get it. They're selling a lot of bullshit. Pardon me, but this place is an inhospitable wasteland. All the waterslides and ski slopes can't conceal the fact that man will be fighting this place forever."

"Perhaps if you were not so beholden to the nostalgia for your precious Earth, you could learn to love this place equally as much, Detective."

"What gives you the impression I love the Earth?"

"If you dislike it here so, why stay?"

"You're a creator of dreams? Well, I solve murders. That's why I'm here."

"Not a very sexy, or lucrative line of trade."

"No, maybe it isn't sexy, and maybe there isn't a great deal of money involved, but regardless, it's a nasty little reality that needs to be tended to in every society."

"Oh, no, no, no, this is just a little inconvenience we've to deal with. This will pass. And let's hope it passes without too much disturbance. I can reward discretion quite handsomely."

There was that familiar word, discretion. "Is this a veiled bribe?"

"Veiled?" the man laughed heartily, his jowls flapping. "Detective, I don't veil anything. Tell me how much you want and I'll see to it you get it." The voice was bent with a kind of cynical pride.

"It's not that easy."

"Oh, I assure you, Detective, it is, quite easy." His tone was unnerving.

"A figure. For me to go away?"

"Yes, a number. As with all commerce, for all business, there is always a number, just the right price. If a job is wanted; a fee is arranged. A preferred apartment; a value is set. A woman desired; a price agreed upon. Everything on Mars has a price. You don't rise to a stature like mine without knowing this, without accommodating this."

"Settling a planet with the currency of bribes."

"Yes, that's right, Detective; Dollars, Yen, Rubles, Yuan and Rupees. There is nothing different as to how man has always settled new lands. In the past, perhaps more physical brutality was required. Now, there is little need for brutes, save for the construction. Otherwise, it's all legalese and paperwork."

"This isn't some novelty that can be shuffled into the thin memory of this place. So long as man colonizes planets, there are going to be murders. You're going to have to figure out a way to deal with it, not just now," Drinkwine said, with a weary tone of experience, "but in the future as well."

"But there's no profit in it," the man responded in earnest.

"Yeah, what a shame."

"Detective, we're creating a new colony on Mars. The people who will come will not be of a criminal or wantful kind."

Drinkwine studied the man, his gaze running down the man's bare forearms, coming to rest on the garish gold watch adorning his thick wrist. "No, the bloom has certainly not gone off the bud of this investigation."

"Detective, the gravity of the situation overrides any falsehood of decorum here, it demands absolute transparency. There are deals pending that require the grand plans for Mars to come to complete fruition—the figures of which, to say the least, are quite astronomical. Forgive me my candor, however revolting it may be, but there is far too much at stake to allow the status of Mars to be tarnished."

The man regarded Drinkwine, his face flushed red for a moment. His eyes burned sharply with threat and floated in pools of anger. Drinkwine thought, to draw a man to anger is no great feat. But did he have any sense of morality? Or was he merely another businessman trying to curb a flood of bad press for their precious investments in paradise?

"Think of a price, Detective. Whatever the figure, it will be in your hands by the set of the sun."

Without another word the man was called away by a disturbance at the table where his family sat. A dispute had erupted between two of the children over an ice cream. They bellowed loudly their privilege, overwhelming the mother who screamed for her husband's assistance, her shrill voice echoing across the space, comingling with those of the skiers.

Drinkwine watched as the man settled the argument with the procurement of more ice cream before looking back at him and motioning with a rubbing of fingers, as if to say; *Think of a price.*

Drinkwine emerged from the chilled atmosphere of the ski slope building into the wall of heat waiting for him just beyond the glass doors. It stopped him in his tracks, the sun quickly evaporating the mist of frost that had formed on the collar and sleeves of his linen suit. He thought of the people who wanted him gone. Well, he wasn't going anywhere. Fill him with all the expensive booze and elaborate meals they wanted, place him in the penthouse suite of the most lavish hotel and offer him substantial bribes. He wasn't going until this damn thing was solved.

From this vantage point the newly completed skyscrapers of Jannah, with their glass façades, were catching the sun with a glistening beauty that hid the fact that all the floors were empty, waiting to be occupied. Others were skeletal framework reaching skyward in a buzzing of activity, engaged in the chase of commerce. That's where Drinkwine was headed; to one of the towering skeletons to speak with a Mr. Smith, an associate, so to speak, of the late Mr. Byrne.

†

The construction elevator climbed the exterior of the building in a rickety scaffold that creaked with rusted moans, the cable rattling as it ascended to the upper floors. Save for the perforated metal grating the elevator was open to the elements. Drinkwine had a rendezvous with Mr. Smith. The name was probably fake, he thought as the lift rose, the result of some dubious past on Earth. No one cared. So long as you could serve the raising of these behemoths of glass and concrete and steel, and provided you would accept the meager wages, they would allow you to come. Greed helped dramatically to relieve the restrictions of the law, providing a steady flow of questionable persons into the workforce of Mars. Drinkwine wondered where these people would go when their usefulness was used up.

It was rumored that Mr. Smith was owed money from Mr. Byrne due his bad luck at cards. Drinkwine didn't put much credence in the scenario, but he had to investigate everything. Besides, there was always the chance of something mentioned that could open up a whole new path of investigation. As the lift continued its ascension the breezes increased. Drinkwine didn't care for heights. In fact, they scared the shit out of him. The creaking rattle and vibration of the lift was only serving to reinforce his uneasiness.

The lift clamored to a stop at the twentieth floor. Drinkwine stepped onto the fresh slab of concrete flooring that was opened on all sides. No warning tape, no barriers to guard against a fall. A person could easily step off the edge into thin air. Nails and screws and scraps of wood and metal littered the area. Clusters of colored wiring hung down from the unfinished ceiling like draping Spanish moss.

There was a man sitting on a box of fasteners, precariously close to the edge, transfixed on a length of wire in his hands. He was carefully stripping the plastic sheathing back with a pair of dikes to expose the copper for splicing. He hadn't noticed the lift arrive and was startled when Drinkwine called his name.

"Mr. Smith?"

Spooked, Mr. Smith accidentally clipped the wire in half, an expletive escaping his mouth. He froze when he saw the detective.

Drinkwine cautiously approached, trying not to appear frightened by the height. He could see all the way to the street below. The vehicles looked like toys. The turbulence created by the canyons of high-rises whipped discarded food wrappers and pieces of trash upward with serious velocity. There was nothing in between himself and the fall to death. Mr. Smith seemed unconcerned.

"Yeah?" Mr. Smith uttered hesitantly.

"My name's Drinkwine, Detective Drinkwine." Flashing his badge. "I need to ask you a few questions."

"About what, why?" Mr. Smith came back anxiously.

"You knew Michael Byrne?"

Smith took far too long to answer. Eyes wide, unblinking.

"Mr. Smith, surely you don't need to *think* about that. Either you knew the man or you didn't."

"He's dead," Smith now blinking nervously.

"Yes, that's right. Somebody killed him."

"I didn't kill him," Smith urged.

"Well, okay. So that's settled."

Smith was woefully confused.

"He owed you money?"

After a moment Smith answered, "Yeah, but I didn't kill 'em."

"How much did he owe you? And what for?"

Smith sniffled, his nose running. "Cards. Blackjack."

"Blackjack?" Drinkwine shot back quickly.

"It's the only game we know."

"I take it Byrne wasn't very crafty at the game?"

"No. I mean, well, I mean…"

"What *do* you mean?" Drinkwine's voice rattled Smith further.

"Jus' bad luck."

"Yeah, plenty of bad luck; the man's dead. How much are we talking?"

"Three thousand duckets," Smith divulged. "That ain't 'nough to kill no man over, not even here."

"Do you know anyone else he owed money to?"

"I's the only one play with him."

"Why was that?"

"The guy was kinda weird."

"How so?"

"Jus', kinda weird."

"So, you weren't friendly?"

"No way. Jus' cards."

Drinkwine looked out over the city. The buildings were creeping a little higher each day. Out on the horizon the desert was stirring with rumor of a dust storm. The taunts unsettled him. He'd had enough dust storms to last him the rest of his natural life.

Smith was sitting there nervously twirling the hacked off wire in his hands. "So, is that it, we done?"

Drinkwine turned to look out over the cranes. He knew he was wasting his time. "Yeah, we're done."

The cable whirred as the construction elevator dropped down through the rickety column of scaffolding. Drinkwine watched the passing floors, catching brief glimpses of workers engulfed in the rain of sparks as they grinded and hammered the metal with a vengeance. He wondered if any among them knew anymore than Mr. Smith. Or was that it? Was Smith the last lead, the mysterious contact, the great clue?

The elevator shuddered to a stop at the ground level. Drinkwine unlatched the flimsy metal cage door and exited. As he crossed the muddied ground, considering his next move, there was a loud metallic snap from high above followed by a chorus of warning screams. He looked up to see a heavy iron beam had broken loose from one of its triangles of cable as a crane was swinging it into place. In a violent upset of balance the beam shimmied and squirmed wildly, smashing against the structure, sending shockwaves up and down the iron maze. The beam was falling, fast. Drinkwine bounded for the street, slipping and sliding across the muddy ground. He could hear the tonnage of errant steel falling from height, clipping the building repeatedly as it came down. The heavy beam slammed into the ground behind him, flattening a generator in a deafening crash. It hit with such force as to upset Drinkwine's balance and stumble him to the mud. The ground shuddered for a moment in the aftermath.

When all was clear, after the remnant pieces of debris had fallen, clattering in chase of the beam, the entire area sat stunned with an eerie silence. After a moment, a worker approached Drinkwine, helping him to his feet. The linen suit was splattered with mud. Dazed, Drinkwine looked at where the beam had settled, pressed a full two meters into the soft ground. It was perched, spear-like, exactly where he had been walking. Shielding his eyes from the sun, Drinkwine peered up the precipice of the skyscraper. Dozens of hard hatted workmen were looking out from the open floors at the commotion below.

Drinkwine looked into the faces of the approaching workmen. Two of them tried to be courteous, swatting the mud off his jacket, making a mess of it. Drinkwine searched out any incriminating malice in the faces around him.

"Buddy, you okay?" one of the workers asked.

"Yeah," Drinkwine answered absently, "fine, fine."

"Shit, you was lucky," another exclaimed.

Was it an accident? Drinkwine thought to himself. Just one of the many mishaps that plagued this place due to lack of oversight? There were few rules in place or governance over these monstrosities with regard to safety. Safety? No, that would impede the progress. The fucking progress. Or was someone trying to kill him? Drinkwine backed away from the gathering workers as they speculated on what had caused the mishap. When they turned with their questions, he was gone.

✝

_____Chapter 15

A S HE STRIPPED THE cellophane wrapping off another pack of Hollands, Drinkwine stared out at the barren reaches of Mars from the penthouse suite. Still shaken by the incident of the falling beam earlier in the day, Drinkwine wished he had a glass of that calming Glenfiddich to settle his wracked nerves. He contemplated the rapidly dwindling stash of his favorite cigarillos. What would he do when they were gone? As it was looking like they would be, much sooner than anticipated, given the increased numbers he'd been indulging. The impending shortfall helped him to savor each smoke. He placed one of the thin cigars between his lips, then struck the flint of the silver lighter and raised it to the tip. He drew in on it, tasting the sweet tobacco. When he exhaled he watched the smoke cloud above his head, forming curling waves before dissipating on the still air. How much longer? He thought to himself.

The evening call to prayer of the muezzin had began, the haunting wail coursing the barren avenues, competing with the rising winds that had begun to mist the sidewalk below with a gathering tide of red. Far out in the desert, the winds coerced the sand into one of its malicious risings. However, tonight's display of tumult appeared to have acquired an impressive anger, stirring a dense wall of dust that rose up into the blushing sky, blotting out the remnant of sun that sought cover below the horizon in anticipation of the impending beating. The wall of sand and dust rose silently, appearing to stand still, lording its presence over the desert.

Drinkwine suddenly realized that the rising wall of sand was not standing still, but in fact was a tidal wave racing with incredible speed across the desert, headed dead-on for Jannah. He watched with awe as the tsunami of sand and dust crossed the intervening space, gathering ferocity, rising up to a height greater than that of the penthouse. The gargantuan wave slammed the metropolis without pity. The crashing force of the impact shuddered through the building. The call to prayer of the muezzin was blotted out by the virulent dust wave that engulfed the towering structure with a much more powerful song; a deliberate affront to the faithful. It was as if the planet had grown impatient with the abuse against it and was now lashing out its anger with self-destructive retribution. The winds lashed the building with laughing cruelty, pouring copious waves of sand into the avenues. Amidst the bedlam, Drinkwine thought; the broom men would have their work cut out for them come morning.

After the initial hit of the giant wave the winds continued the truculent battering. Tonight there was definitely a much more disquieting malice in the winds. They pounded the glass, shaking the large windowpane with an unusual fury. Drinkwine studied it all curiously, trying to decipher the strange language of the planet's enraged nature, wondering how much abuse the glass would tolerate before succumbing to the forces waylaying into it.

Captivated, Drinkwine watched the reflection of the room slowly distort as the window bowed inward from the force of the winds, his reflection twisted comically in the bending pane. Instinctively he took several steps back, away from the large picture window as it bowed further than he thought possible. Finally, the glass surrendered, shattering into the penthouse with an explosion of violence, the winds drumming Drinkwine's ears and tossing everything in devilish play. His arms came up in protection against the slashing shards and flying debris. The winds ripped his carefully drawn notes and intricate maps from the wall, feeding the investigation into the twisting tornado that consumed the room. Drinkwine found himself engulfed in a swirl of papers, assaulted with his own questions and suspicion. The room went black as the electricity was cut-off by the virulent winds. The thunder of destruction pounded his ears as the sand pelted his face and hands and body, smashing mirrors and glass all around him in the darkness. He was caught in a commotion of flying lampshades and silk pillows; a swirling mass of opulence dashed to worthlessness by the anger of Mars. It was screaming at him to leave, to get away from here.

Forearm raised protectively across his eyes, Drinkwine used his free hand to blindly feel his way along the wall in the blackness. The winds turned up their rage against him in angered play, turning all the garish ornaments into projectiles. Deafened by the noise, Drinkwine finally bumped into the doorknob with his hip, its gold plating having lost its worth in the darkness. He fumbled for a moment, wrestling to pry the door open just a sliver against the onslaught and squeeze his body through. It held him like a vise as the wind tried to draw him back into the room for further beating.

Drinkwine finally managed to free himself from the angry grasp of the room, spilling him into the calm of the hall as the door slammed shut behind. The tornado inside the room, angered further by his escape, pounded the door with threat. Collapsing onto the floor, chest heaving with excited breathing, Drinkwine drew himself up against the wall, the faltering illumination of the battery-powered emergency lights strobing the hall in confusion. He watched, horrified, as the winds fondled the door handle from within, threatening to unlatch it and give chase. The winds grew in their frustration at having lost him and thrashed the room beyond with even more violence. The force of the winds angrily blew sand through the narrow gap at the bottom of the door, fanning out across the carpet in a thin veil of red. Through the walls he felt the rumbling reverberations of the rage tearing the penthouse suite apart and pounding the building. The sound of shattering glass gradually subsided as every last available breakable item had been discovered and smashed to pieces by the vengeful winds.

Drinkwine crumpled exhausted against the carpeted floor. Somehow, despite the brutality of the desert, the anger of Mars, and the deafening sound, he drifted off to needful sleep.

†

_____Chapter 16

WHEN DRINKWINE WOKE, ALL was calm. The first light of day was flooding into the hall through the bank of windows. The storm had vanished. The turbulence of the night, with its unnerving violence, had been calmed to absolute stillness. Curled up on the floor, Drinkwine's immediate thought was that he was surprised he'd managed to sleep through the storm. Perhaps it had all been a dream? How could this be the same place that just hours before had been in the grip of such mayhem? Getting to his feet he looked out the window at Mars. It was as calm as the bottom of an ocean. The streets were thoroughfares of deep sand, immaculately combed with perfect dunes. Not a thing moved. The broom men would be useless against this flood of red. They will have assessed the situation and gone off to secure a proper plow. The undulating mounds of sand were casting beautiful shadows from the rising sun. It was quiet beyond quiet. As he rubbed the scratching grains from his eyes he saw where the red sand had fanned out from under the door, glistening in a fine covering across the carpet.

The ornate handle turned easily enough but Drinkwine could only manage to get the door opened a sliver before it wedged itself against a wall of obstructing sand on the other side. Using his shoulder he gradually forced the door open, each effort resulting in a cascading of sand into the hall.

Squeezing through the narrow opening, Drinkwine labored to

climb the sand that had been raged into the room through the shattered window. He surveyed the penthouse suite—it had been transformed into a surreal wonderland of miniature red dunes. The sand shrouded everything with muting brilliance, effectively suffocating the opulence in a supreme burial. The glass of the big window was gone save for several lethal shards that hung precariously. The air outside was as still as could be imagined, with no trace of the virulence that had tried to kill him the night previous. Yes, Drinkwine was certain, the wind was trying to kill him.

Drinkwine saw the corner of a piece of paper protruding from the sand. He grabbed hold of it and gently pulled it from its burial in the dunes. It was one of the many precious pages of notes he had so ardently collected. Digging through, Drinkwine assessed that the majority of his investigation had been stolen away by the prying winds and swept out through the open window, tossed into the endless nowhere of Mars. Perhaps more disturbing, Drinkwine discovered the cellophane wrappings from one of the remaining packs of Hollands. The winds had cruelly robbed him of his one pleasure, sucking his precious cigarillos out the window and scattering them over the desert. He anxiously dug through the sand in hopes of finding a few salvageable smokes. Nothing. He felt urgently for the pack in his inside jacket pocket. Two Hollands. That was all he had left.

Given the circumstances, he drew one of them out and placed it in his lips. He lit it with his silver lighter and sucked the cigarillo to life as he surveyed the room; a strangely beautiful desert of miniature red dunes that butted against blue floral wallpaper. From one wall of the shredded paisley pattern to the other, the delicate dunes had drowned every aspect of anything man-made. If not for the loss of the cigarillos it would almost be cause enough to laugh. Drinkwine just shook his head at the oddness of it all. Happenings according to its own weird.

†

————————————————Chapter 17

T HE HALLS OF THE embassy were quiet and empty. Somewhere
in a distant room someone was tamping the keys of a
computer. Drinkwine had done his best to clean himself up in
the hotel lobby men's room—due the penthouse suite having been
plundered in the night by the ravenous dust storm. His personal
belongings destroyed, he was wearing the single remaining linen suit,
which carried the scars suffered against the rage of Mars in a dusting
of red. With each tired stride, grains of sand could be felt inside his
shoes, irritating his toes as he made his way toward Kurian's office.
He slowed in his steps when he saw a man emerge from the
Ambassador's office at the end of the hall. The man was familiar—
the open shirt and gold chains, pulling up on his belt to hike his pants
up under his hanging stomach. It was the nameless fellow who had
brashly offered him the bribe at the ski slope.

When he caught sight of Drinkwine an enigmatic smile crept
across his large jowls. He was jubilant in his stride, pushing his
overweight frame along with boyish confidence. He didn't offer a
hello, not one word of greeting as he passed within a breath of
Drinkwine—merely maintaining a disconcerting eye contact. That
disturbing smile spoke of mischief. A mischief that no doubt had just
been unfolded in Kurian's office.

When Drinkwine entered the office there was an air of awkward
anticipation among the two secretaries. Their greetings were stilted
and rehearsed. One of them opened the door to Kurian's office,

151

smiling awkwardly as Drinkwine entered.

The feel of Kurian's office had changed. It was as if the furniture had been re-arranged. It had never felt comfortable, but at least there had been a modicum of salutation on previous visits. Now, there was a staleness, a furtive apprehension that permeated everything, right down to the way the sun was dully penetrating the windows, dirtied in the night by the storm.

Kurian was seated behind his desk, the little man looking smaller than usual, dwarfed by the oak centerpiece of his position. He was attired in yet another of his flamboyant wardrobes. Today; a pink paisley jacket and pant with gold vest, a silk ascot wrapped inside the collar. His normally vociferous demeanor, and that persistent habit of pressing his fingertips together as he raised and lowered himself excitedly on the balls of his feet, was absent. In its place was a different manner altogether. His body, usually erect, sank into the deep folds of the chair in a kind of defeated slump. The sprite, seemingly unflappable disposition had finally been usurped by some dark force. He had lost the pretense, the coquettish behavior. Slouching there, arms obstinately draped over the armrests of the oversize chair, Kurian had the appearance of a vanquished king.

The Ambassador didn't greet Drinkwine with words, instead just using his hand to indicate the chair opposite, the gesture only adding to the ominous atmosphere. Drinkwine wondered what the fat man had brought to bear on the situation that had left Kurian in this strange state.

Drinkwine decided to strike first. "I've had a bit of an inconvenience," he broke the placid air. "The storm last night demolished my room."

Kurian stirred uneasily, as if Drinkwine's comments had disturbed a carefully prepared statement. He had something troubling on his mind that needed to be addressed, evident in the fact that he still had not mustered the courage to look at Drinkwine. When at last he did he was surprised to see the detective's disheveled appearance.

Regaining his composure, Kurian spoke, his voice having suffered a transformation to indolence, dropping a full octave. "Yes, I know." The words were slow in coming. "The hotel notified me this morning."

Drinkwine felt a little guilty for his own contribution to crushing the phony sincerity out of the Ambassador's usual effusive demeanor.

Kurian lazily blinked. "We've a bigger situation."

"Oh?" Curious, Drinkwine settled into the chair opposite.

"Yes, it's been brought to my attention," he said, using his delicate fingers to rotate the form on his desk and slide it across to Drinkwine. "Your passport, doesn't have the required one hundred seventy days left before expiration."

Drinkwine stared at Kurian. He was more interested in watching the Ambassador's mannerisms as he dispatched the news than he was in the form.

"It's all right there," Kurian said, indicating the official immigration form, exonerating himself. "And not a thing I can do it about. Not a thing."

Drinkwine casually reached out and picked up the notification. He read it through quickly. He didn't really need the details. It was a trumped up charge. He had to smirk at the thought of all the people who were badgering the Ambassador to get him out of here.

Unfazed, Drinkwine tossed the form back onto the wide desk. It slid across the polished surface and came to a stop directly between them. "How far did you have to dig to drum that one up?"

Kurian's eyes flared from the insult, delirious with anger. He burned into Drinkwine's accusations with perfect contempt. "Detective, I am not a malicious man," he said softly, "just look at these hands," raising them up to make the point. "I am merely Ambassador to Mars. I have a responsibility to enforce the law." Kurian stared at Drinkwine, wishing this could be the last thing said and that he would now simply rise and excuse himself. "You have our sincerest apologies, Detective." His immaculately manicured fingers were trembling. "I'm terribly sorry for what must be a horrible disappointment for you. But we need to govern, to follow the rules—after all, we're not barbarians."

"Yes, so you keep saying." Drinkwine stared with intent, "So who's governing you?"

There was silence again. Drinkwine was surprised at how much anger was brewing in the Ambassador. He was actually entertained by it. "You do realize," Drinkwine broke the tension, "they will send someone else."

Upon hearing those words, Kurian's disposition changed. His face relaxed, in subtle allusion to victory. "Detective," he began, with the slightest hint of a smile at the corners of his small mouth. "If you remove your fist from a pail of water, it doesn't leave a hole."

Right then Drinkwine assessed that the powers above had appropriately used their far-reaching influence to quash any further investigation. How much money was at stake here that this many men could connive to such action?

"Alright," Drinkwine intoned with passive indignation. "So, now what?"

"Fortunately, there is a shuttle leaving for the Moon in twenty-six hours."

"Well isn't that convenient." Drinkwine got up out of the chair. "Actually," looking at his watch, "it allows me some time to wrap a few things up."

"Detective, you're no longer in a position of authority."

Drinkwine turned. Staring into Kurian.

"Technically, I am your superior now." The little man was resting his chin on his clasped knuckles, face framed with painted nails. He'd regained some of that irritating buoyancy. "So, you will refrain from any further meddling into this."

"You mean, this murder?" Drinkwine asked with spite.

"That's right, your petty little investigation has come to its finish," Kurian said with surprising bitchiness. The tone actually suited the absurdity of Kurian's pink paisley outfit.

Drinkwine looked at the silk ascot tied around Kurian's neck, and for a fleeting instant thought how much he would like to have hold of it, throttling the ineffectual Ambassador and snuffing out that fatuous little laugh of his.

He was powerless against the reach and want of these people, and accepted defeat. It wasn't the first time. And it certainly wasn't going to be the last. Drinkwine turned and started for the door.

Kurian's words pursued him, "As regards your personal losses from the storm damage, you'll be required to fill out a Loss & Damage report in order to be compensated."

The words turned Drinkwine around, but Kurian had already dipped his head in feigned reading of some of the materials on his desk. Drinkwine had to smile at the ludicrousness of it all; Mars, the red sand stretching to the horizon outside the window, and the little man, Kurian, situated obstinately behind the massive desk.

†

Moving with hushed solemnity down the hall, his shoes squeaking against the over-polished marble, Drinkwine made for one of the offices where he was to try and make some vague appraisal as to the value of his things lost in the storm. What he was wearing and the few possessions he had in his pockets—including the last Holland—were all he had now. His suits, his toiletries and personal effects were gone. The investigation, with its reams of notes and study, had been systematically made worthless by the savagery of the winds, further dashed by a few indiscriminate strokes of a pen. With the investigation pulled from him he was merely a ghost now on Mars, with no purpose. To think, somewhere out there was a murderer who had just been granted freedom. Adding yet further condemnation was the knowledge that behind the great glass walls of Jannah were a host of individuals that gladly wished him gone. Well, they'd done it... amassed their collective powers in a protection of greed and trumped up a feeble technicality to rid themselves of the bothersome white man from Earth.

It troubled him to have been removed from the case. Equally troubling was his imminent return to Earth. His unhurried footsteps eventually brought him to the office where he was to make a report about his losses. A sign hung from the door on a perfectly braided little gold rope. The dainty circular wood sign replicated a clock, in Farsi it read: *Office closed. Will re-open at...* the hands of the clock adjusted to read: 14:00.

Drinkwine pulled back the sleeve of his jacket to check his watch. Not even ten o'clock. Four hours. He intrinsically knew what to do with the time.

†

The rover churned up the sand in clanking endeavor across the

155

Martian desert. Drinkwine had taken charge of the vehicle under the guise of work, but actually there was a specific task in mind that had nothing to do with the murder of Michael Byrne. The transportation department hadn't yet been made aware of Drinkwine's banishment from Mars, so he used the opportunity to take one last jaunt into the great elsewhere. The hostility he held for this place was now abating with realization that he would be leaving. How funny, he thought, now he was getting sentimental about this fucking shithole of a planet.

As the rover droned out its monotonous rumble of tread, infested by the discordant shaking and creaking of its weathered and beaten body, Drinkwine stared out at the landscape; a great grieving gulf of nothingness, with nothing to distinguish one direction from the other. He thought how easy it would be for a man stranded out here to become disoriented and wander off to certain death.

At last the tedious travel delivered him to the old paddlewheel steamer, sadly majestic in its listing among the dunes. Drinkwine had come to undertake a specific mission. He hadn't come to unravel questions and riddles, he had come here simply to be alone and savor the last of his precious Holland cigarillos.

Somberly climbing to the third deck of the landlocked boat, Drinkwine settled in to savor the view. With slow and deliberate actions he drew the Holland from his jacket, regarding it for a moment before snapping the silver lighter and glowing the tip in the small flame. The scent and smoke of the cigarillo wafted the surrounding area. The reprieve of stillness from the normal buffeting was as if the desert was sad to see him go, and was granting a soft so long to their favorite son.

As he drew on the last Holland, Drinkwine stared out at the endless red sand. The insouciant sand, he thought to himself. For a brief moment he thought how beautiful it was. But that was the trickery of Mars, lulling the visitors into complacency before pummeling them with its repertoire of abuses.

Drinkwine pondered the steamship. It was in quiet decline, without ever having served its purpose. It was like him; an aging, useless dinosaur, slipping toward extinction. Far away, over the ocean of dunes, man was attempting to force a home out of this reluctant land. They were making a fucking mess of it. This place would never be the paradise the developers were promising.

EARTHRISE

As he sat there, savoring the Holland, Drinkwine thought of all the artists' elaborate renderings that were being beamed back to Earth and the Moon, propagating the lie of serenity. The discontent was so palpable on those planets, bending under the weight of overpopulation and the endless waves of crime, that the sellers of the lies had an easy go of it. They pounced on the tired hopes of the naïve and lured them with false promises of new lives on crime free Mars. What a bunch of marketing garbage. And after Mars they would sell Jupiter, than Enceladus, and Titan, all with the same empty promise.

The gullible fools buying in didn't seem to notice that none of the sales people lived here. No, the sales people had never set foot on Mars. But man would continue to impose their will and the red planet would continue its steady repelling of their attempts to tame her. Drinkwine wondered if it was a case of an eye for an eye. He laughed, "An eye for an eye just leaves everybody blind."

The Holland was ashing up. He'd smoked it halfway down. Just a few more precious tokes and it'd be gone. The five-week journey home was going to be a fucker of a trip without smokes. He tapped the burnt ash of the Holland over the teakwood rail and watched it flutter down, settling onto the red sand... the quietly malevolent sands.

†

The trek back to Jannah from the wind blown paddlewheel steamboat—with its forgotten ghosts of love inhabiting the tiny cabins—held a mix of relief and melancholy. Despite the frustrations of the investigation, it had allowed Drinkwine to drown some of his bewilderment and put off the angst of returning to Earth where he would confront the inevitable emptiness of the home that awaited him there. But, on the other hand, he would be gone from here, this dreadful, harsh place. So, they didn't want his help. They preferred to let it all go unsolved, brushed quietly under the other lies they were propagating here. Fine. Let them fool themselves.

The rover's alarm bell sang out with piercing intensity. Drinkwine didn't know what it was. As the desert began its crawl to white, he

157

realized it was a pre-set warning for the daily assault of the sunstrike. He'd not forgotten the frightening reality of the daily routine of deathly pouncing, but had let the time slip away in thought.

The temperature rose with alarming speed, blinding out the landscape in a wave of scorching glare. The rise of temperature was so immediate it warped the rover's metal skin in a creaking of expansion. Drinkwine sank his face into his arms to protect himself from the debilitating heat. His skin crawled beneath his clothes, itching with irritating discomfort. He didn't dare stop. He must wait out the great mistake of the orbiting Myoko mirror, pounding the planet with its misguided and unruly behavior completely unchecked. This pummeling felt more severe than the previous ones, perhaps due to the isolation, the unfathomable distance from cover. There wasn't a single spot of shaded respite from the beating. Head hung, Drinkwine squinted down his eyes against the growing glare. Beads of sweat fell from his face and shattered like tiny glass balls across the floor of the rover. Through it all, the rover chugged along, defiantly groaning against the assault.

Finally, the glare began to abate and the temperature receded with pity. Drinkwine watched the thermometer as it drifted back to the normal roasting. He lifted his head and focused his eyes, blurred from sweat. Well, at least with any luck, that was the last of the sunstrikes he would have to endure. He wiped the streams of perspiration from his face as the rover continued its endeavor back to Jannah.

†

The faint clacking of computer keys let Drinkwine know that at least someone was at work in the vast reaches of the embassy. The sound grew steadily louder as he approached the office where he was to file his claim. Drinkwine wondered what the point was. There wasn't really enough value to warrant the inevitable hassle of trying to follow up a claim across the cosmos, a celestial bureaucratic nightmare that would most likely be misplaced and fumbled in the process. Yet if by rote for following protocol, Drinkwine entered the office.

The young Iranian woman tapping away at the computer stopped her work and greeted Drinkwine with a genuine smile, completely unaware of her boss' scheming and the artful ruse that was forcing the detective from Mars.

"I'm to file a claim, for my personal effects lost in the storm last night," Drinkwine said with a sigh.

The pretty young woman reached down and pulled a file cabinet drawer open, adeptly fanning through dividers with her slender fingers, the nails brightly painted. She pulled a form from a manila folder and set it on the counter before Drinkwine.

"You will please to fill this out," she began, setting a pen alongside. "With descriptions as to what was damaged or lost and what you believe the value to be. Then sign and date it, and make sure you put contact information for any compensation that might be granted."

Standing at the counter, the Loss & Damage form in front of him, Drinkwine's thoughts floated back to the fruitless investigation. A pang of dissatisfaction shuddered through him. He was being put off Mars by a bogus charge. How could they? The killer was being gifted amnesty by the powerbrokers—a killer, roaming free on the red planet. Damnit. How dare they. Resigned to it, Drinkwine pulled his bifocals on and studied the form on the countertop. He read a few lines of text before taking note of a stack of similar forms in a wire tray, already filled out and awaiting process.

The phone rang. The secretary picked it up, answering in Farsi. In her native tongue she asked the caller politely to give her a moment, then disappeared into the back room where Drinkwine heard file drawers being opened and closed in a concerted search.

Her absence gave Drinkwine the opportunity to finger through the stack of Loss & Damage claims in the tray. It was just his curious nature. Some might call it snooping. Actually, he was curious how others had described their various losses to lend him some guidance on how to scribe his own.

There were claims for various personal items that had been lost or damaged, representing a range of value, from small to large. Flipping through, the forms became a stop motion collage of things ruined by accidents and mishaps. Among them, certainly, were a good many falsehoods and phony claims. It was what this place was all about;

corruption, money, greed. If they couldn't be party to the huge pay-offs at the upper levels, such as those of contractors and politicians, the bottom feeders would get theirs by inflating the value of some personal item lost to God knows what kind of unscrupulous calamity. Mars was comprised of one continuous conga line of upturned palms; everyone in it for himself; everyone out for a fix, a scam, a bribe; everyone on the take, eager to make a dollar out of any situation that might present itself, regardless of who might be harmed, or who might lose. It was all being undertaken under the guise of a new and safe place to raise a family. Well good fucking luck.

As the forms flipped past, blurring the various handwritten claims of loss, Drinkwine's eye caught, for one fleeting second, the name Jafar Barr. He fished through the forms to find it again and withdrew it from the stack. In neat, handwritten letters, the applicant's name… Jafar Barr, the man Drinkwine had been in the middle of interviewing when he fainted. Below Barr's name was the word, Agni; Urdu for fire. His rudimentary grasp of the language allowed Drinkwine to decipher that the report was filed with regard to a remote research shed which had burned to the ground while in the charge of Barr. A 'total loss,' the handwritten note explained in perfectly executed penmanship. What a strange coincidence, Drinkwine thought, to have happened upon this, a Loss & Damage report filed by the man he had been with when he passed out.

When the secretary returned and resumed her phone call, she glanced around, looking for the white man who had asked to fill out the Loss & Damage report. He was gone. She settled back into her chair and resumed the call, with one less task to concern herself.

†

Drinkwine flushed through the corridor, stirring the stagnant air with urgency. He was headed for the records room in the main administration building. He wasn't supposed to be here. There were orders for him to be on the next shuttle off Mars. He looked at his watch. That was roughly eighteen hours from now. Happening across the Loss & Damage report filed by Jafar Barr was a strange and unsettling coincidence. He wondered if there was any value to the thoughts presently floating through his head. A coincidence— perhaps nothing more.

Drawing a vague hunch along with him, Drinkwine arrived at the records room. The woman there had seen him before, had seen him with Kurian, knew he carried a badge and, despite his color and nationality, bore some semblance of authority. Drinkwine was hoping Kurian had not sent out any official notification of his being pulled off the case and ordered off the planet. He asked calmly, "I need to see the releases for the interviews."

When she casually retrieved the folder of forms from a cabinet without question, Drinkwine knew he was safe. He immediately began thumbing through, stopping when he found the one for Jafar Barr, scrutinizing the scrawl of notes. As his eyes reached the bottom of the form he had to digest what was there. On the line where the interviewer was requested to sign their name, Drinkwine saw a signature unfamiliar to him. He even flipped through several pages to confirm the discrepancy. The signatures were all identical; the large, rounded D, followed by the scribbled, mostly undecipherable letters that spelled out his name. Flipping back to Barr's form he saw what was an unquestionable forgery. So, Jafar Barr had used the situation of Drinkwine's fainting spell to forge his signature, and in so doing, exonerate himself from the investigation. Clever, Drinkwine thought to himself. But why? It was the first true breath of suspicion, however vague or unconnected, drawn on the murder of one Michael Byrne.

Thumbing through the sheaves of notes that made up Barr's file, Drinkwine found numerous requests and sign-offs for rovers that corresponded with his outings to remote research huts to conduct his duties. There, in his handwriting, was his sign-out for a rover with the destination of the remote station that had burned to the ground. It was eight weeks previous, about the estimated time that the deceased, Michael Byrne, had been laid to rest in the sand. It all lined up with curious implications.

Voice not betraying anything of this disturbing windfall, Drinkwine pulled the woman from her work, "Could I get the address for Jafar Barr, please?"

The woman drew the name up on her computer. As she printed it out she read from her screen. "Oh, but he won't be there," uttering in broken English. "He's on research in the 94th Quadrant."

Drinkwine took the address. "Could I get the coordinates for the station where he'll be working?"

She politely obliged.

With the two printouts in hand Drinkwine exited with a nod of thank you, the woman's eyes curiously following him out the door.

†

The hallways of the long-term residences of the upscale dormitory were devoid of people. The residents, most being of scientific titles, were all off on their various duties, readying Mars for the influx of settlers that would soon be arriving. Drinkwine had hailed a cab from the embassy, once again suffering under the hostile eyes of the grudge master, Robert Haze, who, without a single word, stared at him with seething contempt in the rearview mirror all the way to the dorms.

The hallway smelled of carpet cleaner. So Jafar Barr had forged his signature. And he had been the assigned registrant to a remote research hut when it had burned to the ground about the time that the victim had gone missing. There were too many oddities for this to not have some significance. But was that reasonable evidence to make him a suspect in a murder? Well, either way, Jafar Barr was going to have to explain his way out of the forged signature. That alone would be cause enough to jail a man—well, Drinkwine checked reality; perhaps a white man on Earth.

Once Drinkwine had arrived at Barr's door, he made a quick study of the lock. Producing a small metal file from his wallet he set to tripping it. After some fumbling the handle slid down, granting him access to the room that for a fleeting moment he thought, might possibly belong to a murderer. He curbed his imagination. Perhaps there was explanation. After all, thus far it was only a forged signature and a burned down work shed. Still.

Drinkwine slipped into the room and closed the door behind. The darkness smelled of Jasmine tea. Barr was gone to some remote station and would not be interfering. Drinkwine made a calculated inventory of the room. His eyes scanned the small space, soaking in the strange somberness of the order to it all; the neat stacks of papers and pencils, all aligned with perfection, spoke volumes. Nothing seemed out of place. In fact, the room was so disturbingly clean and perfectly organized as to suggest an unsettled mind. The dresser drawers were layered with perfectly folded shirts and pants and paired socks. The cabinets of the small kitchen held their cups and plates with unsettling order. One wall, appearing like a shrine, was dedicated to the collection of old vinyl records. Yes, Jafar had waffled on in his interview about his hobby; a passion for collecting old vinyl records. An ancient, perfectly refurbished turntable sat under a shield of clear plastic.

The shelves above were filled with old albums, their aged sleeves heavily faded, the edges dog-eared from excessive handling. The tastes ran the gamut; Middle Eastern music, American Big Band classics, Top 40 of the 20th Century. Drinkwine saw the records were arranged by artists' last names and in order of release. Save for the disturbing order of the room there was nothing here to suggest Barr possessed any demons or sadistic characteristics. He was wasting his time. That's what was going through his mind as he opened kitchen cabinets and drawers. Swinging the bottom cabinet open he was overcome by the distinct smell of lighter fluid. Sitting there was a small can with a narrow red nozzle, sweated with a thin layer of misted fluid. Using his handkerchief to lift the can by its nozzle, Drinkwine shook it, sloshing barely more than a quarter of the original contents. Barr had used more than half the contents for something... most likely arson.

Drinkwine's mind raced. Normally, on Earth, he would now call in the findings and be given some backup to approach Jafar Barr for questioning about the forgery and suspicion of arson. But he couldn't do that, not here. No one was going to help. In fact, the clock was ticking on his deportation. He had until the boarding of the shuttle before they would come looking for him. Kurian would most assuredly send a car to fetch him and take him to the space port. It wouldn't be out of politeness, but rather to ensure the nuisance of Drinkwine and his badge, and all he represented, would be taken to the shuttle and blasted off the planet. Drinkwine wasn't sure exactly what he was going to do. For now, the only thing his mind could conjure was that Jafar Barr was out there, in the desert. At this very moment he was at a research outpost, unaware that evidence was amassing that required explanation.

Drinkwine gathered his thoughts and left the room, with one last quick review in hope of seeing anymore damning clues. But there were none. He closed the door behind him.

✝

The agent at the transpo center was taking his good ole time to check out another rover for Drinkwine. Every extra second the man toiled behind the computer Drinkwine took as a possible notification that he'd been removed from duty and was without privilege. Each exhale of the agent felt like it would be followed by a stout refusal. Drinkwine was relieved of his anxiety when the agent absently handed over a key, realizing Kurian had still not yet reported his deportation.

✝

Trekking as fast as the clanking vehicle could muster, Drinkwine watched the city of Jannah as it became smaller and smaller in the rearview mirror of the rover. He pulled out the crumpled Loss & Damage report he'd purloined from the records room. It had the GPS coordinates for the destroyed research hut. It was too much of a coincidence; the hut under Barr's reservation when it burned down, corresponding with the discovery of the body; the forged signature, taking advantage of Drinkwine's unfortunate fainting spell. Well, unfortunate for him, very much fortunate for Barr. What was he hiding from? Still, until proven guilty, he thought—until proven guilty. It was training, to stay with the code of ethics. Innocent until proven. Until proven. Until proven guilty. Damnit. He pressed the throttle to its stop, ensuring he was getting everything there was to

164

get out of the motor, the battery needle in rapid descent against the demands. Drinkwine was headed out into the remote reaches of Mars, toward a new jumble of questions that begged answering against a ticking clock. And he was alone, utterly alone.

Surely, Drinkwine thought to himself as the treads spun up the red dust behind, if the hunch he was presently entertaining turned out to be just, there would have to be some clue that the fire had not taken with it.

The barren plains were still and silent. The meandering dunes had been combed with intricate, delicate ripples left in the wake of the previous day's storm. A faint breeze loitered about the area, gently stirring up a thin plume of dust, harboring threats of escalating the calm into a storm of blinding wrath, ready to have yet another go at him. The landscape was marred by the single lay of the rover's tracks, which the funnel of dust appeared to be studying in its drunken wavering to and fro, ready to smooth over all evidence that Drinkwine had been this way. God, he hated this place. How he hated it.

Chapter 18

THE INTERMINABLE SAND UNFURLED beneath the rover in a maddening crawl. Drinkwine bit down hard, his mind swirling with a host of 'what ifs?' He checked his service weapon for the second time. Less than a quarter of battery life. A bad habit, he often forgot to put it on a night charge. A quarter charge. It made him think of the range of the rover. The dial indicated slightly less than a full charge, and dipping fast given the load he was demanding from the battery to speed him to Jafar Barr. But first, one last stop; the burned out research shed.

After more than two hours of monotonous clanking of treads over the long stretch of rock-strewn hard pack, a dark spot corrupted the landscape of red. As the rover crept closer, Drinkwine saw the remains of what had been an outpost of science; the burnt skeletal structure of a research shed. The fire had, quite literally, burned it to the ground. There were several columns of deeply charcoaled wood that jutted from the sand in varying heights, looking like a muted pipe organ rising out of the ground. There were but a few sparse remnants of wall. The sheets of corrugated steel that had comprised the roof had been ripped off by the harassing winds and tossed randomly into the desert. Toasted black and bent by heat, they were strewn about the area, half sunk in the sand. Mars had already begun the slow burial of the remains. It's what Mars did in its irreverent play; bury all signs of man.

Drinkwine brought the rover to a stop. He carefully surveyed the area before emerging into the heat. As far as the eye could see in any direction—nothing. The only movement was a vague impetus of threat from a soft wind that frolicked nearby. It broke from its boredom to curiously spy on him, lazily attempting to incite the surrounding sand without success. On the opposing horizon, incongruous with the expanse of pale blue, brewed a mass of dark gray cloud. It felt inconsequential. But Drinkwine had learned to not disregard any of this planet's flirtations with the elements. He studied the brooding patch as it lumbered across the sky, upsetting the otherwise clear day and then, without a sound, was illumed from deep within by a soundless bolt of lightning.

He made for the burnt, melted mess that was slowly being reclaimed by the desert. Stepping up onto the charred flooring, Drinkwine took stock. The fire had been intense. The area held that ugly smell the rapturous burn of fire, unchecked, leaves in its wake. The heat that had done this damage, deforming the shed and its contents, had long since cooled, leaving behind strange steel sculptures, bent and worthless, augmented by ugly globs of melted plastic that looked like hideous, cancerous growths.

In the report, Barr had stated that the blaze was the result of a hot plate catching the curtains on fire. Making tea, he reported. Probably some of his Jasmine, Drinkwine mused. Barr had written that it was all he could do to get out of the dwelling before the entire structure had been engulfed in flames and burnt to the ground before a single attempt at extinguishing it could be made. Proof to this point, whether a lie or not, was the fire extinguisher still clamped to its wall mount. How convenient, Jafar couldn't stop the flame from engulfing the structure.

Careful not to land a foot on the protruding nails that had been left behind when the wood around them had been burned away, Drinkwine carefully made his way over and under the fallen, blackened and charred beams and ceiling joists that had once amounted to a shed. They had been reduced to waffled patterns of charcoal that had collapsed in on themselves.

Standing at the center of the structure, Drinkwine made a careful scan, reconstructing what the interior of the building must have looked like before the inferno engulfed it. He contrived where a long workbench had been, the work lamps melted into the morass, the plastic material of the swivel chair burned away, leaving just the charred skeletal framework. The small appliances of the kitchen; the refrigerator, the stove, the dishwasher, had all been fried to a crisp. A latticework of springs was all that was left of the couch in what had been a small living area.

The one personal imprint of Jafar Barr among the shed were the charred remains of what had once been a turntable and a grotesque clump of melted goo that had been some of his cherished vinyl records. The records, once etched with beautiful music in their tiny grooves, were now worthless and soundless and ugly. Barr had obviously brought a small selection of his precious discs from his extensive collection at the dormitory to help wile away the long hours of isolation. He had said in his interview that the vinyl replicated the music with a quality of audio unmatched by modern digital components. He had excitedly explained the care required in the handling of the rare vinyl records; the spinning of the turntable; and the scratch of the needle that magically drew the music out of the grooves of the old recordings performed by musicians who had all since died. Drinkwine recalled that Barr had been unusually fascinated by the notion that all the musicians that had played on the old vinyl discs were long dead.

Drinkwine stopped and automatically reversed his slow, methodical turn of observation when his mind discerned something that disrupted the logic of the shed. A charred metal cabinet, melted and bent to half its original size, was set by the back entrance in such a way that it impeded the natural swing of the door. The placement of the cabinet didn't make sense. This little thing entranced him, so Drinkwine entertained his curiosity. Upon closer scrutiny it became obvious that the cabinet had been moved prior to the blaze consuming the building. Why?

Placing his hands on either side of the charred cabinet, Drinkwine took firm hold and began rocking it away from what little remained of the wall behind. The ash and soot quickly discolored his hands as he shimmied the flimsy cabinet away from the stubby, burnt timbers of frame.

Once clear of the deformed cabinet, Drinkwine studied the charred remains of the structure. Retrieving his bifocals and pulling them on after wiping a layer of red mist from their lens, he patiently scrutinized what little was left of the wall. Barely visible in the layers of charcoaled wood, Drinkwine discovered a tiny hole, a near perfect circle of indentation. Snapping open a small titanium pocketknife from his jacket, Drinkwine crouched down and carefully pushed the sharp tip of the blade into the diminutive cavity.

After some prying, he withdrew a tiny, discolored shot pellet. Rubbing it between his fingers removed its covering of ash. Head tilted back to better focus on it in the sunlight—rapidly declining against the gathering storm—Drinkwine recognized it as one of the 9.1mm tungsten shot pellets from the shells exclusive to the Roches riot weapon. It was a damning remnant of the overspray from the wide spread of the Roches' notoriously lethal cylinder choke. Drinkwine understood he held in his hand the immaculately condemning evidence that tied Jafar Barr to the murder of Michael Byrne. Purely out of curiosity and routine—and perhaps to buy some time to think about his next, critical step—Drinkwine searched out more of the incriminating holes, using the knife to pry the singed pellets from where they had been deeply imbedded. The pattern of tiny holes formed a halo in the wall around where Byrne's head had gotten in the way of the violent burst. In short order Drinkwine held a dozen of the tungsten pellets in his closed fist, tinkling with the sound of marbles.

Rising stiffly, Drinkwine circled the kill spot, reassembling the gruesome scene from the facts now coming together with startling clarity. The corona of pellet strikes made a disturbing shrine above where the vinyl discs had been reduced to globs by the heat of the fire. Judging by the entrance wound, Drinkwine figured that Michael Byrne had been crouched on the floor before the antique turntable. So, he had been listening to some of Barr's precious records. Barr had evidently drawn Byrne into a degree of comfort, distracting him with the exceptional fidelity of one of the vinyl records, rotating at 33½ rpm, the needle drawing beautiful music out of its shallow grooves. Then, with Byrne enthralled in the turning disc and sweet music, Barr had leveled the Roches riot gun at the back of his skull.

Why had he done it? The two men were obviously not in a fracas. In fact, it appears the mood was one of congeniality, simply enjoying some music. What the fuck had poor old Michael Byrne done to warrant Jafar Barr blasting a gaping hole in his head? How strange, to be unaware that you have roused the thought of homicide, your homicide, in the mind of a coldblooded killer. How odd. And what was Michael Byrne listening to when it happened?

Drinkwine noticed the darkening skies that had congregated to watch him, threatening to mature into one of Mars' rare thunderstorms. The clouds seemed to be gathering in celebration of his discovery.

Based on the angle of the entrance wound and the halo of pellet holes in the wall, Drinkwine easily estimated the trajectory, taking up position behind where Byrne had evidently been settled on the floor, unaware his life was about to be ended. Then, drawing on a path of execution, Drinkwine extended his arm, holding an imaginary Roches riot gun in his hand. As the storm clouds swept in, Drinkwine envisioned the fully intact research center—a ghosted image of Byrne squatted relaxed on the floor before the stereo, innocently handling an album sleeve—Barr standing behind, about to take away everything the victim possessed. As he eased back on the trigger the gathering storm announced its ferocity with a powerful series of celebratory lightning strikes, the immediate thunder clasp augmenting the explosion out the muzzle of the Roches as Byrne's brains splattered the wall. The disturbing vision dissolved with the first droplet of rain against Drinkwine's cheek, jarring him back to the burnt skeletal environs of the shed.

Drinkwine surmised that Jafar Barr had attempted to clean up the murder scene, placing the cabinet to hide the pellet holes. He had most likely been shocked by the unexpected mess, the copious volume of blood and brain unleashed with the violent discharge of the weapon and—realizing there was no way to adequately rid the shed of incriminating evidence—had determined that an erasing blaze was his best option. The sky rejoiced with a flash of lightning followed a moment later by a crack of thunder—celestial applause to his breaking of the case. The droplets of rain were few, but large and heavy, splattering against the remnant metal roof pieces like a discordant orchestra.

Making for the rover, Drinkwine's mind was awash with thoughts to chart his next move. There was no question now. It all lined up. Barr had killed a man. He'd blown his head almost clean away, then decided to torch the shed to get rid of the evidence. However, he was intelligent enough to know that forensics would find clues, however thin, if he'd tried to get rid of the body in the fire. So, he'd removed the corpse of Michael Byrne from the hut before burning it to the ground. He'd then taken the deceased out to where science and industry would eventually raise a cover of water and shackled the faceless body to an old root, with hopes the lake would never give up its dead. Very clever.

But then the winds went and ruined his plan. They'd contrived to uncover the caper. Barr had no doubt been nervous upon learning of the arrival of Drinkwine. When the questions started in and Drinkwine began his steady progress to an answer, Barr had made good on the lucky incident of the fainting spell and forged the interview papers to absolve himself. It had almost worked. What if he'd not seen that Loss & Damage report? Drinkwine thought. But, that was how tentative these things were. This was how fragile justice was, too often suffering the luck of randomness and chance, relying on the stumbling onto evidence. Well, thank the stars it had been uncovered. No reason to question the precariousness of it all. He had his man. That's all that mattered. Drinkwine decided not to spend too much time questioning it. Regardless, circumstance had prevailed. He knew who the killer was. He knew where it had happened. There remained the motive. Why? That would have to wait. For all intents and purposes, Drinkwine's job was almost done. There was enough evidence to get a conviction. But there was now the task of getting him into custody.

Drinkwine plugged the coordinates for the remote research outpost into the GPS where, presently, Barr was carrying on with his duties, totally unaware. Or was he? What now drummed Drinkwine's head was if Barr had the Roches with him. He didn't want to consider that a Roches riot gun, in the hands of a wanted murderer, might well be waiting for him at the end of that desert that lay between himself and Barr. Would there be a confrontation? Men do strange things when they are up against a wall, when their freedom is in jeopardy. Drinkwine shook the speculation from his head as he pushed toward the distance, toward where Jafar Barr was ensconced in research. The barren red plains of Mars stretched out before him, leading him ominously to his rendezvous with a killer. Innocence until proven... to hell with it. Barr killed Byrne. He killed him.

The mad rush to make sense of the puzzle brought all the questions flooding back like a festering wound. Why had Barr done it? There was no money to be had. There was no suggestion of any labor disputes or safety issues—aside from what was taken here as normal. Perhaps a failed homosexual encounter? A rejection? Was it jealousy? Was Barr gay? Perhaps Byrne wasn't, or vice versa? Was he fearful of the harsh laws of Islam regarding an accusation of homosexuality? Was that enough to take Byrne's life? Why had Barr lured the victim to the shed, stuck a Roches riot gun at the back of his skull and pulled the trigger, ending the man's life and spilling the very essence of his character on the wall? Every memory, every dream, every laugh the man had ever experienced had dripped down the plaster walls of that shed and were sent to high heaven on the heat waves of an intense and all consuming blaze. All of these things crossed Drinkwine's mind in rapid succession. Why had he done it?

Drinkwine couldn't quite fathom how Jafar Barr would react when confronted with a charge of murder. Best not to imagine the multitude of scenarios that might unfold, as they would all most likely prove to be wrong. Best to just go, and be ready for anything.

It was at that moment, Drinkwine realized with sobering implications, that in his haste to get after the perpetrator of the crime he had forgotten to bring his hat and, worse, water. He hadn't used his head. Damnit. His crime, he thought to himself. Yes, it was his crime. Drinkwine repeatedly scolded himself for his foolishness. That foolishness might well plant him out here in the desert where the sand, in gleeful collusion with the wind, would bury him in an anonymous grave. How could he have been so stupid as to not grab a hat and water? Too obsessed with his work. Tunnel vision. That's what *she* had accused him of. Perhaps it was true. Painfully true. Just a liter bottle of water—something—anything. Drinkwine had to shake himself from the thought. He was drifting now. He felt the sands laughing at him. The heat was already scheming to undo him.

†

——————————————————Chapter 19

T HE DRONING OF THE rover's treads—trading between churning the deep sand and skirting the hard-packed ground—rattled Drinkwine's mind. The GPS shone bright, indicating the long haul ahead at slow speed, teasing and provoking as to where this all might end. The creeping sand played into Drinkwine's obsessive thoughts. Why had Barr killed a low-level worker?

With the plains holding the heat of the day, Drinkwine saw the fresh imprint of a rover's tracks in the sand. The GPS, narrowing in on the research hut, had put Drinkwine's rover on almost the exact course Barr had navigated. Barr was out here. The man who had pulled the trigger with cruel indifference. As he slipped his rover into the track imprints Drinkwine considered the distance he was now from the city, from help, considered how far he was from assistance. He was frustrated by the conspicuous rumble of the treads, which meant there was no hope for surprise.

Squinting into the glare of the red desert the sharp angles of a man-made structure corrupted the rolling landscape of sand and rock. Almost lost in the quivering waves of heat rising off the Martian surface, Drinkwine saw the remote research station where Jafar Barr was currently situated. The signal flag indicating the shed was active hung limp in absolute calm. Once again the wind was fucking with him, this time being nowhere in sight. The wind now could help conceal his approach. But this agonizing stillness and quiet would allow the movement of the rover to be heard well before it arrived at the shed. Barr would hear the whining motor and rattling treads well in advance.

As he crept toward the encounter with the murderer in painfully slow progress, his eyes stinging with sweat, Drinkwine saw movement about the shed, still some distance off. As he surmised, the noise of the rover had alerted Jafar Barr to his presence. The heat rising off the dunes was playing havoc. Barely discernible against the glare, Drinkwine saw Jafar Barr emerge from the shed carrying something. When he raised his hands to his face Drinkwine realized that Jafar was spying him through binoculars. He watched as Jafar retreated into the shed. Was it to retrieve the Roches? Drinkwine wondered. There was still the question of whether Barr had the weapon in his possession and, if so, had he had the good sense to recharge it? If so, there were potentially a dozen rounds in it, each one capable of taking Drinkwine's head off and spreading his precious Harvard education over the Martian sands. The visuals planted in his mind as to what the weapon did to Byrne—and the notion that the same hot flying lead could be aimed at him—was disconcerting. Not the kind of thing a man needs to be thinking about as he treaded closer to confrontation. Drinkwine drew his service weapon from the shoulder holster. He wiped his brow of sweat with his sleeve as he studied the gun, considering its effectiveness against a Roches. Nothing like showing up with a pencil sharpener to a gunfight, he thought. The rover continued its noisy approach.

Against the blurring void and the painfully slow progress of the rover, Drinkwine saw Jafar—distorted through waves of heat— emerge from the shed. If he had retrieved the Roches, Drinkwine knew the range of the weapon would not reach him at this distance. Still, to have a weapon leveled at you is no small event, regardless of the gap. But Jafar Barr instead made fast for the rover parked alongside the corrugated steel structure. The rover leaped forward and whipped around, the inside tread throwing up a rooster tail of sand as it made a tear for the distant horizon of red.

The suspect was making a run for it. Stuck in the pitifully slow progress of the rover, all Drinkwine could do was watch the frantic activity of a desperate man from afar. The man who had killed Michael Byrne was in that rover, presently making a dash for God knows where. Where he intended to go Drinkwine had no idea, for this was the last outpost of humanity on the wild reaches of Mars. What lay beyond this was nothing but the murderous abyss of the red planet. Given time, there was only death from hunger, dehydration, and exposure to the elements. As far as Drinkwine was concerned, for a healthy person to trespass into that certain demise was merely testament to the man's guilt.

A full twenty minutes after Jafar had bolted from the shed and taken off in the rover, Drinkwine arrived at the research shed. The wind speed indicator atop the roof was absolutely still. Not a whisper of movement in the air, not a breath of relief from the heat.

In his haste, Jafar had left the door to the shed wide open. Jumping from the rover Drinkwine barged through and made quick survey of the interior. He was determined not to make further missteps and searched out items that would be useful in the strangely measured pursuit that had just begun.

The first thing that caught his attention was the Roches firearm. It was sitting on the workbench in partial disassembly. It appeared Jafar had tried to repair the weapon, sand having corrupted its workings, rendering it useless. This was good. Drinkwine now knew his killer was no longer armed with a lethal weapon.

Infused with relief, Drinkwine tore through the shed looking for provisions. He found several bottles of water in the refrigerator, scooping them up in anticipation of entering the sweltering desert. He would not make that mistake again. He wondered if Jafar had had the presence of mind to grab any water or take any provisions with him. Hopefully the crush of capture had ruptured any logic and the murderer was headed out into the unforgiving desert unprepared. Oddly, what stroked Drinkwine's mind for a fleeting second was the hope that Jafar would not die before he could learn of the motive for the killing of Byrne. What was the agenda, the motivation behind the brutal homicide?

With the guilt of Barr confirmed, Drinkwine switched to a mode of police protocol in the apprehension of a suspect. He maintained the same calculated approach that accompanied his research, thinking through the probable events. This shift in mindset happened quite effortlessly as Drinkwine put the droning rover onto a course across the plain in pursuit of Jafar Barr. The two vehicles, identical in performance, would gain and lose nothing on one another in the laborious crawl across the nothingness, taking them into more of the nothingness.

Drinkwine calculated how long the two vehicles could run at this clip before they drained their batteries and came to an excruciatingly frustrating halt, far from anything. He wondered how much battery life the two vehicles had already exhausted in the trek to these far reaches. Certainly, one of the vehicles had more in reserve than the other. Drinkwine hoped it was his.

As the slow pursuit unfolded across the endless expanse of desert, the sweltering heat cruelly played on Drinkwine's thoughts. The tracks of Barr's rover screamed of desperation. They strode the flattish red desert divulging unretractable confession. There was no longer any question of who had murdered Byrne. The murderer was up ahead, just out of sight, making some mad play for escape. Escape? How did he expect to escape? He was trapped here on Mars. There was nowhere to run. What did he hope to achieve in this desperate act? Perhaps it was merely to avoid capture and extend his freedom by just a few precious days, a few precious hours.

The insufferable distance conjured a host of possible outcomes. Drinkwine considered that even if Jafar Barr wasn't in possession of the Roches that didn't negate the possibility of violence. Men driven to extremes, given over to the base primal instinct of survival, were capable of anything.

Staring into the deceiving plains, Drinkwine hoped the winds would remain benevolent for now, so that the tracks Barr's rover was leaving in the Martian surface could be followed. If one of the planet's notorious windstorms blew up it would remove the one trace of the killer and his intent. He eased the rover's treads directly into the tracks Barr had laid and settled back in the seat, ruminating on what the outcome of this situation was going to be. If it came down to having to use his weapon Drinkwine assured himself he wouldn't hesitate. Once he had confronted the suspect, he would keep a safe distance. He would toss his handcuffs out to him and have the suspect cuff himself to avoid the unnecessary risk of getting too close and unintentionally granting an upper hand to the suspect. It had all been covered in basic training all those years ago; how to apprehend a suspect when you are unaccompanied. And Drinkwine was unaccompanied, completely and entirely unaccompanied.

All that might happen played on Drinkwine's mind; not enough water; not enough power in the rover batteries to get them back to the settlement. The cell phones, what about the cell phones? Drinkwine checked the signal. It was fading, fast, weakly bouncing between one bar and zero. No way to communicate. He thought to himself that he would get Barr back to the research station and use the radio there to call for assistance. If he called, they would have to send someone. They would have to. Unless those in power decided to take measures to keep this thing under wraps. Jafar was a killer, so what loss if he were to die? And himself? How much was his life worth at this moment to these people? Surely there were those who would just as soon see him expire out here in the quieting desert, leaving the winds to bury him and his trouble where no one would ever find him. The artists' renderings of the city of Jannah could resume their promise; *Crime Free Living On Far Away Mars.*

†

Chapter 20

F AR UP AHEAD, DISAPPEARING now and again against the distance and glare, Drinkwine spotted Jafar's rover in its frantic, albeit slow, escape across the abyss. Drinkwine could see his vehicle was slightly slower, and now, some two hours into the ordeal, the gap between the two was growing. The indicator needle of the battery gauge bounced and hovered jokingly in the red. It would eventually stop its play and strand him. How long could this pursuit go on? The pace was playing with him, agonizing the lawman from Earth with where this all might end. Running his sleeve across his forehead, which was sopped with sweat, Drinkwine took a sip of water. Stay hydrated. It was essential.

The desert was deceiving with its stillness. The winds were loitering, unseen, soon to be joined in conspiracy with the sand, its insatiable friend, to undo the calm. A host of warning lights had been illumed. As Drinkwine had anticipated would happen, the vehicle was slowing. It had been slowing for some time now. The arduous pace had been reduced to just slightly faster than walking. Drinkwine had decided he would run the power out of the batteries regardless of the snail-like pace in order to conserve his own energy for the tortuous journey ahead on foot. He had already consumed a fifth of his water supply, and that was in the shade of the cab, without expending any energy. He had shut off the air conditioner some kilometers back to conserve battery power. The heat inside the cab was stifling. He blinked away each sting of perspiration that slipped into his eyes.

As the rover slowly died, treading the endless sea of sand,

Drinkwine stared ahead into the desert. The heat was retreating as the day began its descent to evening. The cool would be welcome respite from the day's baking. The setting sun raised a pleasant glow over everything, granting a surreal presence to the dunes and rocks. It was almost beautiful, Drinkwine thought to himself. The dryness of his mouth stirred him from the momentary lapse.

With the needle now pegged at the bottom of the gauge, the motor suddenly ceased its turning hum and the rover unceremoniously ground to a halt. The vehicle was now merely a heavy mass of useless steel, stuck up to its axles in drifts of red sand. Drinkwine stared at the instruments, somewhat dumbfounded. Though he had been anticipating this moment, it still came as a surprise. Now, the rolling dunes and scattered patches of rock were to be navigated on foot. He surveyed the area. The death of the rover made the desert more desolate, more remote than any of his previous excursions—if such a thing were possible.

Drinkwine readied himself for the ordeal that lay ahead. In fashioning head protection he mutilated his linen jacket, using his pocketknife to shred it to strips, wrapping them into a headpiece that draped his neck—the excess material to be drawn across his face in protection against the windstorms he was certain to encounter. It crossed his mind to simply return to Jannah, to the air conditioned suites, and wait for the Martian desert to take its toll on Jafar Barr. He would either succumb to the elements and die among the dunes, his body eventually interred in the deep swells of sand, or retreat to the city and give himself up. Even as he considered this, Drinkwine continued his preparations for taking to the desert in pursuit. It was his calling, his ingrained sense of service and duty. He was a cop, after all. It didn't feel right to wait for nature to render punishment. This was a human situation—it demanded a human resolution.

†

The sun had set with a brilliant spectacle of blood red that gradually introduced the ink black of night. Drinkwine was determined to make the most of the cool temperature and rack up the kilometers before the sun would rise with its inevitable beating in the day ahead. The blackness led to a distant seam where the star field domed overhead. That seam was the horizon, and Drinkwine knew for nothing more than to walk toward it, his feet staying within the cascading, treaded grooves left behind by Jafar's rover. Among the stunning array of stars he spotted the Earth, just cresting. The blue orb, one hundred fifty million kilometers away, shown vaguely.

He was tired. To stay awake, to avoid the seduction of the inviting red sand to lay down and sleep, Drinkwine pulled up various mental games to solve. He went through the multiplication tables rather quickly, then the alphabet, first forward, then backwards. Forwards, then backwards. Fuck this, Drinkwine thought. He resolved to let his strides be the entertaining factor here and continued to labor the soft red sand that caressed each precious step with a gentle and tiring embrace.

†

The hours passed. Drinkwine had lost all awareness of time, save that the night sky had made its grandiose nocturnal turn and crossed the stars across the firmament, now introducing the slightest hint of gray. Dawn was approaching. And with it, the assault of the sun and heat would be upon him again. The only reassuring aspect was that Jafar Barr would be suffering the same abuse.

†

The sun was overhead. It had made the steady climb to its perch in the sky to hammer the planet with its fury. Drinkwine conjured the memory of the treated air that kept the lobbies of the buildings of Jannah cool. He thought of the cold air that chilled the building with the fake snow and the ski slope. How he wished he could be there right now, out of this torment. Drinkwine's mind was getting drunk from the sun. He had to concentrate to keep his strides straight and true. His nose had been blistered red. The planet graciously tolerated it all.

Far to the west, against the immense sky, plump gray clouds ran on legs of rain. Drinkwine longed to be beneath them, longed to feel their drops of moisture. When he stopped to have a drink of warm water, he checked his stores. Just one liter bottle remained, and that was already half gone. The other bottle purloined from the research shed had long since been emptied and tossed into the garbage bin of the desert. The scenario gave little reassurance as Drinkwine contemplated the foreboding desert that stretched out before him. His cell phone—the battery teetering just above the red—was his compass. When the battery died, so would he. Those distant rain clouds were taunting him again, trying to lure him into a deception of relief. This is what Mars did; it played with men, coyly drawing them in with its mischief to slowly slaughter them. The planet was predisposed against man, exhibiting extreme prejudice, and rightly so. It didn't matter that he was one of the good ones, Drinkwine thought. He was guilty by simply being human.

The desert had deceived with stillness all morning. Now, it awoke. It didn't take long to exact its nature. It began as they all began, with but a single, harmless stir of dust whipped up by a passing breeze. Drinkwine watched to see if it would spin itself to nothing, dying among the dunes, or turn angry and vengeful. It answered immediately. The wind rose, stirring the sand into a frenzy, the funnel gaining strength, teetering one way then the other in indecision before turning and making headlong for Drinkwine. The gods were probably laughing at it all, he thought.

Drinkwine pulled the excess tail of his headpiece across his face and fastened it above his ear in anticipation of the pummeling he was about to endure. He kept on, pushing through the sand toward some strange duty. The wind seemed to understand his resolve and lured him deeper into the desert where it could pound him mercilessly.

The funnel of swirling sand engulfed the lone visitor with brute force. Drinkwine clamped down his mouth and eyelids but still the grains made their way between his lips and into his eyes. Fuck, Drinkwine thought to himself, pushing on despite the forces fighting him.

The sand and wind, in their bored play, were plotting to undo this foolish human who had dared to enter their domain. They were to exact revenge on him for the destruction the others had done to this place. This was the savage and cruel science of nature, catching up the unwitting, the innocent, in a blind indifference. What if, after all this, he was to die out here having not got his man? His body would be gradually buried in the sand, sweeping his memory into the tomb of Mars. He let out a laugh at the irony of it all. He wondered, as the heat drew the moisture from his body, why the hell was he doing this?

The banging tornado of sand, after having had its play with Drinkwine, leaped off over the desert sprawl to toil elsewhere. Drinkwine pressed on, the tracks of Jafar's rover having been all but removed. He could scarce see the vague imprint of the tracks that the wind had smoothed to almost nothing. Was he keeping pace with Jafar Barr? Was his rover exhausting its battery? Drinkwine hoped so. He wasn't sure how much longer he could keep this up.

"Nine times five is forty-five, nine times six is fifty-five... no," he had to think, "Nine times six is fifty-four, yes, fifty-four, I'm sure it's fifty-four," Drinkwine said to himself. He was drifting. His mind was falling prey to the sorcery of Mars. The mathematical diversion was forgotten upon sight of something up ahead.

There, in the haze of the dunes, was something that didn't belong. Hard, straight edges in an environment of natural slopes and curves. Metal. Plastic. As Drinkwine drew closer to the apparition, he saw it was Jafar Barr's rover. It sat up to its axles in the sand. The driver's side door was open. The killer's rover had died. It had given up the ghost and condemned its occupant to a most probable death as well. Punishment for daring to take on the desert.

As he trudged through the deep sand in approach to the rover, Drinkwine pulled his gun from the holster, taking note of the battery charge. It was dipping well into the red. He wondered if he could even get one shot off before it died too. Everything was dying out here. Yes, the gods surely must be rolling with laughter now.

Drinkwine surveyed the area. There was nowhere to hide, just endless, sweeping dunes of red, quiet and motionless. No ambush here. As he approached the abandoned rover Drinkwine saw the sand around it had been disturbed by a flurry of movement—result of the killer preparing to advance on foot, gathering up what he could before beginning his trek into the great outback of Mars. He looked at where the footprints meandered the dunes and disappeared into the horizon. Fool, he thought. Then bent to the chase.

How long would the winds allow the footprints to remain before deciding to erase the only measure of tracking the killer? Would the wind rudely wipe them away in the cruelest of jokes? Perhaps Jafar Barr had found an accomplice in the sand and wind. Drinkwine could only guess that Jafar, having spent long periods isolated out here in this patent hell, was potentially more adept than himself at dealing with the harsh tendencies of the Martian desert. No creature derives joy from this stretch of nothingness, it is the sole domain of play among the gods, or perhaps evil.

Even more disturbing, what if the two of them should find their end against the harshness of this place having never met up? Two men dying alone, out here, like ignorant animals—one man's fate born of obsessive duty, the other in a desperate attempt to escape apprehension for a hideous crime, a crime no one else seemed to care about.

Drinkwine suddenly felt horribly alone in his principled efforts to bring justice to a crime that had the two of them potentially squandering their lives to the elements. Was it worth his own life? How many times had he been told that the victim was a lowly worker, an unliked, insignificant man. It was in the bringing of justice to the crime against this person that Drinkwine now found himself in the gathering grip of death. But he pressed on. All these thoughts did nothing to slow or detour his stride, pressing on to some irrelevant duty, some ambiguous end.

Staying the course, Drinkwine put his feet directly into the indentions left in the sand by Barr. He studied the increasingly wavering imprints, suggesting that Barr was succumbing to the elements, the heat, thirst. Then, acquainting the calm and quiet, an incongruous chime. It took Drinkwine a moment to realize it was his service weapon. He drew it from the holster to see the warning indicator was blinking. The battery charge was almost dead. The gun was useless. He stared at it, as if it had let him down. The lethal weapon had lost its purpose. It was now just a chunk of metal. He contemplated ridding himself of the additional weight but thought better of it.

Trudging the sand, Drinkwine stared at the footprints that led to nowhere. What was Jafar Barr thinking? What did he hope to achieve by making for the distance? He would die, surely he knew this. He was taking himself, steadfast, into the barren, untouched expanse of Mars. There was nothing out there. Only heat and sand. Did he prefer to die in the wasteland of the planet rather than give himself up to incarceration? Drinkwine didn't want him to die. He wanted to confront Barr to learn from the murderer himself, why he had done it, why he had killed Byrne. The beautiful mystery of killers is that often, once caught, they are strangely quick to divulge their secrets, to purge themselves of the welts of guilt. The more the elements tried to dissuade Drinkwine from his endeavor, the more he was resigned to it.

Detouring from the staggering tracks, Drinkwine investigated the rusted remains of a small weigh station. The makeshift structure had succumbed to the beatings of the winds and was now merely a skeleton of sandblasted siding and oxidized metal. Yet another forgotten outpost of industry laid to waste. As Drinkwine rummaged through the sparse remains, something caught his attention.

There, on the floor, was a length of heavily corroded galvanized pipe. It was perhaps 600mm long, and 40mm in diameter, deeply oxidized and peeling rust-colored flakes. One end was tapped with sharp, chipped threads. Drinkwine reached down and wrapped his hand around it, pulling the length of pipe from its soft bed of sand and pulverized drywall. It had some weight to it. A lethal weight. This, he thought to himself, this could be useful. He wondered of the damage it could do to a skull. It was nature, clawing its way up through his brilliant reason.

As Drinkwine marveled at the galvanized pipe, he stripped the leather holster off his shoulders. Weighted with the dead sidearm it fell to the cement floor with a heavy thud. Draped in his desert rags, the pipe clasped firmly in hand, Drinkwine exited the forgotten outpost and labored off in diligence across the desert.

†

Chapter 21

A DOME OF HEAT HUNG over the desert, the sun pounding the lonely visitor to this Godforsaken place. Drinkwine whetted his lips with what little water remained in his liter bottle. It was hot. As he continued the tireless stride, following the fading imprints of Jafar's staggering footprints, something shone on the sand ahead. Catching the sunlight was an empty water bottle dropped by Jafar Barr. Drinkwine wondered if he was out of water. There was nothing to do now but follow the footprints. He set himself back to the monotonous trek through the sand. "Eight times five is forty," Drinkwine uttered with a throat dry.

The stillness. That's what really got to Drinkwine. The immaculate stillness. Not a thing moved. Drinkwine believed for a brief moment that given the absolute stillness he could feel where the air had been stirred by Barr. Or was it Jafar Barr's scent? Drinkwine wondered, in this void of landscape, could he actually track the scent of the killer, like a wild animal hunting its prey? No, no, no, he was a Harvard schooled detective. He wore fine linen suits and drank fine Scotch. Drinkwine shook the disturbing notion from his mind and trudged on, stopping when he realized he'd been so far gone in his thoughts he couldn't recall the last several hundred feet. He looked at the trail of footprints he'd left in the impressions of those created by Jafar to assure himself he had, in fact, been moving, deeper into that desolation. The desert was luring him in, deeper into the expanse that would swallow him in a brutal beating of elements. These thoughts were upstaged by the disturbing realization that the temperature was rising as the desert began its roasting transformation, driven by the colossal fuck up of the Myoko mirror.

There was nowhere to find cover out here in the open wilds of desert. Drinkwine settled to the ground and prepared himself for the lashing he was to receive from the errant rays. The heat and blistering sun arrived right on time, pounding with Biblical proportions as the entire reach of desert was drawn up into the cataclysmic event. Drinkwine thought his body would rupture from the baking. If the heat didn't get him, perhaps a heart attack would. Roasted alive, like a pig on a spit.

Drinkwine conjured a winter on Earth when he had been taken ice fishing on Lake Erie. Against the pressing heat he tried with all his will to remember the thick ice, the freezing air, the biting cold. How he wanted for that cold right now.

After what seemed an eternity Drinkwine felt the heat ease. Bringing his head up from the cover of sand, he watched as the desert slowly took shape again out of the receding glare. The gods must be having a time of this entertaining spectacle, Drinkwine thought—two foolish humans having entered the devil's playground. He imagined them high above in the clouds, reclined on animal furs, sipping at their drink while being hand-fed grapes by naked nymphs. Cold, plump grapes. Drinkwine had to snap himself out of the delirium. He slapped himself hard across the face to bring himself back. He was drifting, the prelude to death in the desert.

Laboring to pick himself up off the sand, Drinkwine stretched out his arms to try and catch any cooling breezes that might be felt. Standing there, arms leveled, he looked like a tattered scarecrow lording over the barren, wasted plain. With not a thread of air to be found, he trudged on. "Seven times six is...," Drinkwine puzzled over the answer. "Seven times six, is six, seven times...." He was drifting. He knew it. He could feel the desert peeling away his awareness. "I'm Detective Drinkwine, age sixty-one. Married...," the thought was aborted. "No, no, divorced. Separated. Soon to be divorced." He fell into a trance watching his feet sink into the sand with each tired step. "Drinkwine, what an odd name. Is that your real name?" Drinkwine laughed at the years of rude comments. "Yes, damnit, that's my real name."

†

The infinite, ink black of space unfolded with freezing cold. Steady and immovable from its perpetual orbit, the Myoko mirror had re-set its hectares of Mylar panels and settled back into redirecting the sun's rays at the frozen poles of Mars. The satellite was completely unaware of its tortures of the damned far below. It was an innocently malevolent satellite that was unwittingly threatening to take the lives of two men—one, a man of the law, the other, a sadistic murderer. It made no difference to the marvel of technocracy, it had been programmed to do one thing; melt the ice caps and spring forth the precious water for Mars. It was immune to the comparatively petty concerns of two humans who had engaged in some strange pursuit across the wasteland below. It would be here, carrying out its duty, long after those two men had expired. Whether their end was to arrive in the coming hours and days, or whether they lived out long lives back on Earth, or in prison on the Moon, it was of little consequence to the Myoko. It would still be floating serenely four hundred kilometers above Mars for many years to come.

†

As Drinkwine continued into the gathering night he was suddenly aware of the disarming cold that was engulfing the desert. A few hours earlier he'd prayed for cold, now that it was arriving he feared for what he might be met with in the night ahead. Savage place, he thought to himself. What a savage place.

†

The stars crossed the night sky in their imperceptible crawl. Drinkwine, mouth agape, stared up at them as he warmed himself by a small fire. He'd lucked upon a patch of dead branches that had weathered the Martian elements for who knows how long. The dead plants—remnants of man's failed attempts to grow things here—had been spread to these far reaches by the irascible winds. They were one simple little nicety the desert had gifted him. He'd managed to start a fire with his silver lighter, feeding the weak flame with twigs and branches and words of encouragement. He cupped his hands over the licking flames. This place, he thought to himself, with no further comment save a shake of the head. This fucking place.

As Drinkwine warmed his hands against the cold, something far away in the dark spread of desert caught his eye. He studied the black distance for a long while, waiting to see it flicker again. Then, he saw it. Far off on the desert plain, a good fifteen kilometers distance, Jafar Barr had built himself a fire as well. He'd succumbed to the chill and had built a fire. Drinkwine didn't seem too concerned. He figured that as long as there was a fire, Jafar was stopped for the night and would not gain on him. Yes, Drinkwine thought, just keep building fires each night. He was too tired for confrontation, too tired to continue. For now, as the sleep came over him, he considered, there was nowhere for the man to run, save the horizon. The distant fire shown once more as the flames sparked up, the sole thing in a sea of black, and then Drinkwine was asleep.

†

Morning broke with blushing skies as the sun crested the horizon and began its arduous crawl into the Martian dawn. Drinkwine had woken early and sat on an immense dune that commanded an expansive view of the plains beyond. In the distance a thin plume of smoke rose from the dying coals of Jafar Barr's fire.

He traced the lone, dark dot corrupting the otherwise perfect sea of red sand. The speck was Jafar, continuing his desperate, slow escape across the inhospitable desert. Drinkwine had to marvel at the killer's fortitude. He collected up the rusted pipe and descended the dune in pursuit.

✝

Drinkwine had settled into the trace of footprints left by Barr. They waivered drunkenly. They belonged to tired legs in the command of an exhausted and drained mind. The tracks teetered erratically, continually correcting to fall back into some point of incoherent direction Jafar Barr had determined. Drinkwine assessed that by the way the left foot dug unevenly into the sand that Barr was limping, perhaps nursing a strained muscle, an aching knee. It would slow him. He would gradually succumb. The wound would provide Drinkwine with advantage in the hunt.

The sun had climbed high into the Martian sky, bringing the heat with it. Drinkwine tried to ascertain what time of day it was. It was getting near the sunstrike. He raised his arm to discover his watch was gone. He'd taken it off to build the fire last night and had left it sitting in the sand. Fool, he admonished. Fool.

Drinkwine didn't have to wait long to confirm his hunch that it was near roasting time. Time to put the pig on the spit again. His skin was already red and blistered from the exposure of the past two days. His lips cracked painfully with even the slightest movement. His entire body was riddled with rebellion to this endeavor. Only his determination seemed intent on continuing.

At the first hint of temperature rise Drinkwine collapsed onto the sand and pressed his face into the sunburned skin of his forearm. He readied himself for the harsh brutality of the Martian desert, which welcomed the assault of the Myoko mirror like a lusty lover. Those fucking gods must be rolling in the clouds at this, he thought to himself. "Well I'm still here, you motherfuckers," Drinkwine uttered, the profanity worth the further crack of lips as he settled in for the beating, the way a truant kid must accept his punishment.

189

Surely he would die, Drinkwine thought, as he buried his face into the fold of his arm. He felt the heat of the reflected rays blistering the back of his neck and baking his skin. My God, he thought. The sun and heat was draining his body, he could feel himself evaporating. "Shit, shit, shit," he exclaimed, laughing manically at the memory of his mother always saying that when she was angry; "shit, shit, shit." How could he be laughing? Maybe he was going mad. That was it, the desert and sun were toying with his sanity before delivering the killer blow. Well fuck them. Fuck this entire fucking planet.

Drinkwine was suddenly saddened at the thought of dying. He would now be one of his precious corpses with nothing left to say. No emotion, no thoughts, no concerns. Curled up in the fetal position, his face pressed into the fold of his arm to escape the hammering sun, Drinkwine started to cry. He hadn't cried since he was a little boy. But his body was too dehydrated to produce any tears, so he wept dryly.

Was it his imagination, or was the sunstrike abating? Yes, the blast of heat was retreating, returning the desert to its comparatively tolerable baking. He had been toasted raw by the Myoko's misguided wickedness. When he brought his head up he had to acclimate his sand-blinded and sunburned eyes to the red dunes and blue sky, blinking the focus and dull color back into them. As the familiar ocean swells of loping dunes and blanched rock formations came back into view from the receding glare—he froze.

Leaving dainty, perfect footprints in the sand with her splendidly naked feet, a woman was approaching. She wore a thin summer dress that went to just above the knees, revealing smooth calves. She had an elegant demeanor that defied the harsh surroundings. Drinkwine knew the hair, and the walk so well. It was Celeste. She was smiling that coy smile of hers, lips closed, as if stifling some private joy. Shyly, she broke eye contact to look at the sand as she strode closer, ever closer. Yes, it was Celeste, so beautiful. Oh so soft and gentle against the harshness of the landscape. And that smile. That's what he had fallen in love with all those years ago. She had come to Mars to save him. Save him from the sun, the sand, the murderer. She was going to make everything all right again.

When she arrived before Drinkwine, she bent down, modestly holding the dress so as not to reveal too much of her legs. As she leaned in, her body blocked out the harsh sun, casting a cooling relief of shadow over him. She looked longingly into his eyes, tacitly begging forgiveness.

"I forgive you, sweetheart," Drinkwine uttered, "I forgive you."

She smiled sweetly.

He tenderly reached out his hand to touch her. His fingers passed through her hair, invoking the horrific revelation that she was merely another of the planet's mirages. As she vanished into nothingness, smiling coquettishly, her shadow evaporated as well, allowing the sun to slam him with penetrating heat. Drinkwine collapsed to the ground, his tearless sobbing and tormented exhales puffing up grains of sand.

†

The sun seemed to have lost some of its power over him. Perhaps, Drinkwine thought, he was being toughened to the ordeal. No time to get cocky. Especially since he was eyeing the first rumor of tumult in the distance. Maybe if he pretended not to notice it would retreat and leave him be. But evidently the desert wasn't in a magnanimous mood. With dread, he observed as the winds incited the sand, giving birth to one of its dust devils, spinning it into a passion.

Drinkwine watched as the swirling column of dust swayed with indecision, this way and that. Then, as if preordained, it made straight for him. Well Goddamn, he thought, as he tiredly raised the torn linen tail of his headpiece across his face in anticipation of the beating, which caught him up without pity. The calm that had accompanied the day was instantly transformed into a thrashing caldron that descended on him without pity. His body was bullied and beaten in the harsh play of the desert. Drinkwine took a wide stance to brace against the blow but the turbulence bent him at the knees and he had to reach down a hand to steady himself.

When the tornado had had its fun with him it dashed off for parts unknown, leaving Drinkwine battered and bruised in its wake. When he looked down he saw his feet were treading virgin sand. Where were Jafar's footprints? He frantically searched the area and only saw the freshly groomed waves of dunes. The cell phone compass was dead. The sun, directly overhead, had no orienting shadows and Drinkwine was overcome with panic. The dust devil had turned him around and with the sun directly overhead he had no idea what direction he was facing. A desperate fear coursed through him as he tried to make sense of the distant horizons—only rolling sand, in every direction.

He picked up the tracks again by chance, lucking upon the wavering imprints of Jafar Barr's shoes. Drinkwine was calmed by sight of the murderer's footprints. He looked into what they might tell him by their sun drunk swagger. The strides reeked of fatigue and mistrusting direction. Jafar Barr was fading. But Drinkwine was fading too. He pressed on.

Several times Drinkwine had to remind himself what he was doing out here. He was tracking a killer. That's right, he thought to himself, this man, this man Barr had killed someone. Drinkwine wondered for a moment why. It all seemed so unimportant, so trivial. So, a man had been killed. They don't arrest beasts for killing one another. Why man? Drinkwine had to shake the delusion from his head, straining to keep his thoughts tethered to reason. He knew it was wrong, what this man had done, yet, out here, against the harsh plains of Mars, it seemed so inconsequential.

The estrangement from all the industry and commerce unfolding back there in the growing metropolis of Jannah only served to trivialize the murder for Drinkwine. Removed from civilization, from technocracy, the notion of murder seemed simply a routine of nature, absent of guilt, without criminality. An animal is not reprimanded for killing in the wild. So why all the fuss when men do it?

†

Chapter 22

ONCE AGAIN NIGHT SHROUDED the desert with cold. Drinkwine had stumbled onto a small thrashing of errant, dead bush that had once tried to grow here. He had built a fire with the brittle twigs and was warming his hands, staring into the licking flames with eyes drained of life, of spirit—drained of reason. The fire was dying down, the embers glowing orange, occasionally flaking off and drifting up into the night.

On the periphery of the fire was a powdering of ash. Drinkwine was marveling at the black and gray soot. He reached out his hand to touch it, discoloring his fingers. Raising it to his nose he sniffed at it, then rubbed it across the sunburned skin of his forearm. Running his hands through the ash he repeated the ritual on the other arm, slowly covering the white skin. Drinkwine removed his threadbare linen shirt and spread the gray and black soot over his neck and torso. He ran his fingers, thick with ash, through his thinning strands of hair, matting them black. With slow deliberation he spread the grayish, black powder over his face in some strange tribal ritual born in the recesses of a fading mind, gradually concealing him against the darkness.

†

The Martian night hung with a extraordinary beauty. Quiet, ominously still. The serenity belied the cruel nature of this place. A small rise of rock gave view to the expansive valley of blackness below. Clawing his way up the loose shale, Drinkwine arrived at the precipice. He was barefoot and naked save for a ripped and frayed piece of linen covering his groin. The sharp shale had cut his feet, but Drinkwine paid no attention to the blood. His body melted into the night in its covering of ash. He held the galvanized pipe in his hand. He dropped onto his haunches and peered into the chasm of blackness, eyes keenly searching out any movement, his senses peaked. All that shone in the dark were the bloodshot whites of his eyes, his body camouflaged in collusion with the night.

From his perch, crouched and rocking gently back and forth, Drinkwine spied, a good walk's distance, the gleam of a campfire out in the sorrowful blackness. It appeared to be hovering in the vacant abyss. Silhouetted in the shimmering flame was the custodian of the fire, the very evil that Drinkwine had dedicated all of his adult life to, the fire dancing Jafar Barr's shadow erratically against the sand.

Drinkwine absently clubbed the loose shale with the rusted length of pipe. Then, with an adept ease of animal-like prowess, Drinkwine stood, the rusted pipe gripped firmly in hand, and descended the unstable slope of sand, cooling against the night, and walked with quiet strides for the distant flame.

†

Jafar Barr did not look well. All the scientific pursuits and possession of a higher education were not doing him much good out here. He was dehydrated, beyond hungry, and his skin was toasted. His normally perfectly combed hair, pressed to shape with gel, was matted with red dust. His lips bled from blistering. Barr's bloodshot, half moon eyes had given up their almond beauty and were transfixed on the weakly licking flames of his feeble campfire of broken twigs. His mind was partially gone from the battering of the desert. Even the blinking of his eyes seemed to tire him.

Something stirred the wasted specimen of a man and he tiredly gazed into the surrounding darkness. Movement had shifted the still air. The weak flames of the fire did little to illuminate the threat. Something was lurking just beyond the reach of the dull light of the fire. Jafar Barr's tired eyes tried to find it. A presence was out there, pacing back and forth on the edge of the blackness, prowling the immaculate night with malice.

Whatever it was, it was peering back at him. He could feel it. An animal, creeping back and forth in demented strides, watching, breathing, waiting to unravel the quiet in an assault of violence. The desert had sapped all of Jafar Barr's energy and will. All he could do was sit and wait, staring blankly into the pitch black of Mars.

Unsettling the darkness with slow, steady movement, a creature crept into the flickering light of the fire. The creature walked upright, emerging from the embrace of night, naked, save for a loincloth of dirtied linen. The skin had been swathed with ash. The hair was wild and matted. The face, awash in black soot, emphasized the bloodshot whites of its eyes. The creature stood there hauntingly, bathed in the flicker of the disorienting flames. Its right hand was weighted with a rusted length of pipe. The creature made several slow, animal-like strides in its bare feet, catching the light, its face a hideous mask of gray and black, streaks of perspiration augmented with painted lines of human blood, dried against the cheeks in a bizarre cast of tribal paint. The creature's eyes—Drinkwine's eyes—were vacant, defined now not by rational thought, but by the violent indifference of nature. They had lost their intelligence and sparkled with animal simplicity. He stood there, swaying slightly, the club gripped tightly in his hand.

Jafar Barr was mystified by the arrival of the creature. He had lost track of where he was, of who he was. He knew he was hungry, hurting, thirsty, aching—he knew that much. But he had no clear recall of why this creature had followed him into the desert. Oh, yes, he remembered. A man had been murdered. A man. Murdered. Yes, he'd murdered a man and this creature was here to make an arrest. But Jafar was more interested to know if this creature had water with him, for incarceration seemed a fair trade for a drink of water right now.

Barr slowly regained his thoughts. Oh yes, the cop. This was the detective. Bewildered, he thought that presently there were only two beings out here in the far reaches of Mars. He remembered now, he was trying to flee this man. And after all that distance, after all the effort to get away, here they were, face to face.

Jafar Barr did not attempt escape. He didn't even seem that surprised at Drinkwine's appearance. He absently looked the monster up and down in slow deliberation. He hung his head, breathing out a long sigh, then, resigned to it, said simply in painful surrender, "Okay."

True and complete exhaustion had made a mockery of the encounter. There was no surprise, no attempt at violence, no defense. There would be no heroics. Drinkwine, keeping his eyes fixed on Jafar, settled onto his haunches in the sand, cradling the rusted pipe in his ashen arms. The flames danced and flickered between them, licking up occasionally in a flutter and crackle of movement.

All the possible scenarios of this encounter, which Drinkwine had conjured over the past three days in the tiring pursuit across the Martian plain, did not come to fruition. Of all the ways he'd imagined this confrontation unfolding, this wasn't one of them. The moment existed in a pale surrealism bordering on dreams. Two men, one a murderer, the other a cop come to make an arrest, sat spent, exhausted against the elements, sharing this vapid space out here among the nothingness.

Each of the men had to struggle to find any value or reason to place on why they were here. It was all so irrelevant against the remote backdrop of Mars. There was not the energy to fight. No strength. They were simply two men, stranded out here by different ends of the same circumstance.

Finally, after a long silence punctuated by sporadic cracks of the burning twigs, Jafar Barr uttered with a dry and scratched voice, "They're building a tank on the outskirts of Jannah to hold a killer whale. Did you know that?"

The first real words out of the killer's mouth were not what Drinkwine expected. But they seemed strangely appropriate somehow.

"A killer whale will be swimming on Mars," Jafar Barr mused, entertaining himself with the whimsy of it all.

"Do you know who I am?" Drinkwine broke the night in a near whisper, as if careful not to spook Barr, his voice cracked with dryness.

The question stifled Jafar, his face contorting as he searched out the bits of answer floating unconnected through his head. "Yes," he finally said, "you're the policeman, with the odd name."

"That's right, I'm the policeman with the odd name," Drinkwine responded. "And do you know why I'm here?"

Again Jafar Barr fell into a kind of confusion as he wrestled with the question. Then, alighting on a moment of lucidity, "You're here to arrest me."

"Yes, that's right," Drinkwine said, absently stroking the rusted pipe laid across the tops of his thighs, still crouched on his haunches, ready for reaction that might erupt in surprise. "And do you remember what for?"

The flames danced up at the night, the burning twigs cracking and popping. Jafar stared blankly into the fire. "Because I killed a man," he responded in desultory admission.

"How did you get the Roches?" Drinkwine asked.

Jafar took his eyes from the fire and looked at Drinkwine, genuinely puzzled, "The what?"

Drinkwine contemplatively rubbed a grain of sand from his eye and, unhurried, said, "The weapon. The sidearm, how did you come into possession of it?"

Jafar Barr just nodded, he seemed surprised that guns, like people, would have names. "Roches," he repeated, amused, as he turned his gaze back to the fire. "The day they arrived, after being brought up from the Moon, the officers asked if they could use the lab to uncrate them. As they were unpacking them, the officers were called away to mid-day prayer. The weapons were just sitting there. They were still wrapped in shipping cloth and paper, oiled, and ready." Jafar spoke with such ease it was as if he were speaking about someone else. "No one was around. No one. I'd always wondered what a gun must feel like. So I picked one of them up." There was a change in his demeanor. "Do you have water?"

"You took it," Drinkwine immediately steered Jafar back.

"What?" Jafar said, surprised, forgetting his thirst. "Yes. It was heavier than I thought it would be. It felt good—the metal, the handle, the trigger. It felt like power." He stared into the fire. "The shipping orders hadn't been opened. I knew they hadn't checked it against the contents of the crate. They wouldn't know if anything had gone missing. So I took it. I took it, and a box of shells."

"When was this?" Drinkwine asked, never taking his eyes off

Jafar.

"Weeks ago. Weeks and weeks." The memory roused a kind of wonderment. "I kept it in my room. I'd take it out and hold it, just look at it."

"And?" Drinkwine asked, his voice softening to a comforting tone to encourage more confession.

But Jafar Barr didn't need much coaxing, he was so far gone from the ordeal of the desert that he continued absently. "I took it out to the research shed where I was working. I fired it at an empty diesel can. It destroyed it." He left his thought for a moment before returning. "I wondered what it could do to flesh."

"The flesh of Michael Byrne?" Drinkwine's voice stirring Jafar to recall.

Jafar stared into the flames. Distant, his scabbed lips bleeding, he uttered, "I wasn't ready for the amount of damage it would do."

"Why did you kill Michael Byrne?" The words key to Drinkwine's investigation lugubriously slipped from his cracked lips.

Jafar Barr barely registered any emotion. "Was that his name?"

"Yes," Drinkwine responded with an astonished whisper. "What happened? Why did you kill him?"

"Michael," Jafar looked to Drinkwine for help.

"Byrne," Drinkwine offered. "Michael Byrne."

Jafar just nodded a few times.

"How did you know Michael Byrne, Jafar? What was your relationship?"

"He was just a worker who picked up extra money under the table doing odd jobs around the research center."

"Why did you kill him?" Drinkwine asked, still perched on his haunches, fingers massaging the rusted pipe with disturbing gentleness.

"Hmm, why? Why indeed," Jafar Barr uttered, staring absently into the fire. "Just circumstance."

The creature's fingers clamped down around the club. "What do you mean?" the hideous creature asked.

"Because he worked under the table I knew there wasn't a paper trail to link him to me. He was so proud of how he fooled the system," Jafar said, a little laugh accompanying the windfall of confession. "When I realized no one would really know if something were to happen to him, it got me to thinking." Jafar stared into the flames. "I told him I would pay him to move some crates out at the research station." Amusing himself with recollection, "I told him I'd even pay him for the travel time."

Jafar Barr's head bobbed with exhaustion. He stared blankly into the fire.

Drinkwine had to steer him back to the conversation. "And, then?"

Jafar looked up at the creature sitting on the other side of the campfire. "Oh, yes. On the drive out in the rover, to make conversation, I told him about my record collection. He took an interest in wanting to hear the vinyl discs. That's my hobby, collecting old vinyl records..."

"Yes, I know," Drinkwine's voice growing agitated. "So you said in your interview. Then what?"

"He wanted to hear the music." Jafar looked at Drinkwine, "He wanted to hear the old vinyl discs. He'd never seen one before." Jafar Barr tried to rouse saliva into his dry mouth as he remembered. "He was just sitting there, at the stereo, watching the turntable go round, the needle against the vinyl. He had the record jacket in his hands. The music was playing. It was all so easy—to lure him out there—to get him entertained with the records. So easy."

"So, you didn't know Byrne?" Drinkwine asked tentatively, his mind flooded with revelation.

"No." Jafar Barr's thoughts wandered back to remember that fateful day, and the actions that had now brought the two of them together, out here in the desert. "I got the gun and stepped up behind him." Barr smiled slightly. "He was listening to the music. I just lifted the gun—the Roches, you said?—and leveled it against the back of his head. I pulled the trigger and the gun..." Jafar Barr's face contorted quizzically. "I had no idea, no idea. There was so much blood, so much." Barr drifted off. A twig cracking in the fire brought him back. "He fell forward onto the record player, the needle scratched the record. It ruined it."

"Your precious record," Drinkwine eked out, getting angry, fingers tightening their wrap around the oxidized length of pipe.

"The turntable continued to turn," Jafar, amused, "catching on his ear every revolution." Suddenly sobered at the recall. "But the blood. That's what I couldn't fathom—how much blood there is in the human body. You just don't realize," he said, dumbfounded. "You just don't realize."

"So, you moved the cabinet to hide the pellet holes," Drinkwine said with disdain, his eyes moving down to study the rusted pipe clutched in his hand.

"Yes, but when I saw how much blood was spread over the work shed I realized I could never clean it all up." Jafar Barr said it with the enthused tone of youthful mischief.

"So, you decided to torch the shed?" Drinkwine uttered, fingers wrapped tightly around the pipe.

"Yes. But I knew that the fire would never completely get rid of all the evidence of the body, no matter how hot the flame got." Jafar divulged this with a disturbingly matter-of-fact delivery.

Drinkwine was too far gone into seething contempt to take any reward in how exacting his reconstruction of the murder and the murderer's actions had been.

"I realized I would have to get rid of the body some other way. That's when I thought of the lake, the water. It would eventually cover the whole region. That's when I thought of tying his body to the shrubs and letting the water cover it all up."

"And hope that the lake would never give up its dead," Drinkwine said, dumbfounded by Barr's brazen callousness. Anger was coursing his veins, stirring with malice. Forgetting all the lengthy questions he had so carefully constructed and memorized to put to this man, abandoning all the erudite study and paths of psychology to assess the murderer's motivation, Drinkwine found himself asking with painful simplicity, "Why?"

"Why, what?" Jafar Barr responded, staring with empty, shallow eyes at the painted warrior illumed before him in the flickering firelight.

"Why did you kill him?" Drinkwine asked in earnest.

Jafar Barr looked through the flames at Drinkwine; a strange man-beast squatted at the fire, covered in grotesque tribal paint, caressing the rusted pipe in his ashen hands. Jafar seemed genuinely surprised by the question and, after a moment, simply shrugged his shoulders obtusely and responded casually, "I just wanted to see what it felt like."

As if the fire had taken Drinkwine's blood to boil, his bolted reaction to those words came with a frightening urgency of blind impulse. The mind had no opportunity to intervene with reason. The animal leaped with unnerving voracity over the licking flames, the club raised overhead, coming down with a brutal smashing force squarely against Jafar Barr's skull. There was a hideous crush of bone beneath the hammering weight of the rusted pipe. It sank into the brain and flesh with ugliness. Jafar Barr collapsed, grotesquely bent, onto the sand. Drinkwine's mind was slow in deciphering what was happening, as if the swinging ashen arm clutching the pipe belonged to someone else. It rose and crashed again and again, each strike collapsing more of Jafar Barr's skull, accented by the hideously crushing sound of breaking bone.

The blood followed, spurting out in pulsating beats from Jafar's startled heart, the dark crimson hemorrhaging from the cracks in his skull. It was too late, Drinkwine was merely a spectator to this violent display of nature; a mad creature exacting a confused vengeance, the blood splattering in an alarming radius about the fire.

Jafar Barr's body crumpled under the violent fusillade of hits, drawing protectively into a fetal position. He absently raised his hand up, out of instinct, to shield his face, but the swinging pipe smashed it out of the way with a breaking of fingers to strike the head again and again. Strange, inhuman noises were emitted by the bloodied mass of face, each utterance cut short by another blow of the pipe. A wheezing sound corrupted the gurgling of blood erupting in the windpipe, strangling the attempts of screams into nothingness.

The body of Jafar Barr convulsed and twisted hideously out of control in the flickering firelight as the life drained from him. There were sounds that struggled to escape into the Martian night but which were trapped inside the body as it succumbed.

The man-beast stood over the painfully writhing body, its chest heaving with excited breathing. Jafar Barr was motionless, save for a strangely odd and detached movement of his left arm. It rose up, the broken and dislocated fingers opening and closing as if trying to grasp the thin Martian air. Drinkwine stood, enthralled at sight of a dying body reacting to mindless impulses in lieu of lost command from a rapidly fading consciousness. Jafar Barr's heart was still beating, but weakening, with each throb sending a diminishing gush of blood out the many fissures that had been opened up in his skull.

Settled again on his haunches, the beast watched with fascination as Jafar Barr slowly left this planet. His eyes were wide open and he stared at Drinkwine with unnerving horror. Then, in a graceful, synchronized movement, the raised arm slowly came down as the eyelids closed, and Jafar Barr was dead.

Blinking away the rage, Drinkwine felt the heat from the flame of the campfire as he came back into his senses. He became aware of the bloodied rusted pipe weighing down his arm. He stared at the body of Jafar Barr. It was motionless. The skull was misshapen, oblong and hideous. Blood pooled the indentions in the soft red sand created by their scuffle, absorbing the slosh of thick crimson.

Drinkwine sunk to the ground with bewilderment. The only movement was the weak flicker of flames... the only sound his heightened breathing, gradually settling after the burst of violence. He was suddenly acutely aware of the sand, the chill of the night air against his nakedness, and the quiet, the absolute quiet that stretched out in all directions, isolating him in the blackness.

It took a few minutes for his heart rate to return to normal, Drinkwine drawing steady, uneven breaths of the thin air, his thoughts slowly coming to harsh awareness of what had just happened. A moment earlier there had been two breathing, thinking men around the campfire. Now there was only one.

Drinkwine tried to find focus on the depths of blackness he was suspended in out here in the great elsewhere. There was nothing. No movement, no sound, save the licking of flames that danced erratic shadows about the area. The only other human for a hundred kilometers was dead. He was alone, completely alone now. Not an animal, not a single insect. Just sand, and the gathering cold of the Martian night.

Mesmerized, Drinkwine stared at the rusted pipe, bathed in blood, glistening in the light of the flames. He touched it, felt the sticky thickness of the substance on his fingers. Raising his arm, Drinkwine studied the streams of Jafar Barr's blood that ran down his forearm. He opened and closed his fist, captivated by the way the blood pooled into the divots between his fingers.

Transfixed on his bloodied hand, Drinkwine became aware of the distant horizon beyond. The Earth had just peaked above the black rim of Mars to join the dazzling star field, beginning its arduous trek across the firmament. Earthrise. The pale blue orb, small against the canvas of stars, ascended peacefully and without a thread of sound into the Martian night.

†

The Myoko mirror continued its motionless waltz four hundred kilometers above the surface of Mars, silently stirring the cold vacuum of space. The mirror, blemished severely over the years by the constant barrage of meteors that had passed through its hectares of Mylar panels, was unaware of the strange thing that had just unfolded on the remote reaches of Mars. It maintained its majestic and proud stance, despite its crippling of punctures, serenely adrift in its perpetual orbit. Far below, somewhere among the vast reaches of the red planet, a man sat at a fire, clutching a length of rusted pipe.

The End

By the Author

The Plunge of Icarus

Collected Wanderings
(Motorcycle Travel)

Karmic Blues
(Short Stories)

Earthrise

Reader Note: The Plunge of Icarus is also available as a
Cinenovel for the iPad and Kindle.
www.cinenovel.com

ABOUT THE AUTHOR

Jeff Buchanan was born in Dallas, Texas in 1958. The Buchanan family moved to California when Jeff was ten. An avid motorcyclist, he raced motocross in his younger years and spent a season on the professional racing circuit as a mechanic in 1982. Buchanan took up the mantel of directing, following in his father's footsteps, earning a number of awards for writing and directing commercials and producing several independent feature films. Buchanan left the film industry to co-found a motorcycle magazine, serving as Editor-in-Chief. In 2010 he founded Cinenovel, a new genre of visually augmented e-books. Jeff has now put all else aside and, late in the pageant of life, is focusing all his energy on his passion for writing fiction.